Please return/renew this item by the last date shown. Books may also be renewed by phone or internet.

 www.rbwm.gov.uk/home/leisure-and-culture/libraries

☎ 01628 796969 (library hours)

☎ 0303 123 0035 (24 hours)

www.rbwm.gov.uk

Royal Borough of Windsor & Maidenhead

Oldladyvoice

ELISA VICTORIA

Translated from Spanish by Charlotte Whittle

SHEFFIELD – LONDON – NEW YORK

And Other Stories
Sheffield – London – New York
www.andotherstories.org

Originally published in 2019 by Blackie Books, Spain, as *Vozdevieja*
First edition in English, 2021, And Other Stories

1 3 5 7 9 8 6 4 2

ISBN: 9781913505103
eBook ISBN: 9781913505110

Editor: Jeremy M. Davies; Copy-editor: Gesche Ipsen; Proofreader: Christian Müller; Typesetter:
Tetragon, London; Typefaces: Albertan Pro and Linotype Syntax; Cover Design: Setanta Studio.
Printed and bound on acid-free, age-resistant Munken Premium by CPI Limited, Croydon, UK.

A catalogue record for this book is available from the British Library.

And Other Stories gratefully acknowledge that our work is supported
using public funding by Arts Council England.

Support for the translation of this book was provided by Acción Cultural Española, AC/E

*To my Uncle Pepe, faithful
protector of childhood*

INTRODUCTION

The cover of the book in your hand – red and white stripes with an overlaid print from which red, pink, and yellow flowers seem to float upward – is taken from a dress that Elisa Victoria's grandmother made her when Elisa was a little girl. "It was cool and comfortable," Elisa writes. "When I wore it, hardly anyone messed with me." The dress is like a talisman or a kind of armor, a protective layer to ward off at least some of the daily troubles of childhood. In *Oldladyvoice*, protagonist Marina also views certain garments this way, like the palm-tree skirt her grandmother makes her before their Marbella vacation: "Between this and the Minnie Mouse pinafore," says Marina, "there won't be much I can't handle."

But nine-year-old Marina has an awful lot to handle. She feels like a misfit. She's been to several different schools. Her family isn't like others, she knows people think they're weird. Her beautiful mother is enigmatic and troubled. She hasn't seen her father in years, and her mom's eccentric boyfriend Domingo is "more like an older brother with a job than a dad." The social world of her grandma's apartment block is a minefield, and she's tormented by the early onset of puberty, the stirrings of desire in her young body. She has plenty of questions about how she should act as a girl. Or maybe she'd be better off as a boy? She might be enjoying the mild chaos of her grandmother's world for the summer, but she's also waiting for news of her mother's health. Why won't the grownups tell her what's going on? Her greatest fear is that if her mom dies, she'll be sent to live at a boarding school run by nuns.

Marina can let off steam at her grandma's house. She can watch all the TV she wants. She can stuff herself with fried eggplant and croquetas. She can get away with swearing more than she can at home, and her grandma is open with her in a way that her mother is not. Part of this book's charm is its representation of the grandmother-granddaughter relationship as a space of freedom, of the grandmother as a source of refuge and stability on one hand and a purveyor of anarchic joie de vivre on the other. In this homage to the bond between grandparents and grandchildren, the two generations meet on the margins and observe, bemused, as those in the middle go about their lives. More broadly, *Oldladyvoice* is an unsentimental portrait of three generations of women – three Marinas – in a family where men are marginal or simply not there at all. "My inheritance is transmitted only by women, no one else tells family stories, no one else makes important decisions," Marina tells us. "Paternal surnames don't mean anything."

Her grandma's conversation is as unfiltered as Marina's narration. Yet Elisa Victoria always portrays Marina with compassion, because she knows that when you're young, the little dramas can seem as momentous as the big ones. Waiting for news about your mom's illness is excruciating, yes – but so is having to walk past a gang of kids playing

8

table soccer. This awareness extends beyond the social, to Marina's experience of her own body: the scorching summer heat on her skin, the tingling she feels when someone pays attention to her, or that other tingling brought on by lust. The ache in Marina's chest, her fascination with her "hole." The feeling of needing to pee. The feeling of needing to take a shit, and the relief when you finally can. This uncensored treatment of physicality is an essential part of Elisa Victoria's non-hierarchical depiction of childhood, which would be incomplete without sex and other bodily functions. The author has said, "I see all the details of daily life as equally important. From the sleep dust in your eye, to a metaphysical observation. I think you can only get a full picture of the human condition by reflecting it all on the same level." Likewise, Marina's fears and the perverse images that assault her are no more or less important than keeping her dolls' hair looking nice.

Reading Marina reminds me just how deeply felt the perceived injustices of childhood are. She may be small, but her desires – the desire for friendship, the desire to fit in, and to discover her body's potential – are as large as those of any adult. Her keen sense of the wrongs of the world goes hand in hand with her compassion for others. She is wise, tender, and funny. It was impossible for me not to fall in love with this smart-beyond-her-years girl with a filthy mind and an enormous heart. She's the friend I would have loved to have when I was nine. I hope you enjoy meeting her as much as I did.

CHARLOTTE WHITTLE
Brooklyn, May 2021

OLDLADYVOICE

OLD LADY VOICE

My mom's dark flamenco dress lurks on top of the wardrobe. It's green with enormous black polka dots. When she puts it on, she's the prettiest woman on the face of the earth, but it's been lying there for months and I'm fed up with seeing it from my bed. It doesn't bother me too much during the day, but when I take off my glasses to go to sleep, its blurry ruffles turn into a gigantic coiled snake and I have to hide under the blanket so it can't see me. It would be easier to admit that I'm scared of it and ask for it to be kept somewhere else – which would also be better for the dress – or try and explain the vision away, but this doesn't even occur to me. Things are the way they are. It makes no difference anyway. I still see the snake as soon as I turn out the light, no matter how tight I shut my eyes.

There's a loud noise coming from the living room. Mom sleeps in there because we live at my grandma's house and there aren't enough bedrooms for all of us. We lived in other places before, but I barely remember them. I have a room of my own. This makes me feel really guilty. An uncomfortable luxury. The wallpaper is pink with white clouds, but the room is way too gloomy, and I only make it worse by covering the window with stickers. I can't help it, sticking them up there makes me feel rich.

I'm scared, I want to complain, to cry a bit rather than know what's going on. But I hold it in and wait. Mom comes into the room, gathers me up in her arms, and lifts me out of bed in the dark. I take up about as much space as a baby, and it makes me dizzy to be held at the height of her chest. She carries me into the living room like a precious offering. I have trouble opening my eyes. The light hurts. I don't know what's going to happen, and I'm still not wearing my glasses. She's on edge, lost in a mixture of haste and exhaustion. You can tell she's just another scared little girl caught up in one hell of a mess. There are some boxes of toys on the armchair that haven't been wrapped. Grandma is by the front door. I notice she's wearing her blue bathrobe and a really serious expression. She opens the door and three men come in wearing shiny clothes and making a ruckus. They claim to be the Three Kings. Mom isn't happy and doesn't ask me to be happy, and she keeps holding me tight. Her heart is pounding like a bull's. I can't reach the floor. Balthazar pushes his face into mine and says something about a gift-laden caravan that'll arrive later in my honor, with so many camels that traffic will be stopped for miles. Why not now, Balthazar? It's supposed to be now. The dark smudges on his face make me feel sick, I don't want them to rub off on me. I'd rather go see those toys up close and open the boxes now, but I'm not allowed. I have to wait until morning.

In less than five minutes I'm back in bed as if nothing's happened, disoriented and bewildered, imagining an unlikely procession of endless gifts. I get no explanation. Grandma's snores soon punctuate the stillness of the house like an insistent night watchman's. I may not be four yet, but I've got things figured out. Those men can't have been the Three Kings. They smelled funny: pungent, acrid, smoky. Their costumes were fancy, but they were wearing them wrong. They showed up empty-handed. The gifts were already on an armchair when they arrived, and Grandma opened the door to them at the wrong moment. This isn't the kind of royalty I've been taught to believe in, that's clear enough. And anyway, their ringleader was Balthazar. He was the main character, and he was scary. Anyone who knows me knows perfectly well that Melchior is my number-one king.

I have no idea who those three guys are, but all they've done is made me lose sleep and messed up tomorrow's surprise. The real Kings weren't as in tune with me as I was hoping, and they didn't bring what I asked for. I wanted a big stuffed Snoopy dressed as a pilot and a Rainy Day Chabel doll, the one from the commercial where they dance at night, like in that movie I saw some bits of. I love old movies with music and dancing on big stages, where everything's clean and polished, the colors look painted on, and there's never a single curl out of place. I also like the ones set in Roman times. If I could only be grown up and get away from all this confusion. I'd choose a life in black-and-white and the kind of high heels that don't hurt your feet. I'd have a Christmas tree as tall as the ceiling and smother my friends with gifts. Everything would be easier if I weren't so precious. I try to hide it, but it's written all over me. Perfume commercials, TV dances, dolls' houses, Xuxa. I adore all things corny. That thick, tame snake is still looking at me from the top of the wardrobe, but now I have other things on my mind.

A different, bright, yellow light shines on the morning of January 6. What happened last night doesn't bother me much. I'm used to seeing clear skies but today it's like squinting at scenes on postcards from way back in time. I open my presents as if I'd forgotten about them, and I admit that the new toys give off a special magic. There's a St. Tropez Barbie in a bathing suit that comes with a sizeable comb. I admire the comb for quite a while before opening a box with a pink armoire, also for the Barbie. I don't know what I'll put inside, I don't have any dresses for her, but it comes with three hangers and it's nice and roomy. The seven cotton handkerchiefs decorated with mice, one for each day of the week, don't do much for me at all. Maybe the fad for giving hankies as gifts will pass. Things would have to get pretty bad for a kid to resort to using one of those little rags. I'd rather wipe my snot on a dishcloth. But the pink teddy bear is cute. I hug it and jump up and down and stand it next to me to see how far up it comes. They ask me what I'm going to call it. I know exactly. I'll name it after the uncle I worship, my hero, the doctor who looks out for me every time I need looking out for.

"Pepe!" I answer.

"Another Pepe?"

"Yes!"

"But you already have two Pepes."

"Well, another Pepe. This one's going to be Pink Pepe. Pepito!"

"All right then."

The teddy bear melts my heart and now I can even look at the hankies fondly. I take one out and stroke it to make up for the uncharitable thoughts I had earlier. The Monday mouse is dressed as a mailman. Really cute. This didn't turn out so badly after all. The king cake is delicious. A few kids parade their new toys around the patio while I have another helping of breakfast. Some neighbors knock at the door. It looks like a package addressed to me has shown up at Tata's apartment. Tata isn't family, but she lives on the next floor up and I've known her all my life. The word *tata* means something sweet and hard to define, but nonetheless very specific. I think it's something less than *grandma* and more than *aunt*, but definitely more than *neighbor*. If I was alone and faced with some unexpected problem, her apartment's the first place I'd go.

The news of this surprise gift piques my curiosity. I find it in the midst of a tangle of grown-up legs. It's a carrying case full of sparkling princess accessories. A crown, some bracelets, and who knows what else. I glare at it without a word. Being corny is one thing, but being tacky is quite another. An awkward silence prevails among the towering bodies, until Tata asks lovingly, "Do you like it?"

I've been taught not to lie, so I look up and shake my head. Everyone is deflated. I thought I was doing the right thing, but now I feel horribly guilty. Tata snatches up the gift and stalks off muttering about returns. I look at Mom and shrug, not understanding what just happened. She crouches down and says, "Marina, sweetheart, when someone gives you a gift you have to pretend you like it even if it's not true."

"Why?"

"Because if you don't, the person who gave it to you gets sad."

"Why?"

"Because they thought you were going to like it and they feel bad for not getting it right."

"And did Tata get sad?"

"Yes."

"But I didn't want her to get sad."

"I know, sweetheart." She hugs me and sighs. "But do you understand?"

"Yes, but that means no one will ever give me anything I like."

"You tell me what you like, you'll see. And if you don't like something I give you, you can tell me and it doesn't matter."

"Are you mad, Mom?"

"No, it doesn't matter, you couldn't be expected to know what you were supposed to do."

"And Grandma?"

"She's not mad either."

"And Tata?"

"I don't know, but if she gets mad it won't last long, and anyway there was no need to make such a fuss. If the kid doesn't like the gift, then fuck it, what can I say?"

After lunch, I throw the loot onto my bed. I pretend that the Barbie is beautiful and evil like the witch in *Snow White* and that she's trying to destroy everything I own, without any success. Mom comes in to say hi. The wallpaper only looks pretty when she's there. The afternoon light gives her naturally pale face some color. As she comes closer, some reddish highlights glint in her loose black curls. She's wearing pajamas and lipstick. That's her usual look at home, though she's out a lot of the time. She's thirty-one years old and has a whole lot of problems.

"How are you doing?"

"Good."

"Do you like the doll?"

"Yes."

I've learned my lesson. I'll have a chance to let her know what I really want when we're both more prepared, but for now we've had enough. It's not what I asked for, but the Barbie is pretty, and it'll be good for me to practice with. I've called her Katrina, because she has the face of a true villain, and the name Katrina suggests terrible evil. It makes me mad that I'm still too clumsy to handle more valuable presents. I want someone to give me a Michael Jackson cassette.

"But Mom."

"What?"

"Those guys who came last night weren't really the Three Kings, were they?"

"No, that was your father and a couple of his friends. The real kings are magicians, and you can't see them."

"Oh, right. And which one was my dad?"

"Balthazar."

"Well, I like Melchior better."

"Of course. Me too."

It puts my mind at ease to know that the guy last night was my father. You can't ask too much of mere mortals. Who were his friends? No doubt they meant well. I've made Mom laugh, so she gives me a kiss. Her wet lips make it awkward, but my lungs still swell with delight. I wonder how long it'll take Tata to forgive me, how long this excitement will last.

PART ONE

PART ONE

1

I've just turned nine, and Tata hasn't let go of her grudge. I live in a different neighborhood, go to a school that doesn't totally terrify me, and spend lots of afternoons in Amate Park, keeping tabs on what's going on at the pond. It's full of stuff that people throw in. A stroller, a walking frame, a crutch. Sometimes a kid shows up with a remote-controlled boat. One winter, I thought I saw a big fish leaping out of the water. I heard it too, but only caught the last flick of its tail when I looked. I have a theory it was a sturgeon, but no one will back me up. It's a pretty small pond, to tell the truth.

I've gotten taller and more observant. I never forget a thing. I miss Grandma pampering me every day, but now I understand that it's Mom who's the real queen, the only one in this world, and she's getting sicker by the day. I like it better now that we have our own house, even though we have to share with Domingo, the latest weird boyfriend she's found for herself. This neighborhood is a little more modern than the last one, and there's lots of red brick, which makes it more welcoming too. The three of us have reached an understanding by now. Things aren't going too badly. The problem is me, inside. I do my best to hide it, do my best to pretend that everything around me doesn't totally creep me out. It's hard to trust other people when it seems so easy for them to perform their roles. This worries me. I wouldn't even say they're acting, life just seems to come naturally to them, while for me it's an effort. Whenever I talk to anyone my voice comes out weird, my palms get sweaty, and I realize my human disguise is second-rate. When I'm alone I feel like myself, but then I have to fight the abyss of freedom and terror opening up at my feet. I'm constantly craving an ally to keep me company. At school, in the apartment block, in the little plazas.

Today I got up early to go to class, but luckily that's a long way away now. From Friday to Sunday I leave the school routine behind, spending all weekend back in the mild chaos that has always ruled at Grandma's house. It's just me, Grandma, and Canica, a fluffy little dog with a black back and a white belly. She's really sweet. Supposedly Santa Claus brought her, but I always had my doubts about how she arrived, since it was a young guy, about twenty, who actually came in and put her on my lap. I was expecting the real Santa Claus to show up that afternoon and ring the bell, or at least someone in fancy dress. Canica was so small and adorable that I pushed her around in a toy baby carriage for weeks. I'd keep doing it, but she won't let me anymore. She stayed at Grandma's when we went to live with Domingo. We throw some croquetas together in the cramped living room with the TV on. We like mysteries, though Grandma can always sleep afterward and I can't. She's tired; we undress in her room together. There's a flesh-colored slip beneath her cool-looking red dress. I don't understand the point of a slip, which must be really hot just by itself, and Grandma still has to take off multiple layers, the stiffest ones. You could squeeze a whale into all that armor, between the bra, girdle, and panties. They dig into her soft brown skin.

"Help me unfasten this."

I kneel on the bed and free Grandma from the thick shell. It doesn't seem to bother her a bit during the day. She sighs and sits down, and I crouch to pull off her stockings. She sighs again and begins to speak.

"Now, tomorrow . . ."

"What?"

"Hang on, I'm thinking."

A few seconds go by while she squints, her wrinkled index finger at the ready. With her other hand she takes out a cigarette and lights it. She exhales her first puff of smoke and goes on hatching her plan.

"Now, tomorrow I'm going to put my feet in a plastic tub with some salt water."

"Yes."

"And then you can take the scissors, snip snip snip, and cut my nails."

"OK."

"All right."

"OK."

"I look like a hawk."

"That's true."

"I'm going to poop now."

"I'll go with you."

The thought of cutting her toenails makes me uncomfortable and even a little scared, but I think I'm up to the task. She suggests it in a fun way, and there's no point objecting. She does all kinds of things for me quite happily. I follow her slowly into the bathroom and as she turns the corner she loses her balance.

"Fuck!"

"What happened?"

"Nothing, I just crashed into the corner of the wardrobe."

She's seventy-two, short, pot-bellied, and has no regrets. Until recently, the only thing that ever embarrassed her was her own smile in some of the photos where she looks happy. But last year she put her false teeth in for the first time to go to Expo '92, and since then she's been feeling invincible. The only thing that seems to get her down nowadays is that she was sewing me a really elaborate flamenco dress and back in March I told her not to keep going since I wasn't going to wear it and had no intention of going to the Feria ever again. I mean, I get it, dressing up as a gypsy is a huge deal in Seville, and it must have made her mad to abandon a project like that so far along. She gives me an earful about it nearly every day. But apart from that, I don't think she's ever been this happy. She sits down with her cigarette in her hand and I keep her company squatting on the floor. I like watching her take a shit. Sometimes we talk and sometimes we don't, but I'm always mesmerized by her toilet-paper ritual. She tears off two pieces the same size and lays them delicately on her thighs with zen-like calm. She often mentions that she had a Chinese grandma, and when Mom's around she says that actually, on the quiet, her grandma was Filipino, but it's all the same to her, and then there's a squabble. She flicks ash into the bidet. It's three thirty in the morning and the only sound is her slow breathing. I find the plopping sound very satisfying since I'm a constipated kid. There I am, a white-knickered minion at her feet. She's sitting upright and stark naked on a throne she's been enjoying for only a third of her life, relishing the convenience modernity has to offer, the cigarette in her mouth and pieces of white tissue hanging at equal distances off her legs. Now a howl shatters the warm peace of the neighborhood. I shoot a pitying glance up at the ceiling. An unfortunate family lives on the third floor with their disabled son, enormous and lumbering like a rhinoceros crying for its missing horn in the forest.

"Poor little angel, he can't sleep," Grandma murmurs, tilting her head.

"How old is he?"

"Almost forty."

After she's done, she puts on her white floral nightgown, turns on the radio, and we lie down together in the double bed. I try to think about something nice to scare off any ghosts.

"How long till we go on vacation?"

"Hmm . . . I'm not sure, let's count the days. Where are we now?"

"Who knows."

She takes a little calendar out of her nightstand and we calculate as her eyelids begin to droop. Twenty days until Heaven. I stay awake and listen to the humming radio, which keeps me company as I gaze at Grandma's nightgown. It's my favorite but also the one that troubles me most. It gives me a sense of freedom since I associate its pattern with summer vacations, but it also represents the precise moment the dark side of life became clear to me. I'd seen it coming for a long time, of course. Lurking in the silhouettes of *Princess Knight*, in chairs with high backs, in the lights that flickered across

Mom's thighs in the few taxis we'd taken at night, and in Grandma's sewing machine, the same heavy Singer with the same fake mahogany stand it's had since the sixties. Then the dark side finally stuck its paw under the door in 1990, when three key events happened at the Worker's Resort in Punta Umbría.

The first one caused me a kind of unease I'd never felt before. We had a packet of chocolate sandwich cookies in our room. Each cookie seemed like it would never end – dry and hard and difficult to chew. They filled me up straight away, leaving me stuffed but unsatisfied. I decided to handle the problem by eating just the chocolate filling, the part of the cookies I liked, scraping it off with the still intact baby teeth I miss so much. I knew I might get a major scolding for wasting food if I got caught, so I would sneak over at night, under the cover of darkness, lick the cookies as clean as a dog bowl, then leave them discreetly in a corner of the balcony, on the floor. It would've been pretty unclassy to throw them off the balcony, definitely beneath me. But it didn't take long for them to discover my secret cache, and the dressing down they gave me was epic. The lesson was clear: in this life, if you want to eat just the chocolate, you've got to have a decent place to stash the dry cookies.

The second and most important of the three events happened that same night. I was anxious and couldn't sleep after the row, lying in the roll-out bed next to Grandma's box spring, and I started feeling scared about being down on the floor. I crept onto the mattress and pressed up against her. She was wearing the same nightgown then that she's wearing tonight. There were mosquitos wandering across her soft and tanned old skin but she hunted them down, giving herself the odd slap and scratching away the bloody corpse in her sleep. When I finally began to doze off, I saw my first image of the night: a huge army in formation listening to the orders of its colonel, a skinny and shifty character who marched up and down as he yelled. Soon the colonel dissolved mid-speech as if his limbs were made of string, leaving a tangle of flesh-colored vines. When I opened my eyes, I was facing Grandma's sturdy back covered in colorful little flowers and felt suspicious of my own mind, an unexpected traitor.

The third dramatic moment was hardly unusual in itself. Some boy I didn't know decided out of nowhere to hold me under water in the swimming pool and try to drown me. From beneath the surface, I saw the shape of alarmed adults coming over, but even then I didn't think they'd be able to coax the boy out of his fit of rage in time to save me. It wasn't such a big deal, but kids are weak and accidents happen. I thought I'd probably die then and there. No, I wouldn't want to go back to Punta Umbría. This year will be different. This year we're moving up in the world: we're going to Marbella, the capital of luxury and comfort.

It's Saturday. We've had fried eggs and potatoes and an endless feast of croquetas. I got up late and lunch was after the usual time. Grandma's been awake since noon, she's dressed and her eyebrows are already penciled in. I've only just got up so I'm disheveled and in my panties and a T-shirt. There's a movie on TV called *Banana Joe*. I really wanted to watch it, I saw the trailer and it made it look so fun. The jokes and the plot are a little bit disappointing, but the soundtrack more than makes up for that. I chalk up the letdown to my immaturity and pretend like I totally get it, like I can appreciate all the finer qualities that the movie doesn't actually have. Our first dessert is two slices of watermelon. The second is Neapolitan ice cream. Strawberry, vanilla, and chocolate. We scoop some out for each of us, and Grandma puts her feet back in the salt water. She splashes and watches the process. She's been in this position two hours.

"Grab the scissors, honey, it's time."

"OK, OK."

She makes the cutting gesture with her gnarled fingers and says again, "Snip snip snip."

"OK!"

"Well, if you want you can wait for the commercials."

"No, no, it's really no problem."

I feign sacrifice and interest when really the movie's a drag. That way I look good. It's win-win. Her little hawk talons terrify me, which is exactly why I want to get this over with as soon as possible. I kneel and hold her wet foot like an enormous mushy chickpea, a bite of vanilla still melting in my mouth. I rest her calloused heel on my knee covered in scabs from various falls and do my best not to touch any of her nails with my bare hands. The scissors are big and sharp. They're her sewing scissors, but they're all we have.

She smokes contentedly while I conduct the operation.

"You're so good at this," she says. I smile with my mouth closed, swallow the vanilla ice cream and wrestle with the nail on her big toe, the thickest, most stubborn one, curled in on itself in a spiral.

"Jeez," I grunt. "Does it hurt?"

"No, it doesn't hurt a bit. Give it a good chop there, squeeze tight."

I squeeze the scissors with both hands and a chunk of yellowish toenail goes flying.

"Bravo! What did I tell you? You've got talent. Your mother wasn't even half as bright as you at that age."

"She wasn't?"

"No way. She was very pretty and very quick and fun, I'm not saying she wasn't, but you're a real smarty-pants. It's something else! The only trouble is your mother keeps you on such a tight leash that one day you'll have a seizure."

"What's a seizure?"

"It's like a throwing a fit, but in your head."

"Oh."

"In your brain."

"Right."

"You're not even allowed to say jeez. I'm telling you, there's no need for her to be such a drill sergeant. You're no trouble at all."

"Jeez is no big deal, right?"

"How could it be a big deal? I even let you say shit when you're here with me, isn't that right?"

I laugh and carefully snip off a toenail.

"Not fuck though, eh. That would be going too far. You can't say that. I only say it if I've hurt myself or I'm upset over something serious."

"All right, all right, not that one – just thinking about saying fuck aloud is too much. Oops, I said it!"

"Hey! You can't even say fuck as a joke, all right? If it slips out in front of your mother she'll have my guts for garters."

31

Grandma lets out a puff of cigarette smoke and her belly wobbles as she laughs. She opens her mouth so wide I can see her dentures against her palate from below. I laugh too, and lift up her other foot. The second is always easier than the first. You know how it goes. You only have half left to do.

They've just picked me up and I'm back in the red-brick neighborhood. I wish they'd let me have lipstick the color of these walls. It's seven in the evening and I've already got my backpack ready with Monday's books for school tomorrow. I go buy cigarettes with Domingo. Even though he's my mom's boyfriend he seems more like an older brother with a job than a dad. He's got a stutter and is also a know-it-all, which is a tricky combination, but it didn't take me long to get used to it. Other people have trouble understanding what he says, but not me. I'm the one who's spent the most time with him, for better or worse, so he stutters less when we're together. He usually gets stuck on the Ms, Ss, Ls and Ts. The vowels aren't exactly a picnic for him either. He studies me like a nosy imp and teases me mercilessly, year after year. He and Mom have had plenty of fights, but I don't think he'll ever ditch us. Back when Mom figured their relationship was getting serious, she gave Domingo a nudge one day and left us alone on the couch.

"Listen up, little girl."

"What."

"Let's talk terminology."

"What's that."

"About words."

"OK."

"Great."

He cleared his throat and plowed on, feigning confidence.

"You know even though I'm not your father you can call me Dad."

We stared each other down with our poker faces. Eventually some hysterical giggles snuck out of both of us.

"No," I said, "I don't think I need to do that."

"OK, that's clear enough. But, look, I'm just saying, if you'd like to, we can do it that way."

"No. I said no."

"You sure?"

"Yes! It would be really weird."

"I mean, I agree," he said. "I figure it's kind of weird too. I just asked in case you wanted to. And maybe weren't brave enough to ask me."

"I think we're good as is," I said.

And we shook hands on it. I noted a mixture of sadness and satisfaction in him, perfectly balanced. He's one of the few other people I know who are obviously just barely getting away with pretending, but the fact that at his age he still wouldn't admit it unnerved me. After a minute of our both feeling weird, he proposed a new plan.

"All right, well, since we're in agreement and we've got to define the situation somehow, let's go into business together."

He took out a piece of paper and started to write out a contract. I was six at the time. He was twenty-eight. I thought he must be older, since he was balding and had a dark beard, but he had this playful, mischievous, boyish air about him, like a kid just out of high school. His contract detailed his promise to support me until I was no longer a minor, at which point it became my responsibility to support him until his death to pay off my debt. He was offering me the loan with the highest interest in history. Once again, that typical blend of mild humor and cruelty began to gnaw at my stomach. It was a perverse sort of deal. I didn't get whether he was serious or not. Obviously, it would be forever until I turned eighteen, but he was rubbing his palms together greedily like an immortal villain salivating over my soul. From that day on he called me *Partner*, an affectionate nickname that summed up the arrangement to both our tastes. I'll admit I was about as keen as he was on being soppy. We were in the same boat as far as that was concerned. Soon it'll be three summers since we moved in together, but running into him in the hallway still gives me a shock. When we're alone, him and me, something keeps me on the alert, the same kind of suspicion I figure kids with erratic siblings must feel. The difference is he's been given authority over me. I still long for a real father figure, sometimes. But given the choice maybe I prefer Domingo.

As we go out in search of a packet of Winstons, I beg him to take a detour past the toy store, an essential source of comfort to me in the neighborhood. It's closed, but just looking in the window is enough. This year is getting really boring, and the Three Kings are the only religion I can get behind, so that's what I feel like dwelling on. Most kids have already stopped believing in them, and I've been through a few crises of faith myself, but I decided a while ago now to hang on to the few crumbs of innocence I've got left as hard as I can.

"I hate waiting for the Kings to come."

"Why?"

"Because it takes so long, and I'm already thinking about what to ask them for."

"Come on, Partner, don't tell me you still buy into that charade."

"What's a charade?"

"It's like lousy theater."

"Like what?" I cry, playing dumb.

"Like a farce."

I stop dead in the middle of the street.

"Hey, don't mess with the Kings!"

"I'm not messing with the Kings, I'm just telling you the truth, plain and simple."

I'm utterly outraged. "Just because you don't believe in them doesn't mean they're not real."

He gives me a sneer and walks on. I start worrying and rush to catch up with him.

"OK, but if they're not real, then how come they visit you too?" I ask.

"Mother of God. We just buy each other gifts and give them to each other. That's all it is."

"Maybe that's all it is for you, but Mom believes in the Kings and they come to her every year."

"We'll see about that. I'm telling you, I buy her the stuff." I'm dumbstruck.

"All right, all right," Domingo says. "If you'd rather keep kidding yourself, go ahead."

"Oh yeah? If I'm kidding myself, then how do the Kings always know what I want?"

"Because your mom finds out."

"Well, there are times when I don't say anything and I still get stuff."

"Because your mom finds out."

I grumble. I'm pretty sad that it might all be a lie.

"Your mom has her methods," he says. I have no arguments and no hope. I can't believe how insensitive he's being. I keep walking in silence. "I'm sorry, kid."

"I'm not your kid."

"All right then, Partner."

He's clearly in the right. I was the one who brought it up and he gave me an honest answer. I should be grateful he doesn't take me for a fool. But I'll still pretend not to believe him and that I buy the other version. Just for a little bit longer. It's too delicious. We don't say anything else until we get home. Domingo is smoking a cigarette that looks like it tastes of triumph. At the door to our building, the *Banana Joe* theme song floats into my head. I adore that song. I wish they hadn't actually shown the movie yet, so I could just keep hearing it in the trailer.

"Hey, how many Oscars has Bud Spencer won?"

Domingo cracks up. He flicks his cigarette butt onto the street and we go inside. Not a word.

"What's the matter? Why are you laughing?"

"Nothing, nothing."

"But do you know how many Oscars he's won or not?"

"None. I don't think he's won any."

"Seriously?"

"I'm pretty sure."

"But how can that be? Bud Spencer is super famous!"

"If you say so."

"Well, I thought they'd have given him at least four or five."

He keeps on laughing as we climb the stairs and I don't understand why. In my opinion no one deserves an Oscar more than Bud Spencer.

2

I'm the only one in my class taking ethics instead of religion. I've been to four schools so far and it's always been like this. At first, I didn't know what *ethics* meant, and got it mixed up with *equestrian*. I thought they were going to teach me all about horses, and that the rest of my classmates were a bunch of gullible goody-goodies. In the end, I spent an hour a week talking to the teacher about crossing the street at a red or green light, good manners, and simple moral dilemmas. I didn't mind being alone with her, though it made me feel even more like a misfit, a feeling that plagued me like some horrible goblin whispering into my ear. Mom teases me about the equestrian thing but also assures me I can do whatever I want. Believe in God, get baptized, take communion, even ride horses someday. But I already know that God, and want nothing to do with him. Since my second day of preschool, to be precise. On the first day, I was sitting alone in the sandbox in the courtyard, wishing someone would come over and play with me. I was comforted by the fact that I was wearing my favorite dress, the only one Grandma hadn't made me, the only one that was bought for me in a store. The skirt and sleeves had blue and white stripes, and on the front there was an embroidered doll facing backward, wearing an embossed hat with a red satin bow I never got tired of stroking. All of a sudden this little girl ran over, yanked out the ribbon, and went off without saying a word. I didn't say anything either. Grandma noticed as soon as I got home.

"What happened to the little bow on the hat?"

I felt so ashamed I didn't say anything.

"You already lost it? But you liked it so much!"

"Somebody yanked it off at school."

"You don't say. And who was it?"

"Some little girl."

"And did you do something to her?"

"No, I didn't."

"And did you tell your teacher?"

"No."

Grandma leaned in. She was going to tell me something serious. Her gappy, greenish teeth didn't scare me at all.

"Don't you worry, sweetie," she said. "The Lord will punish that little girl."

"The Lord? Is that the same as God?"

"Yes, of course."

The soothing image of a sweet, chestnut-haired, bearded Jesus emerging from behind the clouds filled me with trust. I thought justice would soon be done, that by His design everything would take care of itself, as though seeing a person get punished could somehow help. I went back to school the next morning, as sure of victory as someone with an ace hidden up their sleeve. I spent all day staring at my vicious classmate. I watched that little girl do all the evil she wanted, day in, day out, without learning her lesson, and regretted not taking charge of the situation, being passive, not knowing how to change my approach. Humiliated and cheated, I gazed bitterly at the 1987 Jesus calendar that hung in our living room until the end of the year. There were more calendars after that one, but I never stopped being mad about it. And my opinion of Catholicism wasn't helped by the fact that the nuns used to slap my mom on the hand with a wooden ruler, that they'd instilled an unhealthy amount of shame in her and made her feel responsible for all the wickedness in the world, not to mention that her family couldn't afford to keep sending her to the nice school with the good little girls.

My family's take on religion began to change last winter, when Mom broke it to me that this time things were serious and gave me a fancy children's Bible. To butter me up, she took me to the store and let me choose the one with the prettiest Virgin Mary on the cover. Then she told me there'd be no more drawing until I'd learned the Lord's Prayer by heart. It was all a trick. Six months later, I'm being interviewed at the same Catholic school she went to herself. It's a worrying sequence of events, but I've always been obedient and adaptable. Besides, I like uniforms. I've already gotten used to the humiliation of still believing in the Three Kings, and even though the truth eats away at me I'm learning to cope with contradictions. It can't be all that hard. Anyway, no one was better than Melchior. I'm not nearly as keen on Jesus, so it won't be as much of a letdown. I know right from the start that it's all a big, fat lie. Today will be my first job interview, in a way. I've got to make a good impression on the head of school because if I don't get into the convent who knows what'll become of me. Mom has been tactful but aboveboard from the beginning. She's really sick. Sick enough to have to tell me about it. It's no surprise, there's almost always been something wrong, and even though I completely believe in her, and I've been afraid forever that one day she might suddenly vanish, I've got to get used to the idea that this time it might be different, this time she might get too sick to go on. I haven't seen my dad in five years. Domingo may be my business partner but he's really just a big kid. We signed a contract but there's no way he's ready to take care of a girl my age full-time. We need a backup plan. The idea is to send me to the nuns if things get ugly, but I'm not even baptized. It's urgent. I've been told this in no uncertain terms. And Mother Rosario is making an exception for the sake of an old student who's in a tight spot, even though she knows perfectly well that I ought to be getting ready for my first communion by now. The biggest drag about all of this is having to go to catechism.

I've seen the courtyard, the library, the dining hall, and the dormitories. A pupil my age, perhaps a sweet future companion in misfortune, shows me two Chabel dolls with their own yellow wardrobe, the one I asked Grandma for once, right before she dragged me out of the store for picking something so expensive. The little wardrobe has three doors, a shoe rack, a fold-out mirror, and a ton of clothes, all so pretty and kept spick and span. I tell the girl how much I like it and excitedly reel off a list of toys of my own. Mom interrupts and hauls me out of the room. She's gripping my arm and looks annoyed.

"Marina, listen up."

"Yes, Mom?"

41

"Can't you see they hardly have any toys here? Don't go telling these girls how many you have at home and rubbing it in, OK?"

"I was telling her because if I come and live with her, maybe we can share."

"Oh."

I feel like crying, partly because I've upset the cute little orphan girl, and partly because I've only just realized that I might have to get used to this kind of austerity too.

"Won't I be able to bring my toys along?"

Mom puts her arm around me and leans down to kiss me on the head.

"Oh darling, of course you will. Of course you will."

I hold the snot inside my nose and we continue the tour silently, hand in hand. I'm now up to speed on the situation. All that's left is the ultimate monster, the Mother Superior. Her office is cramped and gloomy and I hope I don't have to go back there, that's for sure. She and Mom have talked a lot on the phone and now she wants to meet me. It's just the two of us. She pulls up a couple of chairs and we sit face to face with her big desk to one side. I'm wearing a checked, calf-length skirt but I squeeze my knees together to show her I know how to sit up straight with my legs closed like a proper young lady. This is partly thanks to those ethics classes. The Mother Superior is stout and looks ancient inside the wimple framing her soft, pale face. She sizes me up through her little round spectacles and greets me with a Hail Mary.

"Conceived without sin," I answer. I've been preparing for this moment for a long time.

"How are you, Marina?"

"Very well, thank you, Mother," I smile, thinking about the yellow doll's wardrobe. Smiling is my forte.

"How are you doing at school?"

"Excellent."

"Do you get good grades?"

"Yes."

"What would you think of coming to school here?"

"That would be nice. I like the courtyard."

"But if you came here you might have to be a boarder. Have you seen the dormitories?"

"Yes."

"You have to pray every day here, you know."

"I know, Mother."

"Do you pray?"

"Yes."

"Do you pray to Jesus?"

Her voice is faint, soft, measured. She knows how to spot a heretic, but I'm highly skilled at the art of winning over an enemy. I also got a pep talk before I came. If my lies are too exaggerated, she'll see right through me. I need to be as sincere as I can within the bounds of the girlish discretion and virginal holiness that's already part of my repertoire.

"I haven't been to church much, Mother Rosario. I'm sure my mom told you. But I believe there's a God and I'd like to learn more about him."

She watches me carefully from on high. I'm nervous, even though I know I'm polite and well spoken and give an impression of credibility, at least at first.

"Do you know the Our Father?"

"Yes."

"And do you like it?"

"Yes."

"Would you like to know more prayers?"

"Yes, I've already started learning the Hail Mary."

"Let's see. Say an Our Father for me."

I recite it, word-perfect, shyly but sweetly, doing my best to be irresistible.

"Do you want to be baptized?"

"Yes, Mother, I'm really looking forward to it."

"And to have your first communion?"

"Even more."

"Very well. You may go now."

"Thank you, Mother."

Back home, they're proud of me for being admitted to the College of the Most Holy Trinity. While my real mother, the one without a capital M, takes a siesta, Domingo and I celebrate the triumph of my charms with a boxing session. First he holds up his palms so I can pound him with my closed fists. Once I've warmed up, he starts to dodge and feint and react with light punches, mostly aimed at my belly and arms. He likes to provoke me.

"My charming business partner! What a performance! You're a young lady now!"

That kind of comment drives me nuts. Really gets on my nerves. He guards himself with a cushion and bears the brunt of all the nervous rage devouring me, until I'm worn out. I love the way he teaches me to fight. His rationale is that I'm learning self-defense while having fun. The reality is that I need all the stress-relief I can get and he knows it. Controlled violence is our greatest ally at times like this. We play war games and draw maps of battlefields, surveying our domain, identifying the enemy's weaknesses the better to wear them down, building cities on the living-room floor and then blowing them to bits. Afterward, we switch sides and the bombs fall on our home, destroying everything we have.

"Green bomb!" he yells. We hide under the dining table. The green ones don't do much damage, it's not too hard to survive.

"Orange bomb!" I yell. We cover our heads and hold on amid the shower of debris.

"Oh no, my legs! I've lost my legs!" Domingo stares down at his thighs in terror.

"Me too! I've lost my legs and arms!"

"Look out, here comes a red bomb!"

"A red bomb? Is this the end?"

"That's right, Partner, we're going to die, but it's been glorious fighting beside you."

"So long, Domingo! See you in hell!"

"May it be so, comrade!"

"So long!"

The bomb falls. We play up the earth-shaking sounds of destruction, milking the pathos of the moment, crawling around and bleeding to death. I make the most of the drama and moan and groan to my heart's content, alternating wails and hysterical laughter. When the dust finally clears, I stand up red in the face with tangled hair, let Domingo collapse on the couch in peace, and pad off to the bed where Mom is sleeping. She's in her panties, resting beneath a thin blue sheet, wearing lipstick, with her hair cut short. I lie down next to her and snuggle up to her puffy flesh, holding my breath so I don't disturb her. I touch her drowsy hands, sniff her aroma, and understand. I understand everything. If she dies, whenever that happens, it'll be OK. I won't hold it against her. I can always spritz her perfume and close my eyes. I've spent years memorizing the sound of her heartbeat. She trembles beside me and lets out a whimper. I move over and stroke her forehead to help guide her dreams to a more peaceful place. It would be awkward if she woke up. I'm not very well trained in affection. Domingo teaches me to fight anxiety with punches and laughter. He tries to steer me away from all forms of tenderness. I guess it's the only way he knows, and it's true that it's quite effective, but at some point I'd like to be able to show my feelings in public. I think about my impending baptism. So infuriating. So embarrassing. But most of all, so boring. I go back into the living room, the straps of my composure laced back up tight, and sit down on the couch next to Domingo, rigid. I'm ready to be an orphan.

"I'm hungry," I say.

"Have you already had a snack?"

"No."

"How about a sandwich?"

"Yeah, but a chorizo one."

"Let's make two!"

We go to the kitchen, where there are always plenty of buns. Domingo makes two sandwiches and leaves the counter covered in crumbs. We take our first bites still standing. He looks me over, musses my hair, hands greasy from the chorizo, then points at me, laughing.

"Way to go, eh? You really pulled a fast one on that nun!"

I laugh too, with my mouth full, and run to the TV to get there first. I put the Miliki and Rita Irasema show on. Rita is really pretty when she wears a bow in her hair.

"Miliki's songs aren't so bad, Partner, but this circus act with his daughter is pretty lame, don't you think?"

"I'm not changing the channel," I protest.

He lingers on the couch a few more minutes, thinking up an excuse to make himself scarce.

"I'm going to make some chocolate milk. Want any?"

"OK. But the Smurfs are about to come on."

"Ugh. Horrible."

"Oh, they're not that bad."

He goes to the kitchen huffing and puffing. Luckily, he does everything at a snail's pace and lets me listen to the whole opening song. Domingo has a special gift for shitting on most TV, especially the kids' shows. He finds something wrong with everything. His nit-picking is contagious and ends up making you bitter. It's partly because he's really persuasive. He sits down next to you and starts telling you that the end of the cartoon *The Little Mermaid* is way more tragic than the story itself because that poor little girl isn't old enough to get married, and that the Andersen version is way cooler, where she dies and gets turned into foam for being dumb, and how Ariel is a poor puppet of the system, and how the princes in these kinds of stories are always a waste of space. He only likes wicked stepmothers, witches, and villains, since they're apparently the only ones with a shred of personality. Right now I know he's dying to give me his spiel about how Papa Smurf is a Nazi, and to say, where did you ever see a village where all the guys have a

47

job and a mind of their own while the only girl spends the whole time doing her hair and deciding whether to wear the white dress that's a bit shorter or the white dress that's a bit longer. To me, Smurfette has an enviable life, but I know he's right and that cartoons are full of corrupting ideas. What bothers me is that he doesn't realize the movies he watches aren't much better. His only criteria are for it to be sleazy and make you want to throw up, or else give you nightmares, and if it can do both at once then he'll be cheering at the screen. He uses a pretty advanced vocabulary with me and never censors what I watch or read. According to him, the only things I'm not allowed to do are swear and wear a miniskirt. And Mom agrees. They tell me it's for my own good, so I don't get too wild, and promise that when I'm a grown-up I can decide for myself. It makes me so mad I could die. Now *The Smurfs* is on. Today I have the right to enjoy a little basic pleasure without anyone lecturing me, I think. I don't want anything more to do with this place. I'm moving to a beautiful far-off land full of bright colors and fancy flowers, where you can live inside a toadstool. Domingo comes back with two glasses on a tray. I don't look at him but I know he's pulling a disgusted face. Well I'm disgusted too, by those no-budget Jesús Franco lesbian vampire movies he loves, and also the chocolate milk he's bringing out full of cream and lumps.

"I don't know how you can stand this nonsense, kid."

"Look, Domingo, if I miss anything Smurfette says because of your whining, I'll kill you."

"This would be unbearable without Gargamel."

"I said I'd kill you!"

"All right, all right. I'm going to lie down with your mother and read for a bit."

"Good idea."

"Fuck me, you've got some nerve!"

"Well, I already missed *Dragon Ball* today because of that nun."

"You're not wrong. Also, *Dragon Ball* is way better than this."

"And don't swear!"

He lights a cigarette with a sour look and disappears into the hallway just as Smurfette comes on. I've learned to draw her shoes with a single line, and draw them all over the place. I don't care if I'm being manipulated, I'm crazy about those white high heels. When the episode is over, I realize both my adults are snoring. I take this opportunity to shut myself in the bathroom and go through Mom's makeup. She has three lipsticks. One red, one orange, one purple. A black eyeliner. Face cream. Light-colored powders, the ones in the container with a palm tree on it. I could stare at that white palm tree on a green background for a whole hour if nobody came to disturb me. I peek into Mom's room. It's cool and dusty. Domingo has lowered the blind and is lying on his back in his underpants. When he turns over to put his arm around her, his right nut slips out.

I creep into the room and tiptoe over to the nightstand, where there's an issue of *El Víbora* waiting for me. It's one I've already seen but I wouldn't mind another look. I memorize its position, an upper corner touching the base of the lamp, under an old book and topped with a cigarette lighter. Success. I go into my room and shut the door. I hug *El Víbora*

49

against my chest and kick with excitement. This session is going to be a real pick-me-up. *El Víbora*, *Totem*, *Creepy*, *Makoki*, and 1984 are all for adults and I'm not supposed to have laid eyes on them, but it's too late now. At this point they're so important to me that they're a basic necessity. All my favorite authors and cartoonists come from these comics, not counting María Pascual, who actually writes children's books. They rescue me, all of them: Liberatore, Tamburini, Manara, Nazario, Charles Burns, R. Crumb, Miguel Ángel Martín, Horacio Altuna, Max, Shelton, Onliyú, Silvio Cadelo, Moebius, Crepax, Mónica, Beatriz, Pons, Jaime and Beto Hernández, Toshio Saeki, Richard Corben, and Otomo, who also made a movie version of *Akira*, which might be my favorite after *Splash*. Those names in golden letters shine in my heart; they show me the path to salvation, just like Daryl Hannah when she flicks her mermaid tail and dives into the deep. Without this formidable army backing me up, I don't think I could keep on being a nice, meek little girl. I just wouldn't care anymore. On some of its covers *El Víbora* says, "Comix for survivors," a motto that seems pretty crass but that I relate to nonetheless. I can grin and bear it through plenty of tricky situations because the pictures in those comics have a dark and liberating force that fills me with hope. OK, not all the pictures. Most of them are cartoon strips and some of those are beautiful, so fun and uplifting. But some are ugly and twisted, and you never know what you're going to get. With the nasty ones, if the story has no appeal and the drawings aren't any good, I flap the comic shut and wish I could puke up the pages like someone puking up shrimp that's gone bad. Then I go to the bathroom to wash my face and hands in a pointless attempt to get rid of what I've seen. But then there are times when the stories are creepy but the captions are well written and I like the pictures. Then I get sucked in, and end up overcome by a strange kind of admiration, and I'm not sure what to make of it. Thanks to the education I get from comics I feel like I'm simmering all the time. I've learned the craziest language, I've gotten to know the world of kidnapping, torture, suicide, murder, mental illness, drugs, and all the more advanced varieties of perversion. They've also introduced me to fantastic stories of merciless superheroines, mutants, cyborgs, flowers that can make love with both delicacy and passion, angry and sad young misfits, possible futures, dreamworlds, distant planets, highly interesting sexual practices, and jokes I never could have imagined. These comics have given me the most intense experiences of my life. If I learned to read so quickly it was down to pure impatience. I couldn't wait to find out everything that was happening in those comic strips. I know they fill my head with ideas I might not be ready for, but they bring me so much beauty and freedom that if I had to choose between comics and dolls I wouldn't know what to do.

Today I've swiped the 1989 Christmas special of *El Víbora* from the nightstand – a nice and juicy issue that fell into my hands a few months ago and then disappeared. It apparently came with a Liberatore poster insert, which I never got to see. Oh, Liberatore, I owe him so much, whoever he is. Am I his youngest fan? Can there be many of us under ten who hide in our bedrooms during our parents' siestas, dazzled by his colors? On the cover there's a girl in panties surrounded by a bunch of guys dressed as the Kings, who've brought her porn and all kinds of dirty toys. I'm so fond of this image. It once represented all I ever hoped for out of life, in my endless innocence, at least for a time. Back when I would apologize to the floor for falling on it. In the end the floor wasn't my friend and couldn't kiss me on the ass. So many shattered illusions.

3

It's Friday. Mom comes to pick me up in the car when school gets out. There's a suitcase and a pretty decent selection of toys in the back. We go straight to Grandma's for lunch. It's a boring drive, and the inside of the car is roasting. We don't have air conditioning. The heat makes my feelings turn in on themselves. It's like it highlights the pain, condensing it and filling it with color. Mom's arm hangs out of the window, a cigarette between her hard, worn-out fingers. Her skin glistens like a pale gypsy woman's. She studies the drivers around her with defiance. She keeps track of the toys I like most, often raises her hand to me in anger, and always has her rifle loaded, ready to defend our trench. All things in life are war, she tells me, pretty much. Being a warrior seems to come really naturally to her. I'm afraid when it comes to having guts I'm a bit of disappointment. Though I think I probably make her proud in other ways. She tells me the world is an ugly, dirty place, full of trials; that people like us have got to be ready to conquer a lot of hurdles, most of them unfair and out of proportion, but that if you can get up the nerve you can handle anything. We could handle a guy two meters tall and wielding an axe if we had to. She could skip right over him. I could climb up his body like a squirrel, make eyes at him, and plunge a corkscrew into his neck when he lets down his guard, just like the killer girl in *RanXerox*. Our relationship is very intense and very close. I was born into a fragile, unstable home. My mom is the only constant in my life. Wherever she is, that's where I belong. She juggles fears, precautions, danger, and all kinds of animal instincts, while at the same time taking care of herself and wherever we happen to be. We're the same, her and me, seized by urges as powerful as trucks and almost unstoppable. If it was up to her she'd succumb to vice in a heartbeat, just like me. We both know it. I wish we could talk about it, but it's too weird. It's really hard to be open like that. It doesn't matter, we don't need to talk about it. It's in the air. She knows I wasn't born to be her daughter, and I know she couldn't have felt less ready for motherhood when she gave birth. It's an accident that we're both here, resisting temptation as a favor to each other. It's really tough. I live in a hideout full of fugitives.

The simple little plaza by Grandma's is a relief. I like going back to familiar places. I feel quite sociable when we arrive. I run into Cristina in the courtyard and it makes me happy to find that she's pleased to see me. We agree to call each other after the siesta to play. I hope I can keep my word. Grandma is smoking a cigarette with a nasty look on her face.

"You're twenty minutes late! The stew is so cold we'll catch our death!" she scolds us from her chair as soon as we come in the door.

"But Mom, how's it my fault if you serve the soup too early? If you know I'm always a little bit late, why can't you just wait half a second?"

"Because it's perfectly normal to serve at two thirty if that's when you tell me you're coming!"

"Well, why the fuck don't you wait until we're here to dish it out, just in case?"

I know how this tantrum ends and it's such a pain in the ass. Mom's in the right, so I suck up to Grandma to make her forget all about it. I give her a hug and praise the menu, which includes croquetas, stewed meat, bread, soda, and dessert. The soup is tepid, which isn't such a big deal given that it's pushing 40°C outside. For dessert it's a choice between rice pudding, apple compote, watermelon, ice cream, or straw-berries and yogurt. I volunteer to bring them out. At this time of day in the kitchen, the contrast between the indoor temperature and the scorching heat from the back patio feels so good it makes me woozy. It's a long and narrow room, one half sweltering, the other relatively cool. The furniture in the kitchen all has a silly-looking plastic texture, with light tones and rounded corners. When I was little, I wanted to know what the silverware drawer looked like from above. As soon as I'm there, I go straight to the cookie cabinet, open it, and inspect the first shelf. I stand on tiptoe and peer at the second. There are Inés Rosales biscuits, long breadsticks, chocolate cookies, and regular bread. Not bad. I can see there's nothing interesting on the third shelf from down below. I wish I could get up there by myself. I put the cookies in the fridge and collect the desserts they asked for. I'll have to make two trips. Two blasts of heat are better than one. It makes you want to take a shit twice as much.

Soon they're both snoring in front of the TV, one in a chair, the other on the couch.

"Wake me up at five," Mom mumbles, her cheeks soft and slack.

The blessed siesta. I've been holding in a turd just for the pleasure of letting it out with the bathroom door open, the light out, and all the peace in the world. I'm sitting on the toilet, my feet dangling. The door is right in front of me. I look at the calendar hanging on the other side of the living room, at the kitchen entrance, and I'm suddenly scared. I try to ignore it for the first few seconds, but soon I'm lifting my ass in the air and turning on the fluorescent light. The pink tiles start glowing just as the turd comes out, splashing me as it drops. What can you do. Even downtime is rife with danger. But it's worth it. I manage to expel the rest of my load and head out to the back patio so I can boil in the shed under the asbestos roof and terrorize myself by pretending I live with a monster that sometimes looks like Freddy Krueger and sometimes more like Don Pimpón from *Barrio Sésamo*. I make believe that I'm cooking, writing a list of household bills, watering the yard, caring for the sick; I take stock of the wardrobe and the trunk. Sometimes, without warning and out of sheer malice, the monster scares the bejeezus out of me. The more distracted I am, the better it works. It's an odd relationship. There are times when I give myself such a good fright that I have to run for cover. These monsters are a great match for all the nasty pictures stored in my memory. They can show up at any moment and it's hard to make them stop. The train of terror, I call it. I don't try to stop it – we know each other well enough by now.

I'm still in a good mood, so it doesn't bother me. We go out into the street.

"Mom, sing me a Diana Ross song."

"Which one do you want? I don't know many."

"Whichever. It doesn't matter. I know even less than you. I've only seen her two or three times on TV."

She starts humming one of the star's oldest songs. The light grows pale and sharp. I'm over my back-patio episode. I look up at Mom and try to store away the tune for use in potential future predicaments. Oh, I wish I could sing that easily in front of someone, without knowing the words, without caring at all. Why do I have to care so much about everything? I try to take in Mom's example, yell Cristina's name, and then we say goodbye in a hurry. My friend appears on the balcony, scurrying cheerfully like a mouse.

"Be right there!" she shouts. I hear the door close and her steps coming down the stairs. It's been a while since we've played together. We're not bad at it, our styles are compatible. She's a good person and I find it touching, I have a weakness for her. She's peppy and her bird-like titter is so sincere and persistent that it's contagious. Her Grandma Lola's balcony is the liveliest and most colorful I've ever seen, it's my favorite thing to look at in the whole plaza. And our families get along. We've never argued. Now Macarena sees us through a window and comes down too. These are the friends I chatter and hide behind the jasmine bushes with, and who save me again and again. Not that I get along too well with Macarena. We've been unconscious enemies ever since our moms were pushing us around in our strollers. One time I slapped her for breaking my glasses and there was a scene. These days she's gotten kind of pretty, languid, like some beautiful little fly. Everything's going fine, but when night falls at around nine, I start missing Lucía, the most mysterious girl I know. Though I don't run into her often, I think of her as a great friend. Partly because of the mystery but mostly because she's the only one interested in talking about dirty things for hours on end. Before dinner, I run my fingers over the clumsy graffiti I did ages ago by her door. In the orange glow of the streetlamps that have just come on, you can make out the floppy boobs, the coochie with a stream of piss, and the high-heeled shoes like the ones Smurfette wears that I drew for her when I was four, with only the help of a blue wax crayon. She never noticed, though, and I never had the guts to show her. I thought I might've gone too far. They're still there, inconspicuous, alongside the greatest compliment I know how to bestow, in capital letters:

DIRTTY GIRL

I'd only just learned to write. I soon realized the message was inappropriate, that I was lucky you could hardly see it. Cristina's mom comes to get her. The rest of us go in for dinner.

I don't go back into the street until Mom comes at noon on Sunday to put a layer cake in the fridge and dress me up and do my hair just how she likes it. I don't complain. It's Grandma's birthday, and a perfect day for a family celebration, not just because there's a dazzling sun in the sky. It's also the day of the general election. I hold hands with both of them on our way to the polling station, and watch as they vote proudly, one for the Spanish Socialist Workers' Party and one for Felipe González, which seems like the same thing to me though Mom insists that it isn't. At the polling station, some people go into the private booths with curtains and others don't. Some people brandish their ballots proudly, like they want everyone to see. It's really hard to tell which party the ballots correspond to. Almost none of the names are familiar. I don't stop looking until I find Felipe González, like I'm looking for Waldo.

We wolf our food down with relish in front of the TV. There are stuffed eggs, meat casserole, apple compote, and rice pudding. Since the whole menu horrifies me, they've set up a buffet of fried chicken and potatoes too, an alternative I never get tired of. Each time Aznar from the People's Party comes on they boo and make disgusted faces. They grumble about his voice, his moustache, and everything he says.

"He's so hideous. He's got helmet-hair," Mom keeps muttering.

When Felipe comes on it's another story.

"My Felipito, look at my Felipito! He's so handsome!" Grandma cries. She's so in love with him her cheeks even get flushed. I've been watching her sigh for him all weekend.

I have no choice but to like the party they vote for and dread its nearest rival. But I'm sure the good guys will win. The days when the bad guys used to win are over, they were just a kind of shadowy prologue to make the story that begins with my birth a bit more exciting. The nine years since my arrival have more weight than all the previous millennia combined, more than the Romans and the Moors, more than the Civil War. They have more weight than the dinosaurs.

Canica orbits us, wagging her tail hysterically. There's plenty of chicken, so sometimes I slip her a morsel when no one's looking. I love being naughty with her. She tries to get her paws near a plate but they shoo her away.

"Fucking hell, Canica, you're such a pain in the ass!"

It's too early to predict the election results and the atmosphere is heated. Such a decisive struggle makes for an exciting birthday, which is great since our family celebrations are usually fairly dull and depressing. I envy those scenes in the movies where people get together and have lively conversations and you can tell they all love each other. I even envy them when they fight. What would I have to lose? My real family has plenty of fights. Mostly, I fantasize about being seen and spoken to. I feel like I'm alone. The election coverage on TV provides some relief.

It's different for Mom and Grandma. They're stressed and all they can think about is their pensions and the country's future. They chain-smoke. Grandma hoards cartons of L&M in a chest in the living room, but Mom prefers Fortunas and sends me out on a mission to buy some. They both used to smoke Buffalos. I loved the picture of the buffalo on the cartons. I don't see it anymore. I wish one of them had kept up the habit. Canica comes with me to buy cigarettes and pees as soon as we get outside. We cross the little plaza and come out onto the street. It's four o'clock and the blast of heat makes us both want to poop. It makes me mad that she can relieve herself here and now and I can't. The kiosk is closed but there's an old lady who lives round the corner who operates a small stand out of a room in her house. We call this local clandestine outfit the Little Window. Stuck on the inside of the glass is an exhaustive selection of rancid candies. They're just there as a reference catalog, but we kids are afraid that one day we'll ask for a strawberry gummy and she'll try to sell us the one hanging there covered in glue and dust. The window is closed. I knock and a woman who isn't the usual old lady opens up. She's wearing a yellow T-shirt and has bleached hair, glasses, and a sour look on her face.

"A pack of Fortunas."

"Who are they for?"

"My mom."

"OK."

It's easy to figure out how old Grandma is because she was born in 1920, a year I associate with ringlets, porcelain vases full of flowers, delicate handwriting, and sepia tones. The candles barely fit on the crowded cake. She'll be blowing out seventy-three. Lighting them is an ordeal. By the time we make it to the last ones and run to the table, the first are already melting down. Only the three of us are here to sing the obligatory song. Grandma purses her lips; it takes her several puffs to blow them out. The layer cake is covered in drips of wax. We cut three slices. The TV is still on, showing the first exit polls, which are predicting a victory for the good guys, the heroes. Mom and Grandma raise their hands to their chests then take out a bottle of Marie Brizard. It's still not a done deal, we can't get complacent, we need to be strong. I have two more helpings of cake. Who's going to eat it if I don't?

The election thing is like soccer games in bars. On those days there's a kind of collective mood that's as fervent as it is exhausting. I guess the fans are addicted to the company, and sports give them a low-stakes excuse to get together and feel less alone once a week. Loneliness and boredom can take you to the most unexpected places. Things get serious at around eight o'clock. I'm told to shut up every time I open my mouth. I was all packed to go home but I've taken my dolls back out and spend the time admiring them on the couch. There are two girls and a boy. Each time I touch their adolescent bodies my palms burn with lust and anticipation. It won't be long now. It won't be long until I can rub up against other humans, just like the dolls do in my hands. I change one of the girl's clothes and dress her up for a party. I give the boy a stylish jacket. I whisper cheap excuses for them to make out as soon as possible.

"Oh, Peter, I've missed you so much."

"I've been dying to see you too."

"What about this? Did you also want to see this?"

I slip off the straps of her princess dress and show the boy doll her tits. He sucks them for a few seconds and then adds, "But what I most wanted to see is this."

I move his hand toward her flat, hard pussy, outside her clothes, and with a tiny, dexterous flourish, manage to make her lift her own skirt and show him she's not wearing any panties. He starts groping her mercilessly and my voice makes a faint, inaudible moan. I turn their heads to imitate passionate French kisses as they touch each other. The third doll has been spying on them from behind the arm of the chair with her leg in a cast. When they see her, Peter and the girl in the princess dress start playing doctors and nurses, providing the spy with all kinds of medical care.

Illness is just another member of my family, one with the power to decide what will become of me after this summer.

Our lease is up at the end of August. All this year, Mom has been getting worse, and faster. When I was born, she'd already been told she was terminal twice. But I'm feeling relaxed since the people they voted for are going to win. Felipe González is going to be president. That'll be Grandma's birthday present. She'll sleep soundly tonight. No one's going to take away her pension. The bad times are behind her. Orphanhood, hunger, her dead brothers, the sisters who fled to America, the lost husbands, all the chaos. I know this because things can only get better since I came into the world. I give Mom and Grandma's lives meaning. I'm their light and I know how to shine. There'll be no more wars or dictatorships now that I'm around. Mom won't be cleaning houses for three hundred pesetas a day again, and she's not going to die.

I'm not going to go to boarding school with the nuns. Though I'll get baptized, in case. Just in case.

4

It's Monday and the whole school is jumping for joy, because we live in a working-class neighborhood and our side has supposedly won. There are Betis and Sevilla fans around here, and people from the United Left and the PSOE, but no one at all from the People's Party. I've never heard anyone say they support the PP. There must be a bunch of them, though. I wonder where they all are? Anyway, it's not like I've done an in-depth study. Changing schools so often is making me less and less sure how to behave. I never know if I should rush to get to know other kids and make the most of the time we have, or if it'd be better not to get too attached in case I have to beat it at moment's notice. Promises get broken when you move, and kids get separated forever. This time, though, I couldn't help getting attached. I've had almost two years of relative good luck. I don't want to do it all over again. Things are going pretty well for me here, even if right now we're doing one of the things I hate most. We're lined up on the soccer pitch waiting to run an obstacle course. One at a time, bouncing a ball as we go. The teacher is young and shows genuine interest in education. I'm relying on him to be merciful, since I have a feeling things are going to go worse than usual for me with this. I give him my sad puppy eyes, but he doesn't notice. He just presses a ball to my chest and gives me a pat on the back, letting me know it's time to set off.

I don't do too badly for the first few seconds, though I'm so nervous I barely dodge the first round of cones. I briefly think maybe I'll come out of it with flying colors and the feeling is sweet enough to throw me off course. When I get to the gravel, not only do I lose the ball but I also give it an accidental kick trying to get it back, sending it bouncing off to the other end of the courtyard. I go and fetch it, relishing the knowledge that at least I've gotten myself out of half the circuit. But when I get back to the group the teacher tells me to do it all over again from the start. I wish he'd just focus on what we're good at and quit humiliating us when it comes to everything else.

I hope Natalia and Juan Carlos, the tablemates I like so much, won't hold a grudge against me for making them look uncool. Just in case, I decide at the last minute to take advantage of the usual commotion over the Play-Doh. Natalia is engrossed in sculpting a dress with a very full skirt. I turn to Juan Carlos, who's set up a churro stand where business is booming.

"Hey, tomorrow I'm bringing something from home."

"What?"

"A book with tits in it. It's mine."

"Eh? Say that again?"

"There are tits in it."

"What do you mean, it's yours?"

"It's mine, and there are some mermaids with their tits out."

"No coochies or anything?"

65

I shake my head slowly. Juan Carlos covers his mouth with his greasy hands. His pale skin contrasts sharply with his dark eyes and black hair. He's skinny and looks great in red, though today he's wearing blue. I'd like to be able to offer my classmates some authentic porn, like one of the *Penthouses* that have occasionally fallen into my hands, or something by Milo Manara, which always goes over well, but I think if I got caught with that in my backpack there'd really be hell to pay. There are limits.

"So are you gonna take it out?"

"Yeah, but I'm only showing it to you. And Natalia if she wants."

Natalia turns an ear toward us, not taking her eyes off the model she's making.

She pouts like a chicken when she's working with modeling clay, a silly look of concentration I sometimes copy. She's sweet and snub-nosed and always good company.

"What are you going to show me?"

"A photo of a mermaid with her tits out."

She says nothing and stays happily absorbed in her work. I have to admit I really admire Natalia. She's fun, unassuming, capable, modest, charming, and straightforward. I wish we could stay friends for the rest of my life. I'm watching her quietly and intently, so she decides now's the time to tell me a secret.

"Tomorrow my mom stops wearing mourning."

We've known each other two years and her mom has been wearing black the whole time, since her grandpa's death. Natalia barely even remembers him. She's confessed a few times that she's desperate for the mourning to end. It's depressing, and she's been fantasizing for ages about seeing her mom look cheerful again, dressed in bright colors, leaving behind the pain and reserve that this severe, funereal style demands – this undeserved, self-imposed punishment. She's had to hear endless debates about happiness, about the need for traditions or how silly they are, about being stuck in the past or moving on. Now, as she adds the finishing touches to her greasy Play-Doh dress, she holds back a satisfied smile. I give her arm a squeeze, as much to celebrate the good news as because she doesn't resent me for being the worst in the class at PE.

"Wow, really?"

"Yeah."

"But how do you know?"

"Because she told me."

"But why?"

"Because tomorrow it's five years since her dad died."

"So she's really going to do it?"

"I think she really is this time."

"So cool!"

"Yeah."

"What's she going to wear instead?"

Natalia looks me in the eye, shaking with excitement, and squeals, "I don't know!"

"That's great!"

We bounce up and down, our butts still in our chairs, and give each other a hug. I hope it's true. The dead grandpa thing has dragged on so long he's not even a grandpa to her, he's just her mom's dad. "Because it's what my father would have wanted, because my father this, because my father that . . ." I've never been to her house, but I picture it as a dark and closed-up lair where cheerfulness has been declared a lack of respect. We've often used the word *depression* in our hideouts at recess, where we talk about possible sexy storylines for our dolls and possible methods for seducing boys in the future. Natalia and I really get each other. My house is also weird, and we dislike the same girl for being a smartass and being so full of herself. When I was new in the class, I tried to win her over by saying that the day before I'd taken a dump and held the turd in my hand. She was horrified and didn't see the funny side at all. She thinks she's the best at jumping rope, in her red sweatsuit.

It's one o'clock and it's been an uneventful Tuesday. I missed seeing Natalia's mom this morning because I was late, and Natalia still hasn't told me what she was wearing. Since moms have come up, she's asked me how mine is doing. She has as much information as I do: my mom's sick and they're always changing her medication. I realize I know next to nothing about it.

"I don't know, now she's started taking some white pills this big, and some other yellow ones?"

"And do they look nice?"

"Yeah, they look great next to the ones with a bit of red. The pale pink one I haven't seen in a while, but the blue ones are still around."

We keep copying down sentences into our lined exercise books. Everyone's forgotten about the book with the big-boobed mermaids and I've been simmering with doubts about the appropriate time to break it out, and whether the idea is an appropriate one. I think my classmates suspect I was bluffing and don't want to bring it up so as not to make me feel awkward. That wouldn't be anything new. I really do have it there in my backpack, though. I don't want to seem like a phony. I want them to enjoy the pictures. There are two. In one, there's a mermaid on a rock, sadly caressing a conch and completely naked. In the other, an underwater scene, there's another magnificent, orange-tailed mermaid, her hair flowing gently due to the magic of a subaquatic current. Fuck it. I turn around, unzip my backpack, take the book over to my usual seat, and hide it under the table we share. What happens under the table is none of the teacher's business, but now that the book isn't under wraps I don't know what to do. Juan Carlos sniffs out the intrigue.

"Whatcha got there?"

"It's that thing I told you about."

"What thing?"

"The mermaid book!"

He has no idea what I'm talking about.

"Don't you remember? I told you about it yesterday."

"You told me about tits yesterday, not mermaids."

"Well the tits are on the mermaids."

"Oh!" This changes everything and he rushes at me head-long, clumsy and ravenous, like a starving puppy.

"Hold your horses, someone'll see you."

"Fine, show me down here."

I do what he says and look for the page, keeping one eye on the rest of the classroom. The first picture is enough for Juan Carlos, who can barely suppress his initial urge to climb onto his chair and rejoice. His panting has attracted a nearby posse's attention. Natalia hasn't stopped writing but she knows exactly what's going on.

"Hurry up, show me before it gets confiscated."

Her steady little hands flip to the famous two pages. Then she grabs the stiff front and back covers in shock.

"But these are photos," she says.

"Yeah, obviously."

Actually, I'm not really convinced that they are. It's a question that's been gnawing away at me. The implications are immeasurable.

"But that means mermaids are real."

The impact of this conclusion takes our breath away. Juan Carlos seizes his moment to attack. He robs us brazenly and shares the proof of his crime with a group of other boys who'd been showing an interest. I spring up to defend my treasure. Goddamn it, this is stirring up too much excitement.

"Give it back already!" I yell.

They pay no attention.

"Give it to me!"

"What? Why should we give it to you?" answers Diego, a very cute little blond boy who I'm about to shut right up.

"Because it's mine!"

Juan Carlos nods. A grave atmosphere settles over the gang.

"I'll let you all see it, but you have to be careful. Those photos are proof that mermaids are real."

"Come on, those are drawings!" For a few seconds there, I had Diego wrapped around my finger. But just as soon as the miracle happened, it all went up in smoke. A magical moment and I've blown it. "They look like photos, but they're drawings," he adds smugly.

Even I don't believe him, but only Natalia backs me up. We're starting to fight so the teacher comes over, hovers above our circle, and reaches out to take hold of the book. We all let go at once, hoping to wash our hands of it so none of us can be blamed. Our superior raises his eyebrows.

"Sir, are these drawings or photos?" Natalia asks.

"Those are drawings, but they're so realistic they look like photos."

"So mermaids aren't real?"

"Not as far as we know right now. But aren't you supposed to be copying sentences?"

We've got nothing to say to that.

"Come on, get to work."

Natalia saved our necks. We got caught with porn, red-handed, and we've come out of it unscathed. It's a quarter to two and we're copying like crazy so we don't have to finish at home.

"Oldladyvoice," Juan Carlos calls out. I hate it when he calls me that. It sounds like an insult, even though it just means my voice is husky and some of the things I say are oldladyish. I appreciate his familiarity, though. Giving me a nickname means he knows me.

"What?"

"Look."

He's taken his dick out. It's peeking out of the top of the waistband of his sweatpants. I'd like to act all uptight but I can't help giggling. Of the four schools I've been to, this is by far my favorite.

Natalia and I are standing in the doorway. The sun is shining, school is out, and kids rush all around us. She jabs me with her elbow, telling me which direction her mom is coming from. I hardly recognize her. I've been thinking for hours that she'd be dressed in red like in the movies, but she's wearing jeans and a white T-shirt. Simple and breezy. It's also the first time I've seen her with her hair down, curly and shoulder-length. She comes over wrapped in a warm sigh. I wish Mom would show up like that one day, looking like she'd been cured. But no, she appears at the end of the street, harried and serious until she sees us, just like always.

We walk along together for a while, bathed in a kind of late spring glory. It feels good to be part of a gang. There's a breeze like at the seaside, so you can wear short sleeves without getting too hot. When we get to Natalia's apartment block, Mom takes the camera out of her purse and snaps a photo of us by a tree. Luckily our moms start chatting and let Natalia and I have a few private moments out in the open. I'd love to prolong my delight and start scheming to see her the same afternoon, to firm up a plan before I leave.

"I can't this afternoon, I have to go to Country."

"To the country? The country where?"

"No, not to the country, to Country."

"What? I didn't know your family had a house in the country."

"We don't, and it's not a house in the country, it's Country!"

"What are you talking about? Are you making fun of me?"

"No, duh! Don't you know what Country is?"

I stare at her with my heart in pieces. She might as well be a brick wall.

"What is it? What language are you speaking?"

Natalia despairs and reaches out to the sky in exasperation.

"Explain it to me, then!"

"Look. Country is like Supermart."

"Oh."

"You know what Supermart is, right?"

"Yeah, yeah."

"Well it's the same, but it's called Country."

"It's called Country?"

Our moms are saying goodbye.

"Yeah, and we're going clothes shopping."

"Ah, OK. What about tomorrow?"

I'm already being led away.

"I have catechism!" she shouts from her doorway, and says goodbye. Fuck catechism. I hope I never have to miss a playdate for catechism. She's still in a good mood, but mine is gone. Why's it so hard to see school friends outside of school?

The grown-ups I know can recall their first communion in detail, pretty much, but no one remembers anything about their baptism. It's so embarrassing. I'm about to go through a ceremony for babies completely conscious. They keep telling me it's nothing to be ashamed of, that it doesn't mean anything and it's just a survival strategy. Mom has bought me some navy culottes and a white blouse with a prissy collar. I wish the day would never come. I'm keeping it secret from my classmates, it's none of their business. But the next day I do tell them we're going to Marbella. I don't usually remember it during first period, but after recess my anxiety kicks into gear and I need something good to think about.

73

"I want to be in Marbella so badly!" I sigh again. I like that Natalia doesn't make me feel like a bore. She even shows some interest.

"When are you going?"

"The fifteenth."

She looks at the ceiling, attempting a thoughtful face, then raises her hand. The teacher sees her.

"What is it?"

"Sir, when is the last day of school?"

"The twenty-second."

Natalia gives me a serious, disapproving glance. "You'll be gone the entire last week."

"Whatever."

"You're going to miss the end-of-year party."

I hadn't realized that. I missed the Christmas one too, and I even learned the carol I was supposed to sing by heart. I'm mad but I don't want to show it.

"Well, I don't care. I'll be in Marbella."

"They might fail you for missing the last week."

"Fail me? Why?"

"For not coming to pick up your grades."

I'm not sure this makes any sense, but I'd rather play innocent and rule it out. How could they fail me for that?

We've had lentils for lunch. I feel the same way about lentils as I do about taking a bath – I'm never in the mood, but I'm glad afterward. Domingo's at work. Mom has started to nod off at the table, her last slice of melon half eaten. I give her a gentle nudge.

"Mom. Mom, come on, lie down for a little while."

"All right."

I guide her to the couch. I put the dirty dishes in the sink without making a sound. I'm sweet and diligent for several reasons. I love her a lot, but that's not the reason that takes up the most space in my mind. It's in both our interests for her to take a siesta. For one thing she's really tired, and for another, this morning I filched a copy of *Totem* from the bathroom and Miguel Angel Martín's signature has been languishing on my bedroom shelf ever since. Sometimes, when I think of the convent, I remember his comic strips and feel somehow protected. I've never seen his face but I've seen his drawings, his writing, and his signature, and that's enough for me to know his work's a thousand times cleaner than the stuff in that children's Bible – cleaner in every sense of the word. How old is he, I wonder? What's his house like? What was he like when he was little? In some schools they organize kids in alphabetical order. My name is Marina Marrajo. If he'd been in my class they definitely would've made us sit together. During roll call in the morning I'd raise my hand first and then he'd raise his. I would witness his childhood sketches, his first use of color, his first ideas. I'd bet my ass he was also a nerd. He's still a nerd. He and I may not have converged in space or time, but we've shared a whole lot of floors and duvets. I know there are lots of kids like me who get frequent doses of inspiration from his filthy comics. They help us stay on the straight and narrow while also being harmless. I don't know where I'd be without them. I behave myself so as not to awaken suspicion. They make me feel lucky, give me a real sense of belonging, even though legally I'm too young to join their club. Not being able to have my own copies makes me anxious but also gives me the occasional thrill. These comics are the meeting place for my gang of imaginary friends. I move among them like a ghost, a stealthy outlaw – tiny, colorless, almost invisible. I'm always raising my hand but no one pays any attention. At my age people are always asking what you want to be when you grow up, so I've given a lot of thought to the idea of studying medicine, and I think I'd like it. It could be fun to get to know the human body and solve its problems, and then there's also the pain and blood and illness. These dirty comics are the best hope for a girl who's just a clone of her mother, and a second-rate one at that. Me and Mom are basically the same person at different times. There are only two pages in our family album, one for each Marina Marrajo. I guess no other option seemed good enough when I was born. It's been thirty years since my grandpa died, and four since I last saw my dad. Paternal surnames don't mean anything, and I'm grateful I haven't been forced to use one. My only inheritance comes from women, no one else tells our family stories, no one else makes important decisions. They're proud that I'm theirs alone, though they kind of regret having given me such an inbred name. They're scared some doctor might get my records mixed up with Mom's and something weird might happen. What they're actually afraid of, though, is that I might find out what's going on, that I might hear someone say a bunch of fancy words and get scared. They won't admit it, but you can tell that's what it is. If the doctor confuses our records I don't think there's any risk of them giving me the wrong treatment. The real risk is that he might let something slip.

I've been in the bathroom for half an hour, memorizing comic strips for when there's a dry spell. I'm dying to wash my hands. The dust on the covers is so gross, it makes your fingers turn gray. If they'd just buy the magazines every month, it would all be easier. But the issues come and go, some of them get loaned out, some are borrowed from other people, they get wet, dirty, ripped, burned, and all I can do is wash my hands over and over. It won't be too long until I can take them with no fear of getting caught, but something tells me that if I ever ask for the money to buy them, they won't be so generous. I could save up and do it in secret, but you never know what kind of day the newsstand guy will be having. I picture myself young and tall and not having to deal with these kinds of restrictions ever again. Every second that passes brings that day closer.

5

I'm usually happy on Thursday afternoons, since what's left of the week from then on is all a walk in the park. The siesta is over and the neighborhood starts to come back to life. I stand on tiptoe and peer into the inner patio. Tamara and her little brother Alberto are playing below. They live at their grandparents' house, don't know their dad, and their mom hasn't called in months. Their patio is really small. They have a toy market stand and a ball. Alberto has scattered his plastic soldiers all over the ground. I often dream about this inner patio. About falling out of the window and doing a tightrope act along the washing lines with all the clothes hanging off them. I let out a little sound, Tamara looks up, and we exchange a sad but cheerful look I've never been able to share with anyone else. She's a year older than me. Blonde, stocky, freckled, and harmless. She goes to a different school. She nearly always wears a pink sweatsuit and an orange headband that's a perfect match for her lips. We usually stay like this a good while, staring at each other with expressions to match the circumstances.

"You coming?" I say.

"Yeah, OK."

She puts her white sneakers on, leaves her brother sitting on the ground, and disappears into the kitchen. I picture her running through the building up to the third floor and try to guess exactly when she'll knock on the door. I guess right, but only because I can hear her steps. I open the door and we go to my room without speaking. There are often long silences between us. We spend most of our time arranging my toys into warm and comforting scenes, observing the result in detail and saying how nice it looks. Our favorite thing is setting up the Chabel store. Then we arrange the dolls and sit back, legs in the air, to enjoy the narcotic effect. Our friendship is steady and practical, we're like a pair of junkies who meet to shoot up together and let go of all our worries. There's no room for boredom between us, or for enthusiasm. We're good at hanging out for a while and that's all. She's definitely one of my least problematic friends. Her brother traded me the last *Dragon Ball* card I was missing. He'd spent ages searching for one I happened to have, and I'd already gotten it twenty times. We were both ecstatic that the miracle occurred in our own building. Card trading can be a dirty business, some kids really drive a hard bargain. At dusk it cools down and we figure it must be dinner time. Tamara leaves calmly. Passing the kitchen, she says goodbye to Mom, who's boiling some eggs. I can't help being happy that Mom's at home more, now she's on sick leave. She used to work a bunch before, even at night.

"See you later, Marina!" Tamara waves goodbye and disappears down the stairs.

On Friday morning my mind is all over the place and the teacher scolds me for messy handwriting during dictation. I spend recess running around alone in parts of the courtyard where I don't usually go. I pass little clusters of boys I know and act like the girls Dash Kappei chases around in the manga. I wish they'd lift up my skirt, but they're not interested. In the end I go find Natalia, who looks at me with a shrug like she's wondering where I've been. I sit down on a step to eat my sandwich with her.

"It's chorizo," I tell her.

"Can I try it? Mine's mortadella."

"Yeah. Can I try yours?"

"Yeah. Here you go."

We trade sandwiches, keen to taste the culinary customs of each other's houses. We take three bites each, then pass the sandwiches back.

"Did you see Bulma's outfit yesterday?" Natalia asks out of nowhere.

"Yeah! That hair is the best."

The bell rings as soon as we take our last bites. It's been a pretty pointless recess. It's time for art class and we get lost in the pleasant peace brought on by certain satisfying handicrafts. We barely speak until two. Color, cut, paste, see how it looks, paint a frame for it, cover it in little bobbles, scrape the shit out from under your nails.

Mom picks me up from school and we speed over to Grandma's house in the car. Mom leaves me in the living room, Grandma waves hello, Mom blows me a kiss, and through a window I see her pass by with her head held high. I run to the other window but don't make it in time. I listen to her steps fade as she hurries down the street. My stomach is churning.

"Come on, honey, sit down and eat. Your food's so cold you'll catch your death."

Lunch is good, as usual. I gulp it down steadily, watching TV. I was a bit sassy on the way here and now the silence is weighing on me. Sometimes I'm really hard on my mom for her bad jokes and her clumsy attempts at closeness. Then if she gets mad and curses me out I fall apart. And I don't know if I'm just slow to catch on, or if I'm being asked to be up to speed on too many things. I'm anxious. Mom gets a new kind of pill every two weeks. The drugs change colors and sizes but the look on her face when she tosses them all in her mouth at once is the same. For her it's an act of faith and resistance. For me, it sums up all the things we don't talk about. There's hope. Hold on. So I keep hoping and I hold on.

"Look, it's the ad for my perfume."

Grandma points with her brown, gnarled finger whenever she sees it. A blonde woman in a floaty white dress emerges into a huge garden and sees a swan gliding across a moonlit lake. I wonder what kind of fit of passion drives so many women to come flying out of their houses in these ads. Frankly I like them all, no matter how tacky, corny, and cheap they are. At least they're way prettier that the rest of the stuff on TV, so I watch closely even though I know the commercial by heart.

"Gloria Vanderbilt," Grandma says, lighting her first cigarette of the afternoon. "They've had the same ad all these years . . ."

"It's not the same one, they remade it almost the same. They just changed the clothes a bit."

"Really? Is that so."

We have this conversation often. What I like best about Grandma's perfume is that about once a year we take the bus to El Corte Inglés to buy a new bottle. The window displays glisten and I'm amazed by the variety of products for sale. The perfume itself is nasty and cloying, but it's familiar and somehow makes sense.

"Want to try something on, honey?"

"Try what on?"

"That palm-tree skirt. I've got it threaded and maybe I can finish it in time for you to take to Marbella."

I get up dutifully and go look for it in the closet full of half-made clothes. I find the patterned fabric. On the way back I stop in the bathroom to pee and strip down to my panties. From then on I act like a mannequin and keep watching TV with my arms held up while she works at sticking in a couple of pins.

"This is pretty much done, eh?"

"Really?"

"Run along to the mirror and see how it's looking on you."

I go to her room and check myself out. I flash my panties at the mirror, my only lover, then go back to Grandma with a skip and a jump.

"It's so pretty! I love it!"

"Of course, of course you do, see how talented I am? Come on, take it off and make sure the pins stay in place. And now do me a favor and thread the needle, cause the cotton slipped out and I'm as blind as a bat."

She'll definitely have enough time. Between this skirt and my Minnie Mouse pinafore there won't be much I can't handle. I love how it doesn't matter a bit that I'm in my panties with Grandma. It's the same for her. Ours is a comfortable scene, far from any kind of competition or violence. I don't want to leave this private little corral, but on the other hand I can't wait to grow up and see if I end up looking like one of the girls in the commercials, see if one day I'll escape from some awfully dull mansion at midnight and breathe in the pure woodland air. Sometimes I think nothing interesting will ever happen to me, that there's something wrong with me and the reason I have trouble making friends is that you can see it in me from the outside, no matter how hard I try to hide it. I remember Jesús, the first boy I liked in preschool. I thought he was my boyfriend just because I wanted him to be, a really convenient arrangement. I sat in the first row with the good little girls while he spent all day standing in front of us by the blackboard as a punishment. We never spoke, we never touched. I made sure I only got up a couple of times a day to sharpen my pencil over the trash can, brushing up against his clothes on my way past. I would crank the grinder and watch his little hands hanging down sadly. To tell the truth I can't remember a single thing he did wrong, but the fact is he ended up standing there over and over, quiet and still, black hair flopping over his listless eyes. I can't remember his voice either. The mood at preschool was pretty tense. We were so little, it was hard to understand who we were or what we were doing there. Come to think of it, I still haven't figured it out. Right when you start getting the hang of school, they pull out the multiplication tables and it just gets more complicated. At first, doing the work was satisfying, but it's getting boring now, and the rewards are fewer and fewer. And this is just the beginning. Growing up seems like a drag, you have to study so much. Whatever happens, I won't be allowed to get bad grades. I'd like to skip the mandatory training process and go straight to the part where I escape from the mansion, my hair blowing in the wind, fed up with stinking of white flowers. The closest I can get is looking at my hole in the wardrobe mirror. Grandma's still rooted to her chair. She spends all day there running the ship, and I know very well that she's not completely asleep, she's just dozing with one foot still firmly in this world. I get up quietly and tiptoe toward the bedroom. I drop my panties, open my legs, part the flaps with both hands, and muffle a giggle. Sometimes this simple act gives me a real boost. When I did it for the first time not long ago and saw the folds of skin open, covered in dark little hairs, my legs were shaky for the next two hours. Should I be thrown in jail for what I'm doing? This forbidden hole is my swan, my castle, a snare of trouble and delight. To tell the truth I don't know exactly where the hole itself is, so far all I've done is open the flaps, I still haven't worked up to sticking a finger in, and I don't know if it'll work like it's supposed to, but just getting a sense of the hollow in there is thrilling. As soon as I could talk, Mom started warning me about the dangers of this cave. She told me some men are crazy about touching little girls down there, and other places too, that you never know who's going to be into it, that they hide their intentions really well because they know it's bad, and that sometimes they'll coax you gently, then once you let down your guard they destroy you. She said I shouldn't trust any of them, just in case, that I should stay on the alert, and that if I ever got scared I should go to a woman for help, not a policeman, since a woman would definitely keep me safe, but with cops you never know. Even now she tells me over and over not to talk to strangers, not to open the door if I'm ever alone, and of course not to get into anyone's car no matter how many candies or toys they offer me. She wants me to take this seriously and makes it clear that if I get into a car with a stranger I'll most likely end up dead. People have been talking about those poor girls from Alcácer for months, and the grown-ups are always bringing them up so we'll stay scared. I think of my corpse showing up in an estuary, how upset Mom would be. I know I have to be careful with my hole. People lose their minds trying to get inside it. I've seen it in the movies, in comics, and on the TV news. These men like to fantasize, just like me, but some of them do more and actually go out to torture and kill. We kids are the juiciest prey. I want to get out of the danger zone, it's all too much. I get down on my hands and knees and look at my reflection in the mirror. I let my hair down and shake it a bit. Illegal pornography, for my eyes only. I've hoarded plenty of riches from this private black market. I need to stockpile material in case I end up at boarding school. I'd be cleaned out there; though if I can find a little mirror, I figure I can shine a light for myself. Things are definitely strict at the convent. I wonder why. I wonder if my future classmates are really bad girls, and if the whole thing might even be good for me since I'll get used to being around people. I'll have to make friends somehow. I'm sure I'll get visitors. They might even bring me gifts from time to time. I'll climb into their laps for comfort. Nothing's as consoling as collapsing into a welcoming lap. So, no, maybe it won't all be bad. I love the uniforms, and without Mom and Grandma watching maybe I can hitch my skirt up short, like other girls. And I'll get to play with the yellow wardrobe. Mom says they really take care of the toys they keep at the convent, all the dolls' tiny outfits are new and kept nice and tidy. And the mirror in the dolls' wardrobe was perfect, I could use it to look at my hole. And I'll take my own things along too, and they'll make the other girls happy. I go back to Grandma's living room, take out my colored pens, and draw three girls walking down the street in the convent's navy and gray uniform. The one with long, blonde hair carries a folder, the brunette with a ponytail has a backpack, and the dark one has her hair in a shoulder-length bob like the Chabel Cleopatra doll. All three are in profile. I've made them too snub-nosed, but I think the brunette looks a bit like me. I lean over the table, rest my head on my arms, and fall asleep like Grandma. The radio is tuned to Antenna 3 and wakes us both with a start.

"Fuck, is it five thirty already?"

"Yeah," I say, stretching.

"Well I have to go buy a zipper to match your skirt. Are you coming?"

"OK."

The fabric store is just around the corner. It's as boring as it is enticing. It's packed with metal shelves up to the ceiling forming narrow aisles full of products in cardboard boxes. I know the contents of all the aisles by heart and scan them for any new arrivals, paying special attention to the lingerie section. The customers take turns asking for what they want, with two assistants helping them from behind a long counter. There's always a big line. I don't get why the place is so mobbed at all hours. Or maybe the wait isn't as long as I think? Grown-ups tend to laugh and tease me when I get impatient, like my sense of time isn't legitimate. Every kid

I know thinks it's a nightmare to wait five minutes. In the end I focus on deciding which knee-patch I'd want if I happened to need one, and that's how I pass the time. I don't get through enough knee-patches for this to be any fun. Why am I such a scaredy-cat, I wonder? There's a ton of nice patches to choose from. We stop at the bakery on the way back and I pick out a Bollycao bar, which is the main reason I came along. Our little plaza is more like an alleyway that you get to through a gap between two stores, a shoe store on the left and a fruit stand on the right. We pass under the shoe store's awning and I raise my hand, brushing the fringe with my fingertips. At one point I was obsessed with touching that awning, like reaching a certain height was going to save me from some kind of ghastly horror. It's true that I felt more powerful the first time I stood on tiptoe and touched it. "The worst is over now," I thought. It was really tough not to understand so many things. It was hard to get used to. At least now I've got an excellent triceratops sticker, and I know all the tricks for getting it out of the wrapper without smearing chocolate on it.

When we get home it's time for *Baywatch*. Two days of full relaxation await me before the letdown of Monday. I give myself over body and soul to my passion for Shauni, relishing every second she's on screen. Then we watch the *Telecupón* raffle even though we don't have a ticket. It's cool to see where the numbers fall, and Carmen Sevilla leaves me feeling warm inside, like spending all summer at a country house. We kids like doing impressions of her, though the gag is starting to get a bit old. It's not her fault, we're just really annoying. She's gorgeous no matter what, like Concha Velasco, who I once saw a photo of, naked, holding an apple.

Sometimes you see them in old movies from back when they were young. If the movie is black-and-white they're polite and demure, but as soon as it's in color they start getting saucy. Carmen Sevilla at my mom's age with reddish hair and false eyelashes. Old Spanish movies don't do it for me, but the actresses do. They're wild, and they've always been so beautiful. They're irresistible. My weakness for them also means I can keep up with Grandma when she goes into a rhapsody about how talented they are. She lights her cigarettes like Sara Montiel. She's a great admirer of Juanita Reina, Estrellita Castro, Marifé de Triana, Imperio Argentina. Imagine calling yourself Imperio. And Argentina for a last name.

After dinner the neighborhood's quiet and we go to bed. Grandma takes her dress and petticoat off over her head and hangs them from the top corner of the mirror. I unfasten her bra and girdle – thick, hard, and flesh-colored. I crouch on the floor and roll down her knee-high summer stockings. She feels so comfy when I take them off that she always lights a cigarette to celebrate. She rests it in an ashtray and puts on her white polka-dot nightgown. I'm wearing a white nightie with a mouse on it.

"I started smoking at fifty because they said it helped you lose weight. Can you believe that?"

"Uh-uh."

"What they didn't tell me is that if you try to give up you get fat again."

"Why?"

"You get really hungry. You're desperate to shove something in your mouth. And you shove food in there instead of cigarettes. But my problem is that I also like to smoke."

"How can you like it?"

"I don't know, honey, I like to light them and stub them out, and there's something classy about the smoke. Ahhh!" she exclaims with a deep sigh and turns on the radio. Grandma listens to the same phone-in show every night. There are regulars, and she's hooked on hearing how their stories evolve, what new topics come up, who's calling for the first time, and who never calls again. It's a lot like watching TV, but somehow it's friendlier. Also more boring. Grandma provides a running commentary, but my mind wanders. I feel safe in this house, but I'm really lonely too. It's my own fault. If no one forces me to interact with other people, I prefer to avoid them, and then I complain. Grandma notices I'm kind of distant and reminds me between her last few yawns that it's not long until vacation, my baptism will be over soon, and she loves me very much. Then she lets out a fart and laughs and I laugh too and stick my butt out, but I don't have any gas. We say good night. She's already asleep and the radio is still on. I keep listening carefully to people's stories in the dark. Through the open window I can hear at least three other people breathing, including Tata and the disabled boy, but I think I'm the only one awake. The radio beeps twice and a show comes on that I've never heard before. I don't get what it's about, I just know that it's dark, grown-up material. What's the main subject? Anxiety? I guess it's not a bad idea to talk about heavy stuff this late at night and help tormented, sleepless folks all over the country feel less alone. But what I don't get is why it's mixed up with creepy stuff about ghosts. Why talk about so many possible kinds of worry at once? It's mean to rub salt in the wound like that. The callers take turns and get all worked up unloading their problems. The goodbyes are really awkward, no one wants to hang up, they're all miserable and need way more support and comfort than the host can give them. I wish I could lean over my enormous grandma and turn off the radio but now I'm addicted. Also, I'm terrified of silence. I hear the two-thirty beep. The host tells a tragic story about two sick girls in the hospital. Then someone calls in to say they can feel their mom's spirit in the house. I cover my eyes. I can't get to sleep until the early morning news starts. Grandma rolls over when she hears it and turns the radio off with a smack. When I'm finally about to embrace the sweetness of sleep, she asks if I want to have churros at around eleven. I say yes, happy to drift off at last.

When I get home on Sunday they force me to take a bath. I am not a fan of change. I've been taught to be ashamed since the day I was born and it's torture. I don't just mean I die of embarrassment whenever I think of showing my coochie for real. There are other things I find more disturbing. For one, as far as I can tell, there's something screwed up about the way we talk, me and lots of other kids. It's weird to feel like I can't say the word *coochie* in front of anyone. The other day I nearly had a heart attack when I said *fuck* out loud by mistake. Sometimes I whisper it, or speak through my dolls, but why can't I be free to say whatever I want? Where's the harm in words? Do you start out cursing and end up dead in a ditch? There's so much fear swirling around about me getting corrupted, I can hardly take a step without shitting myself. But I'm not sure how much of it has to do with the outside world. Until recently, I even thought *mother* was a dirty word. It made me uncomfortable just to think it. *Mom* was fine, but *mother* seemed totally out of place – enormous, filthy, and somehow unspeakable. I got over it, but I remember that phase well. Back then Mom and I were still bathing together. It was ages ago and doesn't count anymore. Mom started getting stricter and more demanding. I don't think it had to do with Domingo, and I don't think it was out of shame either. Her expression changed after she got her hair cut, like she suddenly got older and felt the weight of all of her problems coming down on her. She tries to hide how worried she is. When someone says hi in the street, she's immediately on her guard. Sometimes these people look surprised to see me. Anyway, once I'm in the bath I don't want to get out again. I want to add more hot water and stay here to live in the bubbles, washing my plastic ponies and eating a snack with my raisiny hands. So I throw the same fit about getting out as I did about getting in. Now I'm in the kitchen, hair wet, arms folded across my chest. The clock on the wall has been stopped since last fall but I'd say maybe it's eight in the evening. Mom wants me to eat a strawberry.

"No!"

"Try it, for fuck's sake. See how delicious it looks?"

"No, I don't care."

"But you'll like it."

"I don't even want to think about it."

"Look at this little red chunk, look how tiny it is."

To be fair, it does look good. I take it. I sniff it. It's fresh. It doesn't seem as gross as it did. It's pretty small. I have a nibble. It's good. I'm embarrassed about having changed my mind, but the joy of discovering a new pleasure is stronger.

"It's good!"

"See?"

"Yeah. More please."

Between the two of us we finish them off. How am I supposed to know who I am if I'm always changing? I soon feel tired and confused. It still isn't dark when I have my omelet on the couch and go to bed holding back tears.

It's Monday and I'm so nervous about getting baptized this afternoon that every little thing makes me jump. School is suddenly over, just like that. Mom came during recess and we went to the principal's office. This is my first time meeting the principal but she seems more up to date on my business than I am. She probably is. She was sorry to see me go. It's weird not to have said a proper goodbye to anyone. I thought the plan wasn't that firm, thought I was just going on vacation. Not leaving the school, not for good.

For some reason finishing early doesn't make me happy, much less finishing like this. I'd rather be the same as everyone else – I'd rather my life didn't have such an unpredictable, hectic pace. I'd like to have Mary Poppins as a nanny, not as a mom. Thousands of details get away from me, but my mom isn't like other moms. She's fascinating, like a fairy whose wings have been burned. There are bewildering gaps in her stories. There isn't a single photo of her from between sixteen and twenty-seven. Why not? Where did she come from? What's going to happen? What does it all mean? I can't keep waiting. It's unbearable.

"Mom."

"What."

"Are you sending me to boarding school with the nuns?"

"I don't know, sweetie, let's hope not."

"OK."

"Don't you worry about it."

The smile she gives me is as loving as it is sad. We're approaching a newsstand and I devour the covers of the dirty magazines on the fly. This gives me a burst of energy.

"Want some candy?" she asks.

"All right, a strawberry gummy, but I'll save it for later."

"Eat it now or it'll melt."

"I said no."

I want to save the candy for a special occasion and I squeeze it as we walk home. We pass a man on the street who makes a disgusting hacking noise and spits at my feet. The fright makes me drop the gummy, which lands smack in his gob of saliva. Mom speeds up and makes a sour face.

"Ew, that was gross, Mom."

"That'll teach you. You can't save everything in life for later or it'll get spoiled."

"But wasn't that gross?"

"Very."

"So then why are you blaming me? Don't you feel bad for me?"

"Yeah, but I feel worse that you're such a klutz."

"Jesus."

"And the next time you say Jesus I'll rearrange your face."

"But Mom, I want another gummy."

"For fuck's sake, no. And stop making that face, you look like your father."

It makes me mad that she blames me for looking like him

when it's more her fault than mine, and even madder that I can't see him in myself, that I don't know I look like him, since I can't even remember his face. I stay quiet until the next newsstand. Mom takes a coin from her pocket and buys another gummy in silence.

"Come on, let me see you eat it."

I scarf it down in three bites. First the green part. Then the fattest part. Then the bottom.

"Was it good?"

"Delicious."

"What do you say?"

"Thank you."

"Good girl."

People wonder how Mom gets me to be so well behaved. She's tough on me as a daughter, and as a person too. I don't think it's fair that she expects me to have so much figured out already. Five minutes later we're home. We have an early lunch. I have to get baptized in a few hours. Time for a twee outfit. They put a white headband on me to keep the hair out of my face and load me into the un-air-conditioned Renault 5. I also take my suitcase because tonight I'm staying with Grandma and tomorrow we leave for our vacation in Marbella. It's going to be a rollercoaster. Luckily we'll get the worst part over with first, and it won't last long. The only thing I'm looking forward to about the baptism is that Uncle Pepe and Aunt Amparo are going to be my godparents. The whole family is proud of Pepe because he's a successful pediatrician. I've been told this approximately eight hundred times, and on the drive over the subject comes up again:

"You know what, sweetie? When I got pregnant I was on the fence about keeping it."

"Uh-huh."

"But then I went and talked to Uncle Pepe about it."

"Uh-huh."

"He told me that if I decided to have you, he'd help me out with everything."

"Uh-huh."

"And he meant it." I pay no attention but she looks at me lovingly anyway. "You're the best thing that ever happened to me, sweetie."

"I know that already!"

"All riiiiiiight, don't get your panties in a twist. My point is, Uncle Pepe has always been really good to us."

"Yeah, I know that already too."

"Yeah, I'm sure you know."

"Know what?"

"Everything, right? Don't you know absolutely everything?"

"Come on, for fuck's sake, don't make the kid nervous," Domingo interjects.

"All right. Are you nervous, Marina?"

"No."

This time it's true. What I am is dying of embarrassment. There's a reason no one remembers their baptism. You get it over with when you're unconscious, only just born. At least there aren't any guests. I don't want anyone to see me make a fool of myself. Domingo tries to give me some moral support.

"We're going to a really old church."

"Yeah."

"A seventeenth-century temple. In honor of whom?"

"I can't remember."

"Come on, kid, make an effort."

"But I don't care."

"In honor of San Hermenegildo, the Visigoth king."

"Well, here's your gold star."

Domingo isn't the first boyfriend of Mom's I've known. Before him there were Juan and Pedro. Juan was a young widower with two kids, and all three of them were pretty adorable. The five of us only got together once. It was a long time ago. We kids were as quiet as mice. Juan stared at Mom like she was his only salvation, and looked at me like I was just another cute problem to solve. I even felt hopeful, so when I stopped seeing them around I asked how the story had ended.

"They were too normal, Marina," Mom told me. "They weren't our kind of people."

I laughed, but at the same time it made me mad.

"But why not? Why can't we be a normal family?"

"What can I say, he was looking for a mother for his children, the poor guy had no idea what to do with them. He was nice enough to me, but he looked at you like you were a sack of rocks, you know what I mean?"

"A sack of rocks? But Mom!"

"Look, we had tea with him a few times, right?"

"Yeah."

"Did he ever speak to you? Apart from hello and goodbye?"

"I don't know."

"Well I'm telling you he didn't, not even once. Do you remember anything he said to you?"

"No."

"Well, I don't either! All he could talk about was how to fix up his house and how much he needed a wife."

"Yeah. Well, OK."

"You understand, right?"

"Yes."

"It's OK, sweetie."

"Yeah."

A year later she introduced me to Pedro, a gentleman with money and a white beard. We went to his house in the country for a weekend and I spent most of the time in the kennel with a Doberman ten times bigger than me. It was an old kennel made of stone. Apparently they were searching for me for hours. I remember how good it felt to be in that cave, hiding out with the guard dog, who sometimes left and then came back to snuggle with me in the dark. I wasn't scared of anything, or cold, or hungry, or thirsty. Deep down I hoped they would never find me, that they'd give me up for gone and the Doberman would keep me safe. I'm sure he wouldn't have minded sharing his food with me. It's not that I turned my nose up at Pedro, but the dog was going to be my real dad.

I'm standing next to the altar, wanting the ceremony to be over, trying to hide the fact that I'm flustered and over-whelmed. The church is dark and cool. The light has an orange hue, and the scorching afternoon seeps in through the windows. In addition to my twee outfit, I'm wearing a brand-new poker face.

The priest is short, bald, and chubby. Luckily the ritual is designed for unconscious babies, there are only five people here, and I don't have to say anything. I tell myself it'll be over soon. Black holes slip into my train of thought, caused by my regret about being a bit sassy today. I should be more patient with the things I hate. I never learn. I stare at a stained-glass window at the far end of the church. Will it be beautiful when the water flows over me, or will it be more of a humiliating dunking? What does each option depend on? I hope my hair won't get wet. We'll definitely go to a cake shop afterward. Maybe they'll have ice cream. The priest holds out his hand, and picks up a silver ball on a stick with the other. Time to go up to the font. I tilt my head. A camera flash startles me. I have zero interest in seeing that photo, ever. The water comes in a sudden spurt. I can't tell if it looks nice but I don't care anymore. I stand up straight, overcome with an epic sense of relief. I turn around to face my godparents, who've also been my official guardians since last winter, responsible for me in the eyes of God and the law. Frankly, I think all these solutions are a complete load of garbage. I'm not feeling remotely calm. I put up a good front to keep people happy, but it's obvious that if Mom dies everything will go to shit. Uncle Pepe looks calm and reliable and smells a bit like his office, which I love to visit. He's not really my uncle, he's Grandma's nephew. He went to her wedding as a kid, in 1940. That's when he met her in her village, at twenty, smooth-skinned and lithe and always singing, colorfully dressed, and with a house full of dogs, cats, and birds. They gaze at me with affection, hug and kiss me, and give me a little medallion with an engraving of the Child Virgin and today's date. The smell of my loved ones makes me feel safe. I'll definitely never wear the medallion. Oh well. What matters is that I've gone from victim to sweetheart. That's the secret of religion. They scare the hell out of you then give you a pat on the back. The church door gets closer and closer. Dear Lord, allow this newly Catholic servant of yours not to face the altar again, because this will mean Mom has survived. You have to understand, Lord. You know that with her by my side I need no other gods.

Today, for the first time in my four years, I've come to the Cine Delicias with my dad. I've been here before with Mom. We saw *Snow White* here, just the two of us. All I remember about it is the old skeleton of a prisoner who died of thirst, which went straight to the engine of my train of terror. There was also 101 *Dalmatians*, which was sweet but confusing, and *Beetlejuice*, which was just a desert full of worms. I'm quite a scaredy-cat and find dark movies disturbing – though it's true that no matter how much light there is, I already make it my business to find darkness in the cracks where you'd least expect it.

This time it's different. I'm restless, cheerful, and extremely excited. I was at Grandma's for a visit and Mom let him see me because it's so close. I've never been alone with my dad before. He's wearing a white shirt, brown pants, and some hideously shiny tasseled shoes. He's affectionate but doesn't know me at all. It's weird to be four and have your dad not know you at all. Not that I know him either. I'm surprised by how big he is, the color of his hair, his voice. On the way, he sweeps me up off the ground and lifts me over his head.

"No!" I scream in terror. I don't like getting thrown around or being startled. Maybe other kids do, but he doesn't know me.

"You silly goose, I'm giving you a piggyback ride."

"No, please! No! Put me down!"

He doesn't know I'm shy and reserved, that it takes me forever to trust anyone. I almost feel like he's kidnapping me.

"It's OK, kid. You're going to like it, you'll see."

"No, no, I'm not. Put me down."

He doesn't get it. I've thrown him off his game. He just wanted to act like we were close, and most kids love getting a piggyback. But I hate fairground rides, getting dunked in water, going over bumps. I have enough to deal with already. I'm up by his neck, kicking and screaming and about to burst into tears, pleading with him to stop it and put me down already. He's become an enemy within five minutes, the kind who doesn't respect my wishes, who wants to force me to be like everyone else. He can't get it into his head, he won't give up. He insists I'm going to like it. Maybe he's right, but I'm desperate and when he tries to lift me again the vertigo scrambles my nerves and I kick him in the face. This time he does put me down. I'm sweaty and overwhelmed, standing in the street with a stranger I call Dad. He's completely miffed.

"What's the matter with you, Marina, eh?"

That's hard to answer. I feel like I'm hiding inside myself, all hurt and shy. I hang my head low and respond in a tiny voice.

"I don't like it. I told you already."

"But it's OK, nothing bad'll happen."

"I know that already, Daddy, but I don't like it."

"But why not?"

"How should I know? Not everyone likes the same things."

"But if you try it, you might like it."

"I don't care, don't do it again."

"All right, all right. Fine."

"Promise?"

"Yes, of course."

We're both bewildered. He holds out his hand and I take it. I'm still pleased that he's come to see me, that he's taken me out. The rest of the walk he asks simple questions and I cheer up. I watch him from down below and try to store up the details. I always forget what he's like between visits. We arrive. There's only one movie showing and it's for grown-ups. He buys me a bag of gummy worms and we go into the half-empty theater. We sit down. My dad and me alone in the dark. This is completely new. I'm practically climbing up the wall. I want to bounce up and down on the seats, crawl into his lap, let out hysterical little shrieks, whisper the word *Daddy* over and over, *Daddy*, *Daddy*, *Daddy*, *Daddy*, *Daddy*, *Daddy*. The movie begins. I have no idea what we're seeing. The opening credits roll. Some anemones tremble on the seabed.

"Daddy."

"Shhh, what's the matter?"

"Daddy, is this one scary?"

"No, settle down."

"But it looks scary, Daddy."

"No, no, Marina, don't worry."

"But it's making me scared."

"What is?"

"The music and the bottom of the sea."

"Really?"

"Yeah, really scared. I'm going to hide so the ocean can't see me."

I drop to the floor and stick my feet under the seat in front, gripping my bag of gummy worms.

"Marina, come back up here."

"No, Daddy, you come down here."

I peek out of my hiding place, grab him by the collar, and pull. I don't want the anemones to catch him and take him away. I want to protect him, want him to stay forever.

"Come on, Daddy, hide down here with me."

"Oh, no, Marina."

"But it's more fun this way, who cares about the movie, it looks boring."

"Come out of there and sit properly, we're going to watch it."

I don't know him any more than he knows me, and I don't understand him. It seems like he's into heights and I'm into hiding places. I'd like to keep pushing until he gives in but I suddenly don't have it in me and feel really sad. I do what I'm told. I chew my gummy worms and can't focus on the screen for more than five seconds. I look at him, hoping he'll look back at me in approval just like Mom usually does, that we'll somehow connect after all this time. It doesn't happen. He actually wants to see the movie, as if anyone could give a shit. As soon as it's over he takes me home and says goodbye in a hurry. I'm standing in the living room, clinging to Mom's purple skirt as she brushes my mussed hair out of my face.

"How was it, Marina, did you have a good time?"

"Yeah. Well, yeah."

"Uh-huh. If you don't want to see him anymore, you just have to tell me."

"No. Well, no. It's OK."

"It's up to you."

Grandma was looking dead serious when I came in but now she claps her hands and gets up.

"Well! Who fancies some fried eggplant?"

Mom and I look at each other. Canica wags her tail.

"Me!" Mom exclaims.

"Me too!" I squeal. Mom picks me up, plants one of her loud, wet kisses on my forehead, and all three of us head into the kitchen.

PART TWO

6

Once I'm baptized and fed they leave me at Grandma's house with my suitcase packed and a book for the vacation that starts tomorrow. I've never read such a long book before. It doesn't look bad, and I'm excited to move on to the big grown-up books I've been dying to stack on my nightstand, but this one's a reminder that I'm about to spend two whole weeks cut off from my secret affair with comics. Two weeks of pure childhood. Mom and Domingo aren't coming for the first week, that'll at least make things easier. I'll be sharing a small chalet with Grandma and three of her friends – Abelina, Felisa, and Felisa's husband Paco. Abelina is petite, cheerful, and elegant. Her white hair is always tied back in a bun. Felisa is tall and a little bit sassy, but last year she gave me a Chabel tennis-player doll for no apparent reason. Paco is the kind of meek and affectionate gentleman I always feel like climbing onto for a siesta.

The night before the trip we don't sleep a wink. Each time we try to drift off one of us gets the giggles. My elation about the baptism being over is combined with the fact that tomorrow I get my reward, a kind of honeymoon with Jesus. The feeling lasts until we board the train and collapse into our seats. The clatter helps us to finally relax. We have a ton of word puzzles to do on the way. I've known all four of these old folks for ages and feel comfortable with them, I can't imagine a better summertime gang. Old folks are friendly, we value each other. We make each other happy and watch the teens and grown-ups like we're making fun of how important they think they are. Our faction isn't fully involved in the world, we shelter out on its cushioned edges. From the age of eleven, you pay the price of your worldly passions. Then, once you're in your twenties life starts getting complicated, full of problems that need to be solved on the go. The only reason I really want to grow up is to see my body fully developed and learn how to use it. Will I be able to dance one day? Dancing in a disco with my friends. I'm looking forward to that. And to fucking. Of all the words I know to do with human sexuality, I think *fuck* is the most embarrassing and the most honest. Even though my dolls say *fuck* every day, we kids just say *doing it*, and we know exactly what we're talking about. Doing it. When I do it, when you do it – I want to grow up so bad and see what it's like to do it, to be able to do it with whoever I want. Whatshername's sister already does it with her boyfriend. Can you imagine doing it with Goku? It's still pretty far off, but it'll have to happen sometime. Sex itself doesn't scare me, but the process of getting to it does. I've been familiar with the tingling, the feeling people call being horny, for as long as I can remember. I may have a one-track mind, but I'm also a wimp. In my mind it's a perfect balance, but the reality is different.

"I've got some chocolate cookies and some peanuts in my purse, honey. You want any?"

I take two dolls from the backpack between my legs, pull down the table on the seat in front, and lay them on top of it. I've brought my blonde doll with long, wavy hair, and the dark one with straight hair halfway down her back. I like to dress them in the outfits they came in when we go on a trip, so the blonde is kitted out for a safari and the dark-haired one has a matching pink skirt and blouse. I make them do a slow dance, I'd be embarrassed if anyone saw me play too rough. I sniff the dark one's head and put them away carefully so I don't mess up their hair.

"Yeah, take them both out."

"But which do you want first?"

"The cookies."

Our three travel companions nod off while we chew. I've been eating whole cookies a while and they don't seem as dry anymore. Actually, they're really good. I wish it was easier to get used to new food. I know lots of kids who are really fussy about it. Maybe we'd be less finicky if we went a bit hungry now and then, but you'd have to be pretty mean to use starvation as a training method.

"Whenever I went on a trip I used to take a little notebook and write down all the villages we went through."

I nod. I've heard this story before.

"You know why I don't take it when we go to Málaga?"

"Because you know them from memory, right?"

"Yes. Want me to tell you?"

"OK."

The list is slow and sedative but somehow passes the time. We do word searches between one village and the next. The sun shines in through the windows and makes me even more drowsy, but it's fun to circle the words when I'm not quite awake. In the end, somewhere near Antequera, we fall asleep too.

We arrive in Marbella right on time for lunch. The little chalet is white with a shaded patio. There are two bedrooms. I'm sleeping on a fold-out bed, flanked by the two widows. I love the Workers' Resorts. They have a self-service dining hall where you can choose whatever you want. This puts my mind at rest. And it's fun to go through the buffet and decorate your tray with food. I like the same things as old folks, and savor the moment in the recreation room full of calm and contented retirees. I spread out my arsenal of crayons on a low table and catch Abelina's eye.

"What shall I draw for you?"

She crosses her legs, lifting her chin in thought. Her gold glasses glint in the sun.

"A house with a beautiful garden."

"OK."

I get down to business while they sit chatting in enormous armchairs, sometimes about really dull stuff. I go all in with the greens, sharpening them into an ashtray several times. I draw palm trees, firs, fruit trees, a fountain in the middle, a footpath, songbirds, clouds. It takes about twenty minutes. "For Abelina," I write on the back. I add the date and my signature. It's Felisa's turn and she asks for a vase of flowers. I don't usually enjoy drawing vases of flowers much but they're not too hard. Paco wants an ocean view. Grandma chuckles because she knows I'll give it all I've got. I love hearing their voices, the perfect stories they tell a thousand times over, how open they are to affection. Paco starts falling asleep before I'm done.

"I'm sleepy too," Abelina admits with a yawn.

Grandma takes a drag on her cigarette and looks at me. "Pick your things up, honey, we're going to have a lie down."

It's cool in the shaded patio, and there's a lawn. Grandma's wearing a red dress and I take her picture next to a rosebush by the path. She puts an orange flower in my hair and takes my picture too. She's tired and happy. In five minutes we're all lying down and taking the second siesta of the day. The fold-out bed was easy to open and we've set it up between the twin beds so I'm surrounded and won't get scared at night. The sheets are clean, rough, and cool. The blinds are lowered. No one speaks until Paco starts snoring and makes us laugh. It's always funny to hear someone snore for the first time.

"Is that how I snore, Marina?" Grandma asks.

"Yeah, pretty much."

Her laughter is so soft it seems to blend with her sleep. The atmosphere is more intimate now. I wonder if I'll remember this moment of intense relief among these drowsing old folks. You forget some things and remember others. I find the distinction unsettling. I never know what's going to last. I'm not so keen on the idea of having been born, but I do appreciate being aware of my existence. I find the dark years of early childhood terrifying. Back when I looked like a chubby doll I loathed going up steps one by one, but at the same time learning to do it one after another without pausing on each step made me dizzy. I remember the long, hard staircase and the exhaustion. And I remember the satisfaction of doing it well, but also knowing the road was long and had only just begun. Right when I'm getting good at more things, they start getting harder, and people demand more and more perfection. Does anyone really expect me to keep up this pace without cursing even a bit? Everyone in my family says whatever they want except me. It drives me nuts, but at least with my dolls it's different. Not that I can spout too many obscenities even when I'm alone. I've noticed that if you do you get used to saying things that aren't allowed, and then you're more likely to screw up at the worst possible moment.

All four of them are snoring now. I get up and head for the patio in my nightie. I want to touch the hot, reddish earth with the soles of my feet. As soon as I'm outside and the afternoon sun bears down on me I start needing to take a dump. There's a hard, dry turd in there, pushing its way out like a tank. I enjoy a blast of the shivers and a slight dizzy spell. I clench my insides even though I haven't had a shit in four days. I crouch down and hug my knees. I close my eyes, count to ten, then make a dash for the bathroom. I can't hold it in anymore. I hope it won't hurt.

I get up with a dirty butt, lean over the toilet, and take a look. It's an enormous turd, cracked, the color of copper. I did my best to let it out slowly and wound up unscathed. I remember the first time I ever had diarrhea. What a triumph. I wipe myself a ton until I'm satisfied with the result. When I first started wiping my own butt I used to try and save paper. I've often been told this is wrong and that you have to get it squeaky-clean, and now I take this task very seriously indeed. I flush. I go back to bed and run through the dialogues from the last comic strip I memorized from *Totem*. The secret shelf stuffed between my ears holds quite a few pages now. I need a certain amount of quiet to be able to dip into the archive, and right now I have more than enough. The main character in the story starts speaking. I won't have to get baptized ever again. The sheets are scratchy, the makeshift bed frame creaks, my insides have just come home from school and dropped off their backpack. Vacation is here.

We've taken a siesta and then freshened up. We're fragrant and looking classy for our first night in Marbella. We have dinner at a table with white chairs. The main course always hits the spot. Chicken fillet, potatoes, and a fried egg. I pay no attention to anything else until dinner is over. Now I fancy some dessert.

"Grandma, will you give me some money for ice cream?"

"Of course, honey. Go buy one and you can eat it over there with those kids playing table soccer."

I knew the pressure to socialize was just around the corner. I grumble. Abelina talks to me with a syrupy, dreamlike sweetness that extends as far as her voice and perfume, and is nothing like the atmosphere at the table game they're sending me off to. Just because kids are kids doesn't mean they're nice. In fact, children have an evil streak I'm constantly trying to escape. We don't live by any laws, it's like the Wild West. I can already tell they're going to be mean to me. I go into the bar with the money in my hand and ask for a Mikolapiz. I can't go back to Grandma without giving it a try, they'd only send me out again, and that would be even more awkward. I amble toward the table soccer, ice cream in hand. The players are teenagers, yelling, punching, and clapping at everything. A cluster of younger admirers has gathered round them. I lean casually against the wall in a corner and watch the game. I thought I could feel the crowd's mood shift when I started walking over, and now I'm sure of it. There's a tense and mocking silence.

"Where'd you get that dress?"

"My grandma made it for me."

They can't hide it anymore. This isn't exactly my favorite dress, but so what? I could make fun of plenty of people myself, but I don't. One of them does an impression of me, pretending to hold up an ice cream and making a dumb expression. He puts his legs together, stands as straight as a pole, and repeats what I said with pursed lips.

"My grandma made it for me."

All of them crack up. I don't know what to do. I'm already at a disadvantage because I look pure and naive. I have a white bow in my hair, a giant sailor's collar, and my skirt comes down to my calves. I don't even know how to play table soccer. I stare at the floor. I look at their sneakers and listen to the barrage of cruel and stupid jokes.

"No wonder your granny makes your clothes, you're a little old lady!"

"Old lady!"

"Get out of here, old lady!"

"Ew, no way we're playing with a little old lady. Gross."

I've got to get out of here as soon as possible. I hate the idea of turning my back on them but I have no choice. I walk like I'm crossing a flaming river, like my dress and my ribbon are made of sandpaper. I wish I'd remembered to wear my Minnie Mouse pinafore, I always forget how much these mistakes can cost me. I shouldn't have let Grandma choose my outfit today, even though I love it when she plays with me like a doll. It makes her happy, and I like not having to dress myself or do my own hair. I don't see why this has to mean I'm a pain in the ass to hang out with. I reach the table where Grandma is smoking a cigarette and sit down without saying a word.

"What, you're back already?"

"Yeah."

The grown-ups don't need to know it went badly, they'd only go and yell at the kids, who'd have it in for me even more next time I saw them. I have no intention of trying to talk to those assholes again. Or of ever wearing this dress. You little shits, if only you knew how often I fantasize about torture, if only you knew that if you showed me even a bit of affection I'd let you take turns feeling me up under my skirt. Totally free of charge, you little shits, I wouldn't even ask you for a bag of Fritos. Your teeth and fingers are all I'd need to make me smile like a fiend. All you'd have to do is be nice to me, just a little bit, I don't even need that much. I wish I could say all of this aloud, be serious and hold it together at just the right moment, but I don't have the guts and I'm terrible at answering back in time. When stuff like this happens, I imagine one of them realizing I don't suck as much as they think and coming to find me later to apologize for the fact that their friends are a bunch of twerps, then chatting with me about other things.

I climb onto Paco and finish my ice cream cradled in his lap with my eyes closed. No doubt those kids are still watching me and now I look even worse. Whatever. "Sopa de caracol" is playing on the night watchman's radio. Snail soup. At first

I thought it was a fun song, but now I've been hearing it three years in a row – it came out when I was barely conscious and it's like I've heard it every day of my life. Snail soup, my God, what a twisted idea, is there anything more disgusting you could eat? I've been told it's rude to say certain foods are gross, but seriously, what do you people expect from me? It's my fucking head, let me think in peace. Snails are not food. They're gross in a delicate, fragile way. The poor things are really weird. It makes me sad that they're so easy to break. I hate the way kids smash them up for fun. I wish other kids had only a thin, crunchy shell for protection, I wish they were super slow and had no way to escape. I'd put on Mom's high heels and shatter them like a batch of frozen croquetas. Evil bastards, we're all the same in the end. We kids are more or less aware that grown-ups bust their asses for us, and we milk our innocent appearance while we can. What else are we going to do? Childhood is a fierce struggle to get out of being a potential victim as soon as possible. Trampling on me moves them a few more centimeters away from danger. And I'm starting to get attached to my predators, precisely because they've been on my trail so long. I like to picture one of them as my ideal tormentor, doing to me what I most want done without having to be asked. I'd sooner trust a pack of wild dogs than a gang of kids playing table soccer. I wonder what this will mean for the rest of my life.

I watch my roommates' beauty rituals from the fold-out bed. Grandma puts a net on her head to keep her hair in place. Abelina undoes her bun, and I see her fine, white, waist-length hair hang loose for the first time. She brushes it gently.

She looks like Fauna, the green fairy in *Sleeping Beauty*. She keeps brushing for a few minutes, and when she's happy with the result starts braiding it into two plaits. I have a tingling feeling all over the back of my neck. All three of us are tucked in, wearing white nighties, books in our hands. Abelina has gone for a romance novel. Grandma prefers mysteries. I don't feel like reading right now, so I stare at my book, not seeing the letters, wondering what tomorrow will bring.

The light has been off for a while. The radio is quieter than usual, as a courtesy. Everyone in the house is snoring. I'm not complaining, silence would be worse. Grandma coughs, rolls onto her back, and lets an arm fall down to my head.

"Marina," she whispers.

"What."

"What's the matter, can't you sleep?"

"No."

"How about a bedtime story?"

"OK, slowly."

"All right, slowly. Which one?"

"The one about the seven young goats."

She starts right up, same as always, never changing a single word of the tale. She's told the same stories in the same way to all the children who've passed through her life. My family tree only has one branch. I can only conceive of this grandma, but there's another I've never seen. The picture of her in my head is hazy and I don't usually give her much thought. What's the point? I don't think I'll ever meet her. The wolf in the story wakes up from his nap under a tree with an enormous scar on his belly and a stomach full of stones. The stones make him thirsty and he goes to the river to drink, but he's so heavy he falls in and drowns. I love that part. And the ending too, when the nanny goat finds the littlest goat hiding inside the grandfather clock. The poor thing sees a beast devour all six of his siblings and stays in the clock for hours, frightened to death. It's a fucking awesome story.

"Now the half chicken one."

Half a chicken sliced down the middle, with yellow feathers on one side and guts hanging out on the other. Traveling around, putting enormous things in a sack. Where does this story come from? I love how she tells these brutal tales in her sweet and husky voice, which sounds even sweeter and huskier without her false teeth. And I love how she often starts nodding off and muddles the details, since she gives her last drop of energy to telling the story. It's been a tiring day, we're completely wiped out. Her hand is still hanging by the side of the bed. She snaps awake again with a grunt.

"Want another story?"

"No, it's OK."

"Don't worry, Marina. You know I sleep with one eye open."

"Yeah, I know."

"Good night."

"Good night."

The glint of the gold watch fastened tight around her wrist will be the last thing I see tonight. Five more seconds and I'll be gone. No, six is better. Let it be six.

We get up at nine and the cafeteria breakfast is amazing. Brioche buns, yogurt, ham and melon. I've never seen ham with melon before and it doesn't appeal to me, but I'm still excited to see it. We get to the beach at eleven, with all the gear. Two beach umbrellas, four deck chairs, a few bottles of sunscreen, towels, sunhats, a basket of tools for building sandcastles, magazines, cigarettes. Grandma's wearing a purple swimsuit with enormous flowers and Abelina is in black, her bun done up on top of her head. Felisa is shaped like a tube and wearing a dark-green swimsuit. They're all surprised that the topless foreign old ladies' tits are so dark. It's true that their blonde hair contrasts sharply with their delicate, burned skin, but the talk has a hint of scorn, and I don't like it. We burn ourselves to a crisp too, it's just that we cover our tits. Actually, mine are still out, and I've started arching my back when I play in the sand so it's harder to tell they're starting to grow. I never really like crowds, much less when I'm wearing a swimsuit. Lots of girls my age cover their chests already, and I keep wondering if I should start doing the same. Most of the ones who cover up are more flat-chested than me. Am I behind already? I think they do it to feel more grown-up, to encourage their tits to grow. But all this is no fucking joke. My nipples are bursting with pain and my pubic hair is starting to show at the edge of my panties. I wish I could be fully grown, a young lady already, and skip this whole awkward, embarrassing process. Since I turned nine, it just keeps getting harder. It's not too serious yet, but I've got to work out some solutions. What makes me mad is that I'm supposed to be ashamed when I think the shame has more to do with other people. It's a feeling they make up and force on you, pointed and cruel. Much worse than fear or pain. I wish I didn't care. Some women don't care about getting a tan. Mom says it's a bad idea to sunbathe too much and you should always wear sunscreen. That's not hard to remember. I take her advice with me everywhere. I wonder how she's doing. Yesterday we called her before lunch and talked for a while. She only asked me about the trip and the resort.

I'm going to make a sandcastle on the beach, then once I'm roasting I'll take a swim. I grab the bucket, the spade, the rake, and a floatie just in case. I lay it all out around me and start combing the wet sand. Whenever I'm at the beach and engrossed in building something, I get sad about the plastic fish I lost in Punta Umbría. I buried it like a dog so no one could steal it while I was busy, but then I couldn't remember where it was. I dug holes in the sand until sunset, when they made me leave without it. I thought I'd left a marker. I still get the urge to dig and look but I know it won't be here. Enough already, into the water, I'm tired of my body being on display. I step into the sea with a fury soon tempered by broken shells that stab at the soles of my feet. I try to go further in, splashing around, and get past two or three waves before the next one knocks me down. I stagger out, my back covered in scratches, face plastered with wet hair, and try to spot Grandma. I wave. I can't see her face, but her laughter floats over to me. She doesn't like swimming much but gets in the water to cool off sometimes. She stands and admires the view, the wind whipping her short gray hair. I go back to the sand, lie down in the sun next to Abelina, and close my eyes. Sometimes, when I'm wet and stretch out to warm up, I'm overcome with bliss and the blinding light makes me feel like less of a person and more of a cool, dark cave. The cave is peaceful, I can't hear the cries of the little kids on the beach. Felisa's voice filters in, returning me gradually to my surroundings. She's insulting the actor José Luis Moreno. I lift my head.

"Hey look, Sleeping Beauty," says Abelina. Her sweetness sends me a few steps back into my cavern of peace.

"Marina," Felisa calls me again. "Hey, Marina, how did you like the tennis doll I gave you?"

I sit up and take the bait.

"Ooof, I loved it."

"Did you bring it with you?"

"Yes."

"And you like it, huh?"

"I like it a bunch, there's a racket she can hold in her hand."

"How about that."

"Oh! And she stands by herself, without being held up or anything."

She laughs, contented. She's asked me this each time I've seen her since she gave it to me, and I don't ever mind. It's a fascinating subject. When we go back to the chalet I show her the doll.

Grandma shuffles over laboriously to my right, cigarette in hand. She stands next to me plump and upright, gazes at the horizon, and starts singing a romantic ballad in her gravelly voice:

> Gazing at the sea, I dreamed
> That you were here
> Gazing at the sea, I don't know what I felt
> But when I remembered you, I shed a tear.

She leans over to me still humming, her voice like little bells chiming.

"You have no idea what a hit that song was in 1950 or so."

"Ugh, 1950, I want to die."

"More or less. I must've been thirty."

She pretends to be shaking maracas and I smile, thinking of Mom, long-haired at thirty. I'm holding back floods of tears but I manage not to overflow. The lenses in Grandma's glasses get lighter as the sun fades. High tech.

My days with the old folks fly by and are all pretty much the same, full of uninterrupted freedom. No one put the idea of making friends with other kids back on the table, and I'm truly grateful. Since we got here, I've spent my time exploring alone, making sandcastles alone, swimming at the beach alone, and in the pool with Grandma, since there she'll get in the water. She takes photos of me with all the animals we see. It's turning out to be a nice break. I don't talk much but meet a whole bunch of cats and dogs and my butt looks white from sunbathing facedown so much. The old folks have been dressing up in more deluxe clothes this weekend, and putting fancier flowers in my hair. Tomorrow, Mom and Domingo take over Felisa and Paco's room. I'm looking forward to the cozy atmosphere, though their presence means more effort on my part in every way. My chalet-mates are cheerful and all dolled up and it makes me feel sorry they're leaving. The bright colors stand out against their dark tans and leathery skin. They have gold brooches pinned to their lapels, Paco's gray hair is slicked back, and the women wear red or pink lipstick. I'm wearing a white pinafore, a green shirt, and a headband. I take photos along the way, telling them how lovely they look. I won't care too much if anyone messes with me today. I'll know they're probably wrong.

From now on I'll have to talk better, act better, have better posture, eat better. I'll need to do some reading. All I've done with the book they gave me is think filthy thoughts and stare blankly at the pages. I recognize some of the words, but they're disconnected. I don't want them to think I'm ungrateful. I don't want to have to lie either. It would be pointless anyway, Domingo will tear through the book in two days and come find me to talk about it. The only solution is to read as much as I can tonight. It's two hundred pages. I'm not afraid of getting told off, I'm afraid they'll think I don't work hard at anything. If I'm smart and responsible they'll trust me more and give me more freedom. That's just business.

As soon as we get in bed I start feeling gloomy and the lost dinosaurs of *The Land Before Time* float into my mind. I try to resist this wave of misery and pick up the book, determined. It's really hard to pay attention at first. Too much information. It's dramatic but too clean. Boring, in other words. The dinosaurs stare at me with their long faces from the margins. But my opinion of the book improves when a stone comes to life and starts talking. I was planning to read two chapters, minimum, but the stone part is quite a surprise and I need to know what happens. The main character is a fatherless girl, and apparently the spirit of an old pirate lives in the stone. The story starts drawing me in because when the girl makes friends with the stone she's really being seduced by the pirate. They're getting attached. I imagine Mom choosing this book, knowing I'd fall in love with a stone too, if it spoke to me sweetly.

7

Felisa and Paco are going around the house collecting things and zipping them up, but I get to stay in bed. Grandma is going to the bus station with them. When they're about to leave I get up, run to give them a hug, then go back under the covers. The cheapest, most efficient goodbye. At around twelve fifteen I'm woken by singsong cries.

"Come on, honey, it's twelve thirty!"

"So?"

"So we're going to the pool."

"OK!"

I don't mind going to the pool instead of the beach since it's small and sterile and makes it easier to wait for our new chalet-mates to arrive. It's two o'clock and we're putting on dry clothes in the patio. They'll be here in a few minutes. The best I can manage is leave my hair wild and chlorine-soaked and put on something cheerful. I pick my palm-tree skirt and a white T-shirt that says "Costa del Sol." I lie down in bed, holding the book. It's a nice story but I'm not in the mood for something this wholesome right now. I need blood and guts, spread legs and pussies, torture, screaming. I get nearly all my energy from forbidden things, and the only way to break the rules in this place is by peeing in the water and relishing my own lawlessness by licking ice cream when no one's looking. My relationship with sin has improved a lot since we moved in with Domingo. If I owe him anything, it's the fact that comics showed up in my life. Who cares if we moved out of Grandma's house or bought a Renault 5. The main upsides are that Mom doesn't sleep on the couch anymore, and I have access to dirty magazines. That's all that matters. Things could be much worse. They could be just the way they are, but with all the tits under lock and key. I could be facing lean times at Grandma's, or anywhere else for that matter. If times were lean through all this, I'd have wanted to die already. The idea of death, graphic and gruesome, traps me like a chairlift and treats me to a string of infernal images that always pop up in the same order, never-ending, unstoppable, a train of terror. Here's the blonde in a blue dress getting raped, the head split in two, the giant walking teddy bear, the mouthful of shit, the pussy getting pounded, the splintered bone sticking out of a broken leg. Where does it come from, this train I've been riding for years? From comics, movies, news, smashed-up snails, or is it a mixture of everything? If I'd never seen so many disturbing images, would I ever have climbed aboard? But I'm drawn to disturbing images, just like all kids, so why do they turn on me, torturing me like this? I don't think the images themselves are the problem. I think it's the way my mind puts them together. As soon as I see something new it gets hitched to the back of the train. Then next time there are more cars to deal with. But all things considered, I still feel like it's worth it. If I don't pick one car to focus on now, the train will keep going round and round, doing laps on its usual track. I try to portion out the selection, soften the images. A blonde in blue would be just the thing right now, but I don't want to do anything nasty to her. All I want is a couple of minutes, one minute to decide how much she should look like Kim Basinger, the other minute to set the scene. I switch her dress for a white one and give her a high ponytail. Now she's ready. I talk to her, tell her not to be scared, that she's going to like it. She agrees and turns around. I tie her up against the wall and strip her. Without using my hands. Some days I've tried to appear to her in the shape of a man, a woman, or a cartoon, but what works best is when I come to her as a force that can mold her flesh, so I can see what happens without any interference. My invisible little nine-year-old arm in a gaping, juicy pussy works as an antiseptic for the sight of my mother greeting the women in the patio with exhaustion. She and Abelina are clearly very fond of each other.

"And Marina?" she asks. It's my turn.

"Over here!" I answer cheerfully. I remove my arm from the blonde, let go of the book, and step onto the scene, with the satisfaction of having committed the perfect crime.

We go straight to the cafeteria. Domingo casts a cynical, playful glance around the place. At the buffet he raises an eyebrow at every dish on offer, tray in hand, then picks all the worst-looking ones. Mom seems excited and happy and keeps giving me soppy looks all day. She loves the scene at the resort and the chalet. It's nothing special, but I don't think any of us aspire to much more. I have to admit I adore it here. First, they take a four-hour siesta while Grandma and I play cards on the patio. Then we show them around and take them to the swings and the seaside promenade. I'm a bit frustrated because the day is over and I still haven't had a single quiet moment with Mom. But after dinner she takes my hand and we go to the beach in the dark, just the two of us, to get an ice cream.

"What do you think of Abelina?" she asks as we take our shoes off and step onto the sand.

"I like her a lot."

"I bet you do. I knew you would. Have you seen her hair?"

"Yeah, I see it every night in the bedroom, long and white."

"Are you cold, Marina?"

"A little bit, but it's OK."

She wraps her arms around me. Please don't be dramatic, Mom. If you hold on and keep quiet, that means not all is lost.

"How come there's so much water in the sea, Mom? How can there be room for it all?"

"What can I say, sweetie. That's the way the world's made."

"And how come it doesn't overflow?"

"Well, it overflows all the time. What do you think those waves are?"

"Yeah, I guess so."

"Or hadn't you noticed?"

"Yeah."

I hang on tight to her neck.

"Remember the flood in Seville? And the day of the earthquake?"

"Yeah, of course. There's a book I love, I saw it in Uncle Pepe's office."

"Oh yeah? Which one?"

"One about massive disasters, all over the world."

"Wow, and what's your favorite disaster?"

"The *Titanic*. Well, that and the bubonic plague."

"The plague is the best. Can you imagine? Everyone dying, and knowing it'll be your turn any moment."

"Jeez."

"You know why it's called bubonic?"

"No."

"It's because when you caught it, these buboes appeared on different parts of your body."

"Buboes? Is that a real word?"

"Yep."

"Gross."

"They're like gigantic boils that get full of pus, then they burst and it all oozes out."

She tickles me. I kick and scream. The world is a cruel and unpredictable place. No one is safe. These days I'm heavy but she still carries me to the wooden walkway. We put our shoes on and go back. Even if I was blindfolded I could find her among a hundred thousand moms.

In the morning we go to the beach, and at four in the afternoon Domingo gets the idea to go for a stroll. He has a weird fondness for walking in the blazing heat. It's already evening in the chalet and I've been in the double bed with Mom since we came back from lunch. I hang around her like a meek little puppy. I haven't managed to sleep at all, I've just been watching the light change in the bedroom. She stirs and lets out a whimper. She's awake.

"What's hurting you, Mom?"

"Everything hurts, Marina, I feel like shit." She laughs.

"I'll give you a massage."

"Ooh, yes."

She lies face down and I start with her back.

"But Mom, what does it actually feel like?"

"Well, it feels like there's a bunch of critters inside my body."

"Critters?"

"Yeah, little critters that want to eat me."

"I'll get rid of them."

"Yeah? How are you going to do that?"

I knead her with both hands and start pinching big handfuls of flesh.

"See how I'm getting rid of the critters?"

She holds her breath. I pretend to be sucking the last folds of skin with my fingertips, removing the unspeakable microorganisms that are destroying her.

"Look, Mom. I've got them in my hands."

I show her my fists, shaking my hands in disgust and letting the illness fall to the floor.

"Ooh, Marina. Do it again."

Kids aren't any better than grown-ups, but the grown-ups like to think we are, that we're pure and full of magic. I summon all the fantasy this version of childhood can offer and cast my spell again on that body in its black panties. When Mom turns over and shows her tits I feel a bit awkward, but this is no time for silliness. She's getting eaten up by critters. I throw myself back into my nursing duties, remove each and every critter I can find, then shake them off me far from the bed. I pay special attention to her worn-out fingers, drawing the disease out through her nails. I keep going until the sun goes down and we have to get dressed for dinner. Mom is cheerful and relaxed. The treatment has been a success. I'll do it again at the same time tomorrow, when she's not expecting it. That'll make it more effective.

Mom is reading a magazine under her beach umbrella, and Domingo is reading a book. Grandma stands with her eyes fixed on the horizon. Abelina sits in a deck chair, legs crossed and arms stretched out. All four are smoking. The sun has been baking my pile of dirt for a while, and I've surrounded it with damp, packed sand from the shore. We're here early, for a change, and it's still a calm day at the beach. I'm really tanned, almost dark brown. My sandy legs glisten. The heat is smothering me. Maybe it's time for the first morning dip. I look up and make out a lone, slim creature skipping among the sparkling waves. I think it's a girl but I can't be sure from here. She has short, blonde hair and isn't wearing a bikini top, despite being taller than me. I stare at her, dazzled, short-sighted and squinting. I'm roasting so I go in the water and rinse my legs off. I'm not sure, but I think she wants to play with me. I get a bit closer, just in case. The wind carries her laughter over, and when a wave knocks me down, I send my own laughter back her way. Soon I'm as far out as she is, and together we leap over the same ripples of foam, with no need to say anything for a while. We dry off in the sun, smiling and panting as we watch each other. It's two o'clock, our families say hi and head for the cafeteria together. Her name is Inma and she's ten; she has an older brother, a younger brother, a dad with a moustache, and a blonde mom. I wonder how long it'll take them to notice that we're a bit weird, but they make such a tight, hard knot that there's no room for them to pay attention to other people. At lunch, they talk among themselves, flooding the space around them with information about their own lives. I guess they love each other, that they like being together and filling every gap with the scent of their flock. I don't talk much and pay special attention to how men and boys, women and girls, interact with each other when they're at ease. Big families are fascinating.

After lunch, Inma and I run off to talk about how we both like the liquid on top of lemon yogurt. She got here on Monday but we've only just met. We want to show each other our favorite spots in the resort and see how they look when we're there as a pair. We skip from one place to another, striking different poses against different backgrounds. We're both curious about the roundest chalet with the biggest lawn. I tell her about my two main kitty sightings. There's the lone Siamese cat's hiding place and the corner of the hedge where no one can see you. She shows me a bar with gigantic windows and sea views I haven't been to before, and a hole in a white fence you can fit your whole arm through. Before long we're on the subject of the Mama Chicho showgirls, and then we hit the key spots on the map all over again, singing and dancing and wearing our T-shirts like triangle bikinis, a fancy-dress trick Inma teaches me.

"Who's your favorite *Sailor Moon* warrior?" I ask as we pass the corner of the hedge for the third time. I think we know each other well enough by now for me to broach such a personal subject.

"Bunny," she answers, and I know right away that she gets bad grades and is confident, open, honest, and I'd even say popular. I admit that I'm drawn to Rei, Sailor Mars, but that

I'm actually nothing like her and in fact I'm just like Ami, the shy nerd who knows how to wield the power of water. She says she understands, she knew it the moment she saw me. I ask her how.

"Because of your glasses."

Of course. I'd also had a feeling I was dealing with a classic Bunny. We take the news calmly, reasoning that though Ami and Bunny seem really different, they're the first two to make friends in the series. I'd like to identify with Sailor Moon or Sailor Venus, since I also like them, but they're out of my league. I belong with the brunettes, and not because they're brunettes, but because they seem fiercer. Ami is really fierce, it's just that she carries it all inside her. Once we're allowed to go swimming again with no risk of stomach cramps, we run back to the beach, our T-shirts in our hands. We don't talk much, but play in a physical, frenzied way, something I really need right now.

By nighttime I'm exhausted but the excitement of having been able to hang out with another girl keeps my heart racing. Three days ago I felt like an old lady. This week I have a mom, a friend, a Siamese cat that lets me stroke it, and I've just finished chapter six.

The next morning Inma's family don't show up for breakfast in the cafeteria. I'm told not to make a big deal of it but can't think about anything else, I woke up really wanting to hang out with her again. But I'm happy anyway, she's bound to show up sooner or later, and I'll still be able to talk to her. Our time at the beach drags on. I'm getting impatient. The only thing that soothes me is being near Abelina. I watch her movements. Sometimes she makes a sweet but insightful comment about the magazine she's reading, or shows you a picture of a pretty dress. She keeps me anesthetized until lunchtime. I can never remember Abelina's connection to my family, and I've asked so many times I feel bad for forgetting again. I guess she's another friend from Grandma's senior citizens' social club. I went with her a bunch of times when I was little. It's kind of a saucy old-timers' club, though most of the women prefer not to mix with men anymore and just want to drink coffee and anisette and dance with each other. I also met Grandma's boyfriend back then, another Paco. He used to come over a lot and sit on the couch. He was tanned, with white hair. He was nice but I knew he would've preferred me to get out of the way. If there was something good on TV I ignored the hint; if not, I went off to the bedroom or the patio. His visits got more frequent, then fell off until he stopped coming. One night I asked Grandma what had become of Paco. She told me he'd wanted to sleep with her and she wasn't interested. Simple as that. He wanted more from her and she wasn't going to agree, so it fizzled out. I pictured old people fucking that day, and when I understood their two perspectives – wanting and not wanting – it made me sad.

Inma is at a table in the cafeteria with her parents and brothers. She lifts her right arm to wave and I see that it's in a cast. Everyone in her family starts telling the story at once. She likes being rough with her little brother, and this morning, while they were playing in bed, she did a somersault, crashed into the wall, and sprained her wrist. It happened just a few hours ago and the plaster cast is already covered in drawings and messages. Her life must be so much fun.

"What are you going to do now? Will you be able to swim?"

"I don't know, not much."

"The cast really suits you."

"Suits me how?"

I think it looks good on her. It's flattering and makes an interesting accessory, but I get that my opinion won't be too well received so I say it's because of the drawings, which is also true.

"Want to come to the pool with me? I'll be able to swim better there."

"Sure. Are you a bit sad?"

"Well, it makes me mad, but it's OK. Tomorrow I'm having a birthday party at the bar I showed you. You should come."

"Really? Tomorrow's your birthday?"

"Yeah."

"Are you turning eleven already?"

"Yeah."

The age difference makes me feel dizzy and proud at once. But I can't miss Mom's afternoon massage. We go our separate ways. Domingo heads to the pool with Inma's family and the old ladies. Mom and I go to bed. When I get to the room, I look for a way to keep track of time and decide I won't leave her until the shadow on the patio reaches the sixth tile from the sunny wall, and only if she's asleep by then. This mental contract includes the clause that if she falls asleep before then, I'll keep on with the treatment until the time's up. In fact, I prefer it that way since everything's easier when she's unconscious. She lets out one of her whimpers and then starts snoring.

Inma is waiting in the pool but she seems down. I guess it's hard for her to have a good time if she can't run free like she usually does. She quickly gets bored of talking and playing quietly. I feel guilty that I can't offer anything more, but then I get an idea so obvious that I'm mad I didn't think of it sooner.

"Do you still like playing with dolls?" I ask with the meekness my nine years owe to her almost eleven.

"Yeah, sometimes. It depends which dolls."

"They're Chabel dolls."

"Don't you have any Barbies?"

"No."

"I prefer Barbies, but I guess I don't really care. As long as they're not Nenucos."

"I don't like baby dolls anymore either."

"All right then."

I hope it's this easy to arrange a fuck when I'm older. Inma has made it clear in this exchange that she needs her games to be sensual not to get bored. She's about to suck on the last candy of childhood and step into puberty. I understand her and can tell things are about to change, that the bubble of fantasy around us is waiting to burst and spray soap in our eyes. But what makes me mad is that she looks down her nose at the past, like she's forgotten she was just as much of a person two summers ago. It bothers me how quick people are to trample those who were their equals just as soon as they climb up a notch. They build up all this unjustified hatred and then take it out on newbies who never did anything to them. It's vindictive. The worst part is I've probably done it myself and don't even remember. I can't choose my memories no matter how hard I try, no matter how much I want to capture what goes on in my mind and around me. Not to mention all the things that escape me precisely when I'm trying to pile up so much information.

The walk to the bungalow where my dolls are relaxing involves a certain amount of sexual tension. I usually say *chalet* since I think that's closer to what they are, but according to Inma they're actually bungalows and she won't let me keep using the wrong word. I had to check the spelling in one of the brochures in the reception. I wasn't sure if it was *bungalou* or *bungalot*. My money was on *bungalot*, which seemed vaguely related to the T in chalet. We've arrived.

"Where shall we sit?" I ask.

"Is anyone here?" she wants to know, coming in with her cast held to her chest.

"My mom, she's asleep."

"I think the patio's best. Bring everything out here."

I pick up my little stash and carry it over, not making a sound. I'm about to give this girl an imaginary smooch. I don't know what kind it'll be. She's eighteen months older than me, has two siblings, is on Team Barbie, has one arm in a cast, and categorically rejects Nenuco baby dolls. These signs of her wildness do not disappoint. She picks the blonde. She grabs the boy with the other hand and without further delay starts rubbing their heads together. She couldn't care less about the plot or their outfits, all that matters to her is smooshing one bit of plastic into another. I've never seen anyone play this rough, not even the kids in preschool. She almost seems a bit angry, and the plaster cast doesn't hold her back from inflicting gratuitous violence. The dolls don't speak or get

dressed or go anywhere. When I try to straighten one out,
she just charges on. Her injury doesn't slow anything down.
She's raping them.

"Hey, Inma, wait."

"What?"

"You're really messing up their hair."

"But they're better with messy hair."

"No, they're not better with messy hair."

"What do you mean they're not?"

"I'm telling you they're not."

"I'm going now. My birthday, Saturday at six at the bar!
Bye!"

"OK, bye!"

She bolts. Like a golden lioness in her prime, unable to
rein in her own energy. Sometimes kids communicate in the
most unexpected ways. Her weird goodbye doesn't bother
me at all. It was as practical and appropriate as can be. I sit
on the hot floor, comb the dolls' hair and put their hats on
them, the best fix for brutalized bangs. Mom appears in the
bungalow doorway in a swimsuit.

"Hi, Marina."

"Hi, Mom."

"Did Inma come and play with you?"

"Yeah."

"And how was it?"

"Good."

"What does good mean?"

"It means good, more or less."

"Why?"

"Because she was really mean to my dolls."

"You don't like that one bit, huh?" she laughs at me. She has a sassy kind of charm when she's just woken up that's hard to resist.

"No, Mom, I really don't like it."

"Not even a teeny bit, eh?"

"Not even a teeny bit."

"Sweet Jesus, how did I end up with such a fussy little girl."

"Well, that's how it is."

"It's OK, sweetie, it's good to take care of your things. What I don't get is why you're such a mess when it comes to everything else."

"Enough already."

"And do you want to go to her birthday party?"

"I think she only invited me to make up the numbers."

"And what does that mean?"

"OK, all right, I want to go."

It wasn't a big deal but I can't help feeling sad and let down. I grab the pirate-stone book, sit on the floor, and arrange the dolls next to me with their hats pulled over their heads. Life is full of crude twists and turns. I leave it all behind for the other world, where every night I sink deeper roots, and feel relieved right away. I can't tear myself away from the book even to go to the patio and eat the fish Grandma just fried for dinner.

It's Saturday. I got here a while ago. I was expecting a gang of ten or twelve friendly teenagers, but there are about forty people at the bar – big brutish men, big brutish teenagers, and moms with squawking babies. I came by myself and it's like I'm a ghost. Almost no one knows me, no one speaks to me, and no one sees me, but I'm trapped here body and soul until the party's over. I sit down in one chair, lean in a corner, order a soda, drink it in a different chair, then finish it in the same corner as before. We sit by the windows with Inma at the head of the table and sing. I hold a balloon and wave it around. Her family turns amber as the sun sets over the sea and a booming "Happy Birthday" makes the windowpanes shake. Inma's dad takes out an enormous camera and aims it at her as she blows out the candles. I smile at the lens, posing stock-still so I don't mess up the photo. Inma puffs, lifting her cast in the air in triumph. Then I realize the contraption's a video camera and when they watch the movie at home they'll see how retarded I look. I've never even seen a video camera, how was I to know what it was? I'm glad I came anyway, even though I wish it would end. I'm curious about normal families and how they mix in this shallow way with people, so often and with so much ease. Are they always this frivolous or are they especially happy today? This much sheer joy must be pretty rare. I think they'll remember today with a sweet kind of sadness. They're on vacation in a nice place, one of their puppies is getting over an injury, there's a cool breeze and a beautiful sky. I don't mind being part of this memory. I'm feeling relaxed. I gave Mom her massage before I came over, and I have a dark tan that makes me look healthy and sturdy even though I haven't touched my slice of cake. I'd rather drown than let a spoonful of custard pass my lips. They'll understand when they see the video. Retarded ghosts don't eat custard.

I still wasn't sure about the party when the time came, so I said they should pick me up at around eight, just in case.

Sometimes other parents won't let you leave unless they can hand you over to a designated adult. Not today. They brought the cake out at seven and I've been waiting for half an hour, watching the sun disappear over the sea. Domingo appears. I can tell it's him by the way he walks when it's hot.

"How goes, Partner?"

"Good, but it's really loud and the cake was a bit of a letdown."

"Was it disgusting?"

"Yeah, pretty disgusting."

"Disgusting how?"

"Like, slimy-disgusting."

"I'll take care of it."

"The more you talk to me, the weirder everyone thinks I am. It's driving me crazy."

"What can you do? People are quick to judge."

"Yeah, true. How've you guys been?"

"Good, nothing new, just that your grandma gave me an earful for taking a book from her nightstand."

"Well, that's fair enough."

"It isn't either, goddamn it. At this stage you'd think the old lady wouldn't begrudge me something like that."

"But if she lets you take her books you end up messing them up or losing them."

Domingo laughs. "Yeah. Maybe she's got a point."

"I don't get why you go out of your way to annoy her. She likes lending you books, she just wants you to take care of them and give them back."

"I don't know, I think it livens us both up a bit."

"Livens you up?"

"Yeah, doesn't it? It's funny when she gets mad, and it's probably good for her health. Rejuvenating."

"Come on, you don't even like her books."

"They're nearly all total garbage, that's what makes them so great."

"They make you laugh, right?"

"A whole lot."

"No wonder she gets mad."

"But you sort of understand my perspective, right?"

"Yeah, and I understand hers too."

"Well then. Truce."

We march back at a military pace. I tell people Domingo is like my dad, who I don't miss at all, but that's not true. It's just so I can look strong, so my family won't seem weird, so I can give the impression that Mom's done a great job and everything's fine. But though Domingo's nothing like a dad to me, I know he's an improvement on most of the dads I've seen, starting with mine. Maybe if I'd spent more time getting to know my dad it would've been different. Maybe other kids have a sense of belonging in the lap of a stable, nuclear family, and that makes up for their dads not being perfect. Domingo and I are already as close as we could be, we've both made an effort to find ways to be friends, but at the same time something always keeps us apart and we end up hitting a wall. We might be on the same team, but we're vying for attention from the same coach – my mom. Obviously, he'd rather live alone with her; I'm just an interesting nuisance that was part of a package deal. It's the same for me. But it's naive to think this couldn't happen in other homes. I've seen it with my own eyes. Parents who hate each other, rifts between them and their kids, breakups, punishments, stupid demands, a total lack of understanding. But when you fantasize you picture the best-case scenario, that's the whole point of fantasies. When I see families in the movies I get sad, especially anything to do with dads, siblings, or grandpas. I can't accept that I'll never have them, I'm always choking back the frustration. I guess everyone has stuff they have to come to grips with in life. I mean, a lot of families don't let animals in the house, and if they do, sometimes they're not allowed on the couch or the bed, and you can't give them a kiss, and if they break something they get a beating. There must be kids who turn green with envy when they see cute dogs on TV, and that never happens to me. But when I see dads, siblings, or grandpas, but mostly dads, I feel a void in the pit of my stomach, that hollow kind of hunger that won't go away no matter how many ice creams you eat. It happens to me with snow, on a smaller scale. A Christmas scene on TV, the family all bundled up, the twinkly lights, the snowmen with carrot noses. Sure, it looks perfect, but Domingo is right: you can't let the movies hypnotize you, no matter how pretty things look. They're just peddling a cheap dream. Snow can be fun all right, he says, but then you realize it's freezing and dirty and the cold cuts right through your hands. I've never sat on my dad's lap, just like I've never seen snow, but I know people who live in the north fantasize about southern summers like it's all an oasis of palm trees and happiness, when at the end of the day it isn't much more than a dried-up puddle filled with poor frogs dying of thirst.

When we get back, Abelina is packing her suitcase on the bed. I don't want her to leave. I go over and tell her this, channeling all the afternoon's nerves into the sheer fabric of her dress. She lets out a tuneful bleat and presses my face to her belly. Grandma's in the bathroom but we can hear her gushing about the sweet Siamese cat prowling around outside. I recognize the smell of the product she's using and the sound as she pats it onto the areas in need, reaching beneath her boobs, into the folds of her armpits, and between her thighs. I'm wearing my Minnie Mouse pinafore and my hair is loose. Mom's just showered and put on a white dress. She takes my hand and we leave again.

"I'll bet you didn't like the cake and you're starving."

"Yeah."

"Come on, let's go get an ice cream."

"OK."

She has a camera in her purse and suggests we stop at the swings, where there usually aren't many people. This makes me happy. Until now only Grandma has taken my picture, and each one seems to capture a different girl. The version Mom sees is much more charming. If she does end up dying, these portraits will help me remember who I was. I pose in the little wooden house, on the swing, and on top of the slide. My mouth is covered in chocolate and I give her a toothy smile. There's something indecent, hilarious, and pathetic about my smile. Last year I broke my left front tooth playing statues in Tamara's living room. I realized I was about to beat her little brother and felt triumphant, drunk on my own success. Tamara counted to three and turned around looking passive and subdued. I leapt forward with so much force that I slipped and saw the floor rise up to meet me. Two bloody chunks of tooth bounced across the tiles. Tamara's brother picked them up and we ran to the bathroom mirror to inspect the damage. None of us really got what was going on, we just knew it was weird for a tooth to bleed. I shrugged and they walked me to the door. Alberto handed me two clean pieces before I left.

"Here, I've got the pieces, in case they can stick them back in."

"Thanks, Alberto."

Tamara and Alberto's grandparents never found out what had happened. I trudged up the stairs to the third floor. It was a Saturday morning and Mom opened the door and gasped.

"Marina, sweetie, how could you split your lip again?"

"I don't know, Mom, I got overexcited playing statues."

"But what happened, why don't you ever protect your head with your hands?"

"I don't know, I always forget!"

"Let's see, show me."

I opened my mouth as far as it would go and looked at the ceiling.

"Jesus, does it still hurt?"

"A little."

"I'm calling the dentist."

Putting my hands out to break my fall and protect my face has never been my forte. But that day, I felt especially cursed. The sight of a smashed-up mouth is always a turnoff, and this was already my second scare. First I'd messed up my milk teeth; now I'd broken one of the most important permanent ones. The first time, I was five. It was nine fifteen in the morning and I was late for school. There were no kids left in the courtyard and I was dashing to class with a knapsack on my back, a chocolate doughnut in my left hand, and in my right hand a drawing I wanted to show my teacher. There were two steps up to my classroom, the perfect number for me to trip on the first and split my gums on the sharp concrete of the second. I remember weighing up my options as I fell, I remember my hands in the air, I remember deciding not to squash my breakfast – even though I knew that brand of doughnuts tasted like Play-Doh – and not to ruin my work of art, but to sacrifice my little face instead, mainly because I thought nothing in the world could be less important than my face. A tiny but powerful section of my mind was secretly curious, and didn't want to intervene but passively accept the course of events. It compelled me to injure myself, not out of some perverse inclination but out of a strong thirst for knowledge and experience. It all happened so quickly. There was no mirror that time, just a lot of blood, then pain that came over me little by little and spread nonstop. I was terrified the agony would only get worse. I picked myself up with my precious, blood-stained objects, and struck out alone across the courtyard, perfectly poised and dripping with red. I walked down the corridor, opened the classroom door, and tried to speak, but my mouth didn't work. The other kids got up and came over, eyes popping out of their sockets, reaching toward me like I was some harmless ghost. The teacher flew into a panic and led me to the faucet where we washed our hands and got water for crafts, telling me over and over not to swallow the blood and trying to shoo my little classmates away from the scene. They called Mom at work. Tensions ran high and as class began I was still spitting blood into the sink. The kids

145

stared as I bent over, hiding my suffering, and the teacher's voice quavered like a custard tart. Forty minutes later Mom showed up, screamed blue murder, dragged me out of the classroom, and cursed the people in charge for not calling an ambulance. I wonder how I looked at the time, no one let me see, not even the doctors. I had no idea until they showed me some X-rays at the hospital. They handled it well, laughing at how you could see two rows of teeth through the split upper gum instead of one – the milk teeth hanging down, and the permanent set peeking through the gaping flesh. They told me I looked like a shark, which made me less scared. When I showed them how brave I was they seemed proud of me. Nothing makes me feel better than that. I like doctors. I like them so much that when they examine me and patch me up, their gentle, soothing attention makes up for all the pain. I hate the world enough to not want to stick around, enough that the idea of getting deathly ill and living out my final days in the harsh, cold surroundings of a hospital actually sounds pretty good. Physical pain is the only pain that counts, so part of me is always happy to hurt myself; I've already been wounded by the world, so why shouldn't someone who knows the body inside and out get paid to give me comfort, ease the affliction gnawing away at me? But I never fake feeling sick, not even on Sunday nights, and when I'm sad I put on a brave face and try to look strong. My smile is taking forever to heal. In photos of me there's always a weird, bright-pink patch, crisscrossed with taut and lumpy scars. They took me to the dentist and gave me veneers that lasted just a few months, until I bit into a really crispy fried potato and they fell off. Just like with my dad being gone, I don't really care about the gap, but I can't quite stop caring about it either.

I try to look sweet and obliging on the swings, though some people think it's uncool to do what your mother wants. It doesn't matter, barely anyone's looking. We're about to leave, and we're both consumed by this sappy longing that's hard to put into words. She's going away tomorrow and I don't know where she'll be or what they're going to do to her, but they're going to try to make her better again and she doesn't want to let on that it's necessary. She doesn't want me to see her unwell, or go to the hospital. I wish she could understand that I'm not remotely afraid of hospitals, but it's like when other moms say their kids can't watch a French kiss on TV. There's nothing to be done. But the thing is, you can see a French kiss lots of other places, whereas I'm not going to the hospital because no one'll take me and that's the end of it.

The film runs out with the daylight and we go to dinner. We stop by the squat little bungalow to pick up the rest of the gang, and the place seems prettier to me than ever. The table-soccer kids have been replaced a few times over, but they're all as bad as each other and I know they're pointing at me, saying I'm the biggest freak they've ever seen. It makes sense, they saw me reading on the beach this morning, now they're seeing me reading at dinner, and on top of that I can't stop kissing my mom on the cheek. Hate me as much as you want, it's all the same to me. Now I have only two goals. The first is to finish the book before we get back to Seville. The second is to find the right time to give Mom her last massage, so she can leave with seven instead of six. I doubt

147

it'll change anything, but that's how I want it to be. The kids pass by our table and look down their noses at me behind the grown-ups' backs. What's your deal, tough kids? Too old for a Minnie Mouse pinafore?

8

Six of us rather than five go home from Marbella in the car, Mom and Domingo in the front and the other three of us in the back, with the unexpected company of the lone Siamese cat on my lap. Grandma decided to keep him, on impulse, at the last minute. On the way back, we stop in the village where Mom was born. I'm always excited to go there but it never lives up to my expectations. I've heard so many stories and idealized the place so much that there's no space left for what it's really like. This is where my grandparents lived without a toilet, this is where they raised a cat called Noni who lived to twenty, this is where they laughed and cried. I'd like to come here and for it to be 1950. The grown-ups order coffee and sweets. I know by now that the chocolate milk in bars is not to be trusted, so I usually order juice. I vary the flavors and I'm so used to them being gross that they're not gross to me anymore. Actually, with a chocolate cream roll, this thick, lusty peach nectar is pretty tasty. The drive is slow and boring with Mom at the wheel. But it's also nice, I guess. She's never in a hurry, it's exasperating. The trip constantly gets interrupted. She needs to stop all the time. To cool off, to smoke, to have another coffee, to go to the bathroom, to check out some sunflowers up close. I have a good time on

149

the drive, except when they start arguing up front. Then we in the back exchange glances that say we feel eons away from problems like that. There haven't been too many squabbles today. By the gap between the shoe store and the fruit stand, Mom promises she'll bring more toys soon, and good news about her health. I didn't get to give her a last massage, to get the last critters out. Her skin is taut and she hasn't got many wrinkles, but I know she's completely worn out, obsessed with providing for me. I don't know when I'll see her again. The feeling I get when I see the car drive off knocks me sideways. Two weeks in Marbella with those loyal old ladies aren't the real summer. It all begins here: my shadowy hide-outs, my steamy adventures, seeing the future come toward me from inside my lair. Based on her own experience, Mom thinks growing up with Grandma leads to ruin. She knows it's my vice, that if she died I'd rather be shut away here forever, that's why she'd prefer to leave me in stricter hands. Abelina's gone. What I'll miss most about the last two weeks is her sweet, soothing voice and the swish of her polka-dot dresses. And I'm a bit mad at my book. I finished it at around four in the morning and all my satisfaction at having got to the end was drowned in a sadness I wasn't expecting that felt like losing a bunch of friends or being abandoned by my true love. I don't even want to look at the cover. All I want to do is watch TV and dip fried potatoes in egg yolk and not think about anything. During dinner, though, the characters in the movie we're watching get onto the subject of death. I still don't fully grasp that I won't always be trapped in this prison called childhood, that at some point I'll grow up and have to face even worse problems. I feel dull and cranky, like a blank chalkboard. I keep belittling the characters' suffering and Grandma frowns. She looks affronted.

"Hey, honey, less of the teasing, OK? This stuff is serious."

"What, death?"

"Yes, of course, death."

"But everyone has to die, right?"

"So what, if everyone has to it doesn't matter?"

"I don't know."

"Well, when you're nine you don't think you're ever going to have to die."

"But Grandma, I thought you weren't afraid of dying."

"Wanting to have a good time is one thing and not caring is another. Get it, smartass? Even people who commit suicide *care*. And what about the people they leave behind?"

I keep my mouth shut. I wasn't expecting a dressing down, but it doesn't surprise me either. No one's free from this horror. One day I'll fully understand all of life's conundrums. Sooner or later I'll see this woman die. That's life and she knows it. It's easy enough to see, even from where I am, that all the adults I know will have to die. But what about the babies at Inma's birthday party? In theory, they'll see my generation die, when my classmates are old and tired and scattered across the world. And there'll be more babies, year in and year out. I'll only overlap with some of them for a few months. They'll see a part of the future I'm not even prepared for. Will I ever be a grandma? Will anyone see me die? I can't imagine raising children and letting them see me on my deathbed. Who says dying alone isn't better? How many people have families as life-insurance policies? Why is everyone obsessed with not dying alone? They never stop talking about the Persian Gulf on TV. I don't get the situation no matter how hard people try to explain it, but I can't help thinking about the war movies I've seen, the atomic bomb, and the train of terror that runs me down, brings me a taste of every torment I'll have to face if there's a barbarian invasion. Being a member of the latest batch of kids doesn't make you immune, though our lives are so uneventful in terms of physical violence that people think we're humanity's greatest hope, like not having been starved and being forced to go to school is going to make us all into superheroes. This cheap training is no kind of privilege, we kids all hate it. Being good or bad at things makes no difference, it's all the same shit. We try to be cheerful since we have no choice and we know what's in it for us, but seriously, this isn't the way. We feel like they're wasting our precious time, like our brains are being colonized by a bunch of second-rate bores. That's why I feel so much for rebellious kids, even if sometimes they pick on me. Deep down I get them, I'm on their side. Getting the best grades in class just means I'm the most fired up, the one who's really itching to burn the school down. But it's hard to fight back. They take all the good things we had away and fill the gaps with useless trash. They break down our defenses. I'm afraid I'll run out of space in my head. They hardly teach us anything useful that might help us figure life out, understand each other, deal with each other. All they do about that is step in when a fight breaks out and ask who started it. Look, I want to get out of the system as much as anyone. I just toe the line because I know there's zip on the other side. Mom has been there and come back to tell me how tough it is, how people abandon you, go after you, punish you. I've figured out that teachers sometimes talk nonsense, that they don't actually know all that much, even if they mean well and make an effort to treat us kindly. A lot of the information they give us is random and confused, you can't count on it. I do what I'm told since I think the system has to be beaten from within. Teachers are never too well prepared and it's easy to follow orders, to learn how to satisfy their whims. I'm obedient but don't want to forget what I already know. When I start running out of space in my head there's going to be trouble.

The movie on TV gets harder to follow, until it's too much and we change the channel. There's a talk show starting, one with two sides that spend the whole time discussing things. But today they're talking about love and that's always fun. Grandma and I join in loudly and say what we think, like a couple of extra panelists at the table.

"That's not true, you can't be that shitty!" she yells. Sometimes we agree and sometimes we don't. We're stubborn but we always hear each other out, and sometimes we even change our minds. The panelists discuss things like passion, affairs, and seduction strategies, and the debate is soon full of sexual content. Since I'm with Grandma it doesn't matter a bit, we're living our lives so far from the world of flesh we're immune to it.

"Grandma, do you think you were good in bed?" I ask after a few seconds' thought.

"What do I know, honey, that's not something you can know, the people I slept with would have to tell you."

"Yeah, but I can't ask them."

"True. It's too bad, honey. Your grandpa would've liked to meet you."

"Yeah, you think so?"

"Of course, honey, you're so smart."

"But why would that matter?"

"Well, it would've made him happy to see how bright and what a good girl you are, but you also have what he had."

"What?"

"I don't know how to explain it — you think a lot. Not like him, he was so tormented, but in another way. You're quick and sharp in a way I don't think he ever was. You get things. And your hands remind me of his somehow and I'm not sure why."

"My hands?"

"Yes, delicate and pretty like that, the way you move them when you're nervous. I think they'll be like his when you grow up, but don't pay too much attention to me."

"And did he think a lot too?"

"Did he ever. Maybe because he wasn't right in the head, poor thing. It started to show in his face. He was always handsome, but when he was twenty he was a quiet, good-looking boy, and then the other, darker side started to show."

"Right."

"Your poor grandpa, honey, he wasn't well, we all went through so much because of him. Times are different now, you know? If he'd been twenty or thirty today, I think things would've been different. Think of what they knew about people's heads in the forties and fifties. They didn't know a thing."

"They know a lot now though, right?"

"Of course, honey, and they'll know a whole lot more one day. Back then people's heads were a mystery. They didn't know a thing about making them better. There were the

154

people who sent you to the priest so he could get the devil out from inside you, and the people who sent you to the nuthouse for electroshock therapy, God damn them to hell."

"What's electroshock therapy?"

"Something nasty they did back then if you weren't right in the head. A dirty trick that left you worse off than you were before. It was a shame, honey, but don't you worry, they hardly do it anymore, and if they do it's different and they do a better job. Plus it would be very unusual for it to happen to a girl like you."

"OK."

"Poor angel, with the doctors these days it would've been so different for your poor grandfather. He was so unwell and it all ended so badly. But he wasn't a bad guy, he was just in a muddle, you see what I'm saying?"

"Yeah."

"He used to say he could sing like Joselito, who sounded like a goldfinch, and one time when we were very young and we'd been married nearly a year, I was making myself a flamenco dress for the village fair – it was a really pretty dress, you know how I've always made pretty things, and it had a high neck, all done-up like this, and dark brown. You know how I've always liked bright colors, but at the time I was terribly modest and I thought now that I was a married woman it was more decent to be discreet."

"Why?"

"Because I was very naïve and silly, and I didn't want anyone to have a reason to badmouth me. And one day your grandpa comes along and sees me sewing that awfully drab dress and he looks at me like this and says, 'Who's that flamenco dress for, Marina?' 'It's for me,' I said, with my sweet little lips. And he asks me, 'And how come you made it so plain?' and I tell him, 'Oh, I don't know, honey, I thought it was the right thing to do since I'm married.'"

"And what did he say?"

"Well, he answered, 'Look, Marina, if you like the dress as it is that's all well and good, but if it's about what people might say, what do you care? Tell me something: If we hadn't gotten married, what kind of dress would you make yourself?' And I answered him right away, without even thinking about it, 'Me? Scarlet and with a low neckline.'"

All grandmas say scarlet instead of red. It makes me laugh. Her belly wobbles gently.

"Back then I only weighed fifty kilos but I've always liked the same things."

"And what happened?"

"I made myself a scarlet dress with white polka dots and a neckline that showed my cleavage, and I wore it with a green shawl my cousin Pepita lent me, and we went to the fair together and had a wonderful time. And you know what I did with the dark-brown cloth?"

"No."

"I made myself a skirt that was tight around the hips and pleated at the bottom that I wore with a yellow flowery shirt, and since I was nice and dark it looked ever so pretty on me."

I stare blankly at the TV while she lights a cigarette, pleased with the end of her story. I try to peer into the forties to see them stroll arm in arm through the fair, Grandma with a cinched waist and plump cheeks, curly black hair at her neck, the ordeals of childhood behind her, still childless but with a big family, taking care of lots of animals. There are only a couple of photos left of that hazy time. The memories are in color for her, but I can't see them no matter how much she describes them. When she thinks about all that, she can picture the fair exactly, and her dress, and my grandpa before he wasn't right in the head. Grandma looks at me and stubs out her cigarette. She's thinking of saying more.

"Now I'll tell you something. When I was widowed I was very beautiful. Look, get up for a second and hand me that coin purse on the table by the couch."

She wants to show me a photo she keeps tucked away. I've seen it lots of times, but I get up and pass her the purse. She takes out the photo, puts on her spectacles, and caresses it.

"Look, honey, no wonder I had plenty of suitors. What do you say?"

I look. Her hair is backcombed and her eyebrows are penciled in, like a country girl's. Her slight smile has a hint of mischief, a bit like the Mona Lisa's. Now she tells me about her second husband.

"Around that time I met Manuel at the bus stop. He was crazy about me as soon as he saw me. I was off to a house to do some sewing and we started chatting to pass the time. And then at some point he said, 'Miss Marina, I've been thinking. Here we are, both widowed, and frankly I don't like being alone.' When he said that I saw it coming, see how quickly it happened? He was still being so polite, but since the subject of how sad it was to be widowed had come up already, well, he didn't want to wait."

"Yeah. That's pretty crazy."

"So he says, 'Life's no fun when you're alone, and I'd like to spend the time I have left with a pretty woman like you. What I most enjoy is taking the car and going to the countryside, and I have five dogs. What do you think?'"

"He won you over with the five dogs."

"He was very simple and a bit of a brute, but he mentioned the countryside and the dogs, and since I could tell he was head over heels, I thought it seemed like a fun idea. And he said right there that if it went well, we could see about getting married and all the rest, and I told him that seemed all right to me. And you know what?"

"What?"

"Two husbands are better than one. I always have both of them with me right here."

She shows me her ring finger with two gold rings that look almost the same, one for each husband, and plants a kiss on them both at once. She takes off her spectacles and goes back to the matter at hand.

"Anyway, honey, the point is I don't know if I was good in bed, but nobody ever complained, that's for sure."

"But you didn't talk about those things, right?"

"Not much, as I recall, but I was always enthusiastic, d'you know what I mean?"

"Yes, yes."

"But the enthusiasm's all gone now, at this age I just want to do my own thing."

Now she has a revelation, claps her hands in the air, and cries, "I know what we'll call the cat!"

"What?"

"Felipe!"

Talking about fucking must've made her think of Felipe González. You're never too old for Mr. President.

I've had a hellish night imagining a gang of Persian Gulfs running rampage through my school, delirious from the sound of the radio and the stifling heat, the cat pressed up against me. I try to focus on my excitement about getting to see Canica, who's been away from us for more than two weeks and has no idea what's going on. Now we're in the waiting room at Animal Advocates, which offers boarding and grooming services. She's upstairs, where they've been giving her a trim. Two weeks of being held hostage and on top of that they give her a bath and cut off her hair, poor thing. I wonder if she's scared. I can hear her paws tapping hysterically on the floor above. Grandma laughs, she knows the dog's been let loose and is thrilled to hear her voice. Canica charges gleefully down the stairs and comes over barking and leaping, running around in circles, ears back and tail wagging. She licks our faces.

"Oh, poor little Canica, poor, poor little thing," Grandma comforts her, stroking her head. Being recently shorn makes her joy seem a tad pathetic. She looks like a different dog. We put on her leash and go out into the street. She can't believe her luck. On the way we buy churros and two bags of kibble, one for dogs and one for cats. We pass only old people. At this time of day the best cartoons haven't started yet, I'll even get to see some of the ones I usually miss. It's nice to get up early in the neighborhood. If only I could do it in a good mood every day.

It's after three thirty, I'm not sure if it's Thursday or Friday. Maybe it's Monday? How could I lose track so quickly? The dog and cat hit it off as soon as they met and spend all day curled up together, napping. The most blistering heat of the year has settled into the houses, making everything perfectly still. It's unpleasant and even unsafe to be in a rush. Time drags on. Lunch is laid out on the table, the blinds are down, the living room dark, the fan on a chair. Someone comes to the door. Grandma gets up and opens it. There's a woman telling a long story that's hard to hear with the TV on. She must've come to collect the maintenance fee or the water money or the latest Readers' Circle book. Grandma asks her to wait a minute and goes into the kitchen. The woman steps furtively inside. Without making a sound, she bends her knees and reaches an arm down to the coffee table. Now she sees with a start that I'm sitting here and locks eyes with me. She smiles faintly but warmly. Maybe she knew me when I was a baby? I get that a lot. She's acting suspiciously. A force radiates from her eyes and smile, making me freeze. She grasps something on the table. As soon as she closes her fist the look on her face is transformed. She can't get out of here fast enough. She retreats to the door, hunched over and walking backward. She gives me a last sweet look before slipping away without a word. Grandma appears in the living room with a glass of water.

"Where's the woman who was just here?"

"I don't know, she left."

"Didn't she say anything?"

"No, who was she?"

"I don't know, she came asking for money and said she was sweltering and, oh! My coin purse! She took my coin purse from the table!"

We look at each other, stricken with terror. A thief came in and looked me right in the fucking face without blinking. The door's still open. Grandma closes it quickly.

"And how much money was in it?"

"None, I'm just sad about the photo I showed you from when I was fifty, back when I was so good-looking."

After the shock has passed there's nothing much left to say, so we have lunch. It doesn't come up again until six, when Grandma takes her fan and goes off to the hair salon. She wants to look good for when she gets her picture taken for a new ID. She loves having an excuse to go out and run errands. I've only ever seen her be lazy about making the bed or cleaning the kitchen. It's time to poop, and I long to look at the label on Grandma's conditioner, but she's taken it with her so they don't charge her extra for any products. It's the same one she had back when Mom and I lived with her. There's actually tons of it left – by the time it runs out I might be fucking, and that's forever away. You don't see labels like that anymore. I love it. I'm kind of obsessed with it. I probably won't be fucking until the next millennium. I'll be sixteen in the year 2000. Centuries are a big deal, which one you get has a major effect. Most of my life will happen in the twenty-first century, weird as that sounds. This is just an in-between chapter, the last one for old people now, and a dark prequel for the kids who've just been born. I've been told over and over that time moves slowly when you're young and then it starts zipping by like crazy. Is that for real? Does being a kid take longer than being old? Why couldn't it be the opposite? That would be more relaxing.

I've just wiped my butt when someone pounds on the living-room window. Either someone wants to mess with me because they know I'm alone, or it's Lucía. It's Lucía. Finally, Lucía.

"Come in, hurry!"

"No, Marina, you come out here!" she calls and then vanishes, laughing, not waiting for my reply, a string of kids of various ages trailing behind her. What does it take to be popular?

I put on my Minnie Mouse pinafore and go outside, wondering what kind of elegant whimsy she's planned for us today. You never know what's going to happen with her. The little plaza is hopping, full of moms and their broods. Everyone looks free and easy and cheerful, so it must be Friday. Lucía is standing in the middle of a ring of people, singing a song. She's eleven and she's been wearing the same blue pinafore since she was six. She's tall and thin and the skirt is shorter on her than ever. Her skin is really tanned and her lips are red.

"Are you wearing lipstick?" I ask, and everyone laughs at me.

"Here we go again!" Lucía cries wearily.

"What's the matter?"

"My mom gave me a kiss on the lips and everyone's asking me the same thing."

Her diva act is so convincing that no one dares to argue with her, to interrupt the captivating flow of her performance. I accept the tale meekly and try to get up to speed. My social skills aren't exactly at their best. So her mom kissed her on the lips? I still haven't been kissed on the lips. Not by anyone. I don't think I'm the only one in this crowd who feels that way. Lucía's stories have a hint of perversion about them and the smut is on the increase. If she stays a while I sometimes get lucky and we end up alone in an entryway. When she shows up, everyone treats her like a princess, but then her suggestions get a bit twisted and people start leaving. There've been times when her familiarity has been too oppressive even for me, and I've had to run away. But we always come back and she knows it. We make her feel like a witch with a magic pleasure wand.

"Want me to show you my panties, Marina?"

"What, I don't know, OK!" I answer.

"She's not wearing any panties!" the others yell, collapsing into another fit of giggles. Lucía finds it so funny she falls on her butt, and explains from the ground:

"I didn't have any clean panties today so I wore one of my mom's bodysuits."

She undoes her shirt buttons and shows me. It's navy-blue lace and matches her pinafore. You never know if she's telling the truth or just spinning out some fantasy to thrill her audience. I admire her style but sometimes she makes us feel bad. When we were little I thought we might be alike when we grew up, but we're not. These days she treats me like a baby most of the time. I prefer Natalia's manners a thousand times over. They're a world apart. But when Lucía gets really feisty she sometimes masterminds truly epic games of kiss-in-the-ring, and even if I end up wimping out, I always want to be there for the beginning. She's a warm and imaginative friend but the problem is that when people give her a lot of attention she gets drunk on fame and it makes her insufferable. We haven't seen each other since November and her talent for lying has gotten out of control. She rubs our noses in the fact that we're just kids, when she's only eleven herself. I'd like to have someone to count on, someone I could see often, someone to talk to. But with Lucía, it's always sporadic and rushed.

Now she's sitting on a bench telling whoppers, who knows why. The littlest kids stare at her, jaws hanging open. She says she's been granted powers by aliens, that she was born on another planet, that she can't feel cold or heat. Maybe some of it's true? She definitely has some sexual experiences under her belt. I don't think they have much to do with losing her virginity, but they're definitely really, really filthy, filthier than regular fucking. What's the point of virginity anyway, it's just a cheap fetish, right? I haven't had many opportunities to experiment and I've usually failed. I would be dying to keep going but then I'd get crippled with shyness, something held me back and made me say no. When someone gets their butt out I can't help laughing, it's like all my other feelings get cut off. Are they being censored? Have I been programmed to react like this? Or have I just not been in sync with the playmates who've propositioned me? Would my body work if I liked the way they came on to me more? The first time, the boy was nine and I was four; the second, the girl was six and I was five. I had a couple of streaks of good luck but since then it's been like a desert. I'm always hungry for it, but when opportunities appear, I hide. I have a feeling a bunch of boys like me but none of them ever comes over to me, and when I go over to them nothing happens either. Maybe it's all a misunderstanding, just fantasy and lust. But sometimes I also wonder if pouring my deepest longings into comics is what dries me up. They give me such relief from my social frustration, but maybe they're getting me into a vicious cycle. Comics and magazines with tits are generally inoffensive, I feel lucky to have them around, but often I'm scared to turn the pages because if the next scene turns out to be really cruel and nasty my eyes burn and it's like they're melting, and when they drip, it stains the pictures forever. But when the stories are appealing, my body short-circuits, my heart beats faster, I stroke the pages, sniff them, suck them, look at them up close and from far away, and feel like I'm about to come. Not that I know what that feels like, but I get the general idea and think it must be a bit like this. People in my generation are either boring dimwits or Machiavellian pigs. I don't know where I fit in. I guess my place is in silent rooms, and there must be lots of others like me, holding their breath alone, without anyone knowing.

Grandma appears in the gate to the street, hair stiff from all the spray, hands on her hips.

"Ah, you're here. I'm going to buy candy, are you coming?"

I get up and run over. When I reach her she asks if I've noticed how pretty she looks. I say yes and we go to the store and buy orange, lemon, peppermint, and Vampire candies. Grandma puts it all in the plastic bag she's using to carry the eighties conditioner.

"I bring the conditioner because if I don't they want to use the one at the salon and charge me two hundred pesetas for a little glob like that, see? Absolutely not."

"Yeah, I know."

"I've told you that already, haven't I?"

"Lots of times."

"Well, now we've added another for your collection."

After dinner I'm the first out on the street, leaning against a water tank on one side of the little plaza with two dark-haired, well-dressed dolls in my hands. I think it's all the kids' favorite spot on this street. It's the perfect height to work as a stage for us. Playing at shop-keeping or bartending here and putting things on top of it is strangely enjoyable. It's also really dark here at night. I wish I could get far away enough not to hear the neighbor ladies, but I'm not allowed. I do the dolls' hair and arrange them around the metal padlock, listening to the ladies chatter about really boring stuff.

"Do you like ironing?"

"Yes, I do."

"That's lucky!" several exclaim all at once.

"Yeah, it's really lucky, cause no one else likes it, right? And it's the chore I like best of all. Cooking, though, I really don't like."

The ones who love cooking now laugh proudly. Grandma's in the same camp as the show-off chefs. On the other hand, she's not very tidy, something I'm grateful for. She doesn't mind that I'm disorganized and lazy too, so it's win-win. We never fight.

Lucía comes over in the dark and jumps the wire surrounding the water tank.

"So you came down early," I say.

"Yeah, I came down with Poppa and Nana, they're going to dinner."

She points to them and shakes the skirt of her pinafore. She moves with speed, skill, and verve. She puts her face up close to my dolls and looks them over.

"You made them so pretty."

"You like them?"

"A bunch."

She's in a good mood. We're alone. I can't believe my luck. I pluck up the courage to say the bravest thing I can say out loud without choking.

"Do you want to play with me before the others get here?"

She makes an impish face, a face some have never seen, but which certain others have seen a lot more than I ever could. How far will her mischief go? I'd do anything to be able to watch, to be a fly on the wall. Within a few minutes, the dolls are grinding against each other. When it comes to this, Lucía has always helped me give vent to my urges. She's already pretty bored of toys and has a different kind of hunger, but we're still on the same level with dolls, and together our fantasies unfold like the colors of the rainbow. It's obvious to her that this is important to me, that I'm relishing it. So she shows off, makes me cream my panties, and feeds her enormous ego in one fell swoop.

By the time more kids start showing up we're breathing fast and have to cut things short to start a game of hide and seek, the only one we can enjoy when there's a wide age range in the group. I've just crouched down to hide near where the neighbor ladies' chatter is coming from, and I relax my butt to let out a fart I've been holding in since we were over by the water tank. But what I feel coming out through the hole isn't gas, but something hot and runny. I touch the fabric of my pinafore at the height of my butt. It's moist. I've shat myself. Just a little. That's all I need. Luckily it's dark and the party is breaking up. Lucía is still playing but without much enthusiasm. The little ones get sad, feeling abandoned in their innocence. She's leaving tomorrow and I don't know when I'll see her again. It's truly annoying to never have anything planned. I can't really say I like her all that much, but Mother of God, I miss her a lot when she's not around.

9

There are some stores I don't care to go to at all and others I always want to visit. The bakery is excellent in more ways than one, but in general it's just a question of whether I like what they sell, like at the sewing supplies store, and of whether the people who work there are nice to me. I get hooked on anyone who can give me a tingling feeling. You have to practice making yourself receptive. Some people get a kick out of offering kids what I interpret as consolation for having been born. When I feel it coming on I try to loosen the bones in my neck and let the strange breeze blow in. Once the channel is open it starts spreading upward, and from there it flows into all the other places. The best place to be is mid-current, but you never know where it's going to show up. These people are like a ray of light shining through you. I pay a lot of attention to the way they cast the spell, to its recurring patterns. I've noticed it can start as an interview or as a tutorial. The grown-up notices you, shows genuine interest in you and your situation. They try to get to know you without any cheap drama; they're sincere and give you the best of themselves. It happens a lot at the doctor's, that's why I like getting sick so much. You don't just get to skip school – a prison covered in colored cardstock and the little white handprints of kidnapped children — they also take you to see an expert, someone who examines you carefully, tells you how to get better, helps you stay alive. It can also happen at the bakery or at a neighbor's house, it just has to come from someone sensitive who you don't know all that well. The first time anyone hypnotized me like this was in the little plaza at Grandma's, in front of Block 5. I was sitting alone on the ground when the daughter of a really grouchy old neighbor walked absentmindedly out of the door and saw me. She was about twenty, had smooth blonde hair with a fringe, and was wearing jeans, boots, and a leather jacket. She spoke to me like she'd been in love with me for months, and finally there I was, right in front of her.

"Hey, hello."

"Hi."

"You're Marina, right? Like your mom."

"Yeah."

"What are you up to?"

"Nothing, looking at some sticks."

"Looking at some sticks, huh?"

"Yeah."

"And what are you doing with them?"

"Arranging them from smallest to biggest."

"Ah, of course. Looks like you're doing a great job."

"I think so."

"Do you know what my name is?"

"Yeah," I answered.

"Oh, really? Let's see, what's my name?"

"Your name is Amor."

I knew this because someone had told me, because I used to watch her when she passed by, and because when her mom held court in summer I always listened until she mentioned her daughter. There have always been two young women in the plaza who can send that same shiver of well-being down my spine, even though we almost never run into each other. Amor and María de la O. I've spent lots of time taking note of their white-magic ways, in case I can use them to give solace to children in need when I grow up. Will I inherit the powers of a fairy godmother?

Amor smiled, sure of the power of her enchantment, and kept asking me simple questions while she adjusted the gears on her old blue motorcycle. I remember her hair glinting in the noon spring light, and the precise movements of her hands, like it was my vertebrae she was adjusting. As the tingling rose, the questions got more personal but stayed classy. What kind of toys do you like, what are you best at in school, what's your favorite color, your favorite smell, your favorite food? Can you ride a bike? Do you like churros? Nesquik or Cola Cao? I answered her, meek and calm, immersed in a completely new and refreshing sense of well-being, blinking slowly, savoring the feeling of every millimeter of bone caressed by her confident voice. Being by her side infected me with her self-assurance, made me feel as perfect as her. She was in no rush to leave, she touched her cogs without hurrying, turning around often, brushing her bangs aside to keep looking at me. Though her voice was soft and low, it crossed the several meters between us and reached me clearly. I didn't want the moment to end, but after a few minutes she stood up, said goodbye with another smile, wheeled her motorcycle to the plaza's entrance, started the engine, and went off down the road. The time had slid by in slow motion. I closed my eyes and focused on the memory of her, how she looked and the words she used, trying to hold on to that tingling feeling. I knew if anyone showed up and spoke the spell would be broken, but I got to stay alone, sitting on the ground, bathed in sunlight. I was entranced and grateful. I lay down like a cat next to my stick collection until Grandma peered out of the window and called me in for lunch. Sometimes, when I'm nervous, I think of Amor and run through this memory from the beginning. Her motor-cycle is still there, broken-down, half abandoned. But now the phone is ringing and I run over to answer it.

"How's it going, Marina?"

"Hi Mom. Good."

They're still talking about the war on the news but the drought is starting to get more attention. My stomach is pretty much the same. Last week all the mailboxes had stickers of faucets with fat drops of water dripping from them, inside a red circle with a line through it. Summer has lost what was left of its charm. Time is taking forever to pass, the days melt away, my wait gets longer. The only upside is that the street is empty till evening, and I like the feeling of having it all to myself, at least at first. But the novelty soon wears off, and the quiet doesn't make up for the sizzling heat. I switch the phone from one ear to another every few minutes, blowing on the hot and sweat-coated plastic while I'm at it. Mom's in the hospital, that's where she's calling from. I'm not supposed to worry, things are going according to plan.

"Mom, was it this hot when you were little?"

"Well, I'm not sure, it's been a long time. But this heat is something else."

"I'm boiling."

"Yeah, me too."

"Really?"

"Yeah, it didn't bother me too much before. Now I drink water all day."

"Yeah, it makes you really thirsty."

"I remember one other summer when I had a really hard time with the heat, when I was a bit smaller than you. You know that photo where I'm with my friend Nati in María Luisa Park?"

"Yeah, with the pigeons."

"We were both wearing dresses as short as fuck. There was an east wind, and we could feel our heads getting burned and the heat prickling our arms."

"I've seen it a bunch of times. You're both squinting."

"I remember looking at the camera, being that size, peeping out of that little body. You understand what I'm saying, don't you? I haven't always been a grown-up."

"Yeah, but sometimes I forget, it's like that time never existed, it's really hard for me to imagine. Doesn't that happen to you with stories from before you were born?"

"I don't know, maybe a bit. I hadn't thought of it like that."

"The time from before doesn't count, I don't know why, just like it doesn't count after you die. It's the same place for me. I think of the sixties and there's something I can't understand, it's like being told stories from the year 3000."

"Right. But the thing is, you do remember yourself when you grow up. You know more and you're older, but everything else is pretty much the same."

"But what's up with that, Mom, how come so many people seem like they don't remember anything? When do they forget?"

"I don't know either, I wonder about that a lot."

"Those people are a drag."

"You don't know the half of it. And they're not just a drag. A whole lot of them are assholes too."

"I think they say they can't remember because they were naughty as kids and they'd rather make like it never happened."

"You think so?"

"Yeah, and I think they decide beforehand, so they can have a free-for-all and then say, oh, how was I to know, I was only a little kid, and kids always get forgiven, and their moms get taken in by all their little Bart Simpson faces."

Mom holds the phone away from her ear to say something to Domingo, who's there with her in the room. I imagine the bare, white cell with metal equipment and an uninspiring view out the window. I was born in that hospital and that's what I think it must be like, but no one's let me go back to check. I've been told that my dad couldn't stop telling jokes while Mom gave birth, and that he was really funny too. She remembers some of the gags but I've never heard them first-hand. I partly have myself to blame for missing those jokes. It's not like there was some disaster and my dad just vanished, it's that no one invites him over anymore because they realized his company wasn't good for me, that it made me sad and a little bit angry and loopy. The last time I saw

174

him I tried to hide how upset I was, but it must've been pretty obvious since a few days later I heard Grandma and Mom in the kitchen talking about it. I guess it was to be expected, since he always showed up unannounced – he specialized in making promises he never kept, and even though I looked forward to seeing him, all this stuff made me really nervous. Sometimes I feel guilty for not having been able to hide it. It's not that I miss him, I just can't get used to the emptiness.

"Domingo, you wouldn't believe the stuff the kid's telling me," Mom whispers.

"Watch out for that kid, she's an agent of Satan!" I hear him say.

"Well, none of this makes sense to you because you were a bossy kid too, always messing with people and getting in fights."

"It makes me so mad when you get all holier-than-thou, Marina. You have no idea how great it is to get in a fight. And I always made sure to only fight with scrappy people like me."

"What about that neighbor from when you were little, when you kicked his trains over every day and it always ended in disaster?"

"But we were having a great time, both of us."

"How do you know, if he never started it?"

"It was an intense thing we had going."

"You were the only one having a good time, Mom, because you always won. Say I like playing in the street and some kid comes along and kicks my stuff around. What then?"

"I'd tell you to beat him up and tell him to go fuck himself."

"See?"

"What?"

"That if you look at it from the other side it's not nice."

"But sweetie, life is all about who fucks who over first. I don't know what'll become of you if you don't get it into your head that that's how it works. You have to stand your ground and make sure things go the way you want."

"Well, I'd rather wait for them to go right for real, for someone to be my friend because they like the same things as me, not because I forced them. There's no fun in that."

"All right, fair enough, fair enough. Don't get mad."

"All right."

Mom has darker hair and lighter skin than me, whereas I came out more like the color of honey. She'd like me to be a clone of her, just with fewer contrasts – the difference in color is the only one she can accept. Then again, I do feel like her concern for me is sincere, and I think she wants to know me and learn from our contradictions. But even there I'm sure that for her the relationship's based on vanity. It's like this in every home: parents love their children because we're small copies of them and they find this mysteriously meaningful. It's usually an accident that we exist, but they're always getting that misty-eyed look and saying we don't understand, until they're blue in the face. I don't need Domingo to play the grinch to figure this out for myself. But I also wonder if they might be right, in their way. It's weird to imagine having kids; I prefer not to think too much about it. Kids running around the place looking like me, me grown-up and worn out but engrossed in the magic of my offspring. Giving birth, a baby tearing me open, all covered in blood, hanging from a cord attached to my belly. Why do they have to be so ugly? Why are they so gross? Other mammals aren't like that.

People object if you bring this up; it's seen as some kind of insult to the species. No one wants to be told their baby's disgusting. How do they manage to love us so much? Some kids are loose cannons, bundles of pure fucking evil. Can they be taught to be different? Do bad kids turn out that way because their parents are also bad, and they pass it on without realizing? I'd hate to be a mom and find my ten-year-old children smashing up snails for fun. And they'd better not give me some line about how they don't know what they're doing either. They know perfectly well, that's exactly why they enjoy it. I remember kids smashing snails all my life, ever since the first autumn my memory could store anything, and the cars in the train of terror started getting loaded up. I was really little, chubby and clumsy, with curly, coppery hair. I looked on the horrors of the world with rapt attention, eyes wild with disbelief. Sometimes, when it rained, I'd go out to the back patio and hear a crunch beneath my shoe. I would howl in distress and try not to move so I wouldn't disturb what was left of the corpse or have to look at the slimy mess stabbed all over with tiny bits of shell.

I hang up and go to look for the photo of Mom at María Luisa Park. I bring it to the table.

"Grandma, did you take this photo?"

"Let's see. Wait a second, I don't have the right glasses on."

She peers over the rims of the lenses, turns her lips down, looks.

"Yes, I took it."

"Do you remember taking it?"

"Of course I do."

"And did you make the dress Mom's wearing?"

177

"Yes, look how cute it is, I made it out of some scraps."

"Did you like wearing short dresses like that when you were little?"

"Oooh, I loved it. It was the twenties and the dresses were ever so short, the way we girls wore them you could almost see our asses. It was great fun, but it could also be tricky. You had to be careful where you sat. Have I told you the story about when I farted?"

"I don't think so."

"Haven't I? Well, I was a little bit younger than you and my aunts had come to visit, and I was ever so happy. We'd had macaroons for tea and I'd been sitting in one of those wicker chairs for a while. Well, when I got up, my little ass had been stuck to the chair and you could see the pattern of the weaving perfectly. I went and bent over to show everyone, and let out a long, whiny fart like this, piiiiiiiiifffffft, and everyone laughed at me."

"Did they laugh a lot?"

"They laughed their heads off, and my chubby cheeks went bright scarlet. I was mortified."

"That's really funny."

"Yes, but imagine being in my shoes. I wanted to die."

"I'd be embarrassed too."

"You should've seen what a cheerful little girl I was, and what a shame it was, how I got when my mother died."

"How old were you?"

"Nine, just like you."

"And what did she die of?"

"They said it was her liver. But the worst thing wasn't that my mother died. The worst thing was that from then on I had to run the whole house. The cooking, the laundry, the floors, everything."

"But if you were the youngest, couldn't somebody else be in charge?"

"No, because I was the only girl left in the house, my sisters had all left home and only my father and two brothers were left."

"They were all older than you, right?"

"Yes."

"And couldn't they cook and clean?"

"No, honey, it wasn't like that in those days. There were lots of boys working at whatever they could, and lots of girls keeping house. That's how things were done."

"Yuck."

"And then, wouldn't you know it, the war started. You know what made me angriest about the war and Franco?"

"What?"

"The priests. I feel sick just thinking about them. It's fine with me for people to have any religion they like, but I can't stomach priests. They were some nasty pieces of work. Thieves and snitches. They got me so scared."

She sticks her tongue out in sheer disgust and a shiver runs through her.

"You know who was really keen on priests and going to mass and was against the Socialist Party for years?"

"Who?"

"Tata. But when my Felipe got in and they gave us our pensions she changed her mind pretty quick."

"And what was Mom like?"

"Your mom? When? Because for quite a few years she wasn't anything to write home about."

"Before, when she was little."

"Well, when she was a little tiny thing she was ugly as sin because she was born too soon, and people laughed at how ugly she was, but then she got cute as can be. She was very bright, she had an answer for everything, and she's always been shameless. Like when she says she's going to be here at eleven and turns up at one. Look at today, she told you she'd call this afternoon and in the end you talked to her after dinner."

Grandma clenches her jaw, making a familiar grimace. All three of us make it. One of my earliest memories is of Mom and Grandma yelling at each other in this very room. Grandma slapping Mom, Mom slapping her back, grabbing me by the arm and dragging me into the street to catch the bus and spend the night at some girlfriend's house. Then they'd make up and we'd come back. When we arrived, Grandma squeezed me so hard against her chest it was like she wanted the hug to go right through me and reach Mom too. Somehow it worked, because loving me was like loving her by proxy. They couldn't stand each other before I was born. As Mom's illness progressed and I got bigger, they laid down their weapons and buried them deeper and deeper. You can still feel the tension but there's a truce around me that hardly ever gets broken. The marvel of my existence ties them together.

"What your mother's always had is a short fuse and a strong will, but she behaves herself around you, doesn't she?"

"Yes."

"It's really something. When she got pregnant no one would've given a penny for her chances, and now look."

"Look at what?"

"How seriously she takes it all. She's very strict and serious about some things."

"Yeah, Grandma. The thing is, she's nearly always right."

"Well, that's what I'm telling you, that no one expected it, absolutely no one at all."

"Because you didn't know her well enough."

"If you like. Shall we go to bed and turn the radio on?"

"OK."

"Do you want a bit of ice cream first? Just a sliver."

"Oh, yes! Yes!"

I clap. A little ice cream always helps settle the mind. Still enjoying the cool chocolate taste, I rock myself gently in bed next to the multicolored furball Canica and Felipe make when they're all curled up, think about the sad Diana Ross song from the movie about lost dinosaurs I sometimes remember, and fall asleep.

"Marina."

"What?"

"I'm going to the bank, honey, you coming?"

"What time is it?"

"Ten thirty."

I hide my head under the pillow. "No."

"You don't feel like it?"

"No, I'm dying of heat and boredom."

"OK."

I go back to sleep.

"Marina."

"What."

"I brought you some Donettes."

"Three or six?"

"Six."

This changes things. I sit up.

"What time is it?"

"Half past a monkey's ass."

I always laugh when she makes that joke. No one swears with more style than she does. Oh Lord, let me get my hands on the forbidden section of the dictionary. Dear Lord, allow this servant of yours to soon be in possession of a potty mouth.

As I sit in bed chewing, I try to work out how many days it's been since I went outside. We're deep into July. The reservoirs are drying out and there's less water in the faucets by the day. I wonder if the same thing is happening inside of me. In my mind the June heat looks yellow, the first half of July is orange, the second is red, and August is purple. It's a fun enough way of seeing the summer as long as no one forces you to go out when it's hot as hell. I don't think you can live a normal life in Seville in summer, but normal people don't have a three-month vacation, like kids. I'm afraid of being a grown-up and being forced to go out and have a routine that's ridiculous for this part of the world. Certain specific activities give me the fear. Like going to the bank. There's always a really long line of pensioners, no matter how early it is. When we go there it's always late, and it's a long way. Going to the bank is a deep purple. If only there was a bit of dark green to look forward to, but Mom's feeling weak these days and doesn't even want me to hear her voice. All I can do is stay here and wait for a call from

Domingo, who reports right on schedule like it's a routine military job. It's starting to get a bit unreal and I just want to talk to my mom, but apparently that's not allowed. Mom's feeling frail and on edge but Domingo says he's sure she'll be better soon. It's odd the way he chooses what to tell me. It's for my own good, but a lot of the time he gets it wrong. It's like he's a robot, programmed to give and receive information, and since he's a robot he can't conceive of doing things differently. He can't remember anything that's of interest to anyone else. For example, he gives me endless packets of raisins just because he loves raisins. I don't know a single kid who likes raisins. I store them in my nightstand out of pity, because it makes me feel bad to tell him packet after packet that I won't eat them. Then whenever he has a snack attack he asks me if I have any raisins left and I offer them to him gladly.

"Who is it? Domingo?" Grandma asks from the plastic chair in front of the TV.

"Yes!" I answer.

"Well, you tell him he's got four of my books and he's got to give them back. Tell him I won't forget. I keep a list!" she shouts with righteous anger, while lighting a cigarette and taking a deep first drag.

"All right, I'll tell him."

"You tell him, eh?"

"Yes, OK. Dom, Grandma says you have to give her four books back, she hasn't forgotten."

"Tell him I keep a list!"

"She says she keeps a list."

Domingo chuckles.

"He says he knows, Grandma, he'll bring them next time without fail."

"We'll see if he does!"

I make a face at Grandma so she'll be quiet, then cut Domingo off before he can plow on again.

"Enough nonsense already," I say. "The wait is driving me nuts. When do you think I can see my mom?"

"She's guessing at least two weeks."

"That long?"

"I'm afraid so."

"Well, OK."

"Hold on, Partner, you'll see how it all works out. There are some of those doctors you like who wear green, and they pulled a few nasty tricks on your mother this morning. She's pretty out of it now, but it looks like it all went well."

"Really?"

"Yep, looks like it."

"Were they really wearing green?"

"Indeed they were."

"And did they put her under?"

"Yep, that's why she's still so out of it."

"And were there also lady doctors in green?"

"Yep, there were one or two."

"Ooh, that's what I want to be when I grow up."

"We'll see. It's pretty gory. Might not be your kind of thing."

"Well, tell me more, what's the room like?"

"Well, it sucks, but it gets the job done."

"What do you mean it sucks?"

"It's really crummy."

"What color are the walls?"

"White."

"And the sheets?"

"They're white too. And the bed props up automatically so your mother can sit up straight."

"Oh, really?"

"Yeah, that part's pretty cool, actually. I wouldn't mind a bed like that at home, where you press a button and it moves by itself."

"So cool. And what's the food like?"

"The food is genuinely lousy, but your mother doesn't complain, she likes things a little bit bland, so it's fine for her. She's a very disciplined woman."

It's heartwarming to hear how Mom likes the food. I like her bland food too, it agrees with me. There may be lots of breaded fillets and croquetas here at Grandma's, but I wouldn't want to give up Mom's chicken and rice, her boiled potatoes, or her lentils for anything in the world.

"I wish I was a grown-up and already through with school. I'd love to be there to make Mom better while she's asleep and be there when she wakes up," I say firmly but a bit anxiously. Domingo laughs.

"That's a great idea, Partner. I'll tell her for you."

"OK."

"Meanwhile, patience."

"Yeah, I guess."

"You might even get a little gift when all this is over."

"Oh, really?"

"Yeah, we'll see. Everything's good with your grandma, right?"

"Yeah, yeah, of course."

185

"I'm even a little jealous of you, spending all day there doing nothing, no one telling you to shower, and delicious stuff coming out of the kitchen all the time."

"Yeah, that part is good."

"How long since you last brushed your teeth?"

"Oof, how should I know."

Domingo thinks this is hilarious.

"All right then, focus on that. The situation has its fun side, right?"

This is good advice. I've got to show that I can be calm and keep it together through the new wait that's just begun. I can even do it without thinking a single thought. When I really decide to make my mind shut down, it's pretty easy. I become dull-witted, inattentive, and get used to the situation I'm in, just like I got used to hiding out with the Doberman. At this point there've been so many houses, so many times Mom's gotten sick and disappeared, so many rough patches, that I don't know whether to be relieved that she's still holding out or worried that this means she won't hold out for much longer. There'll be lots of days like this. The first one isn't the worst, even if it feels like it is. I need to save up my patience, deaden my senses, at least for a while; if I don't make any room for my nerves they won't show at all. And maybe in the end I'll get a reward like Domingo said. I hope he won't be in charge of choosing it, though, that's for sure.

Grandma and I give ourselves over to a routine existence in the company of the radio station. We guzzle the afternoon schedule down greedily, and I let myself feel wrapped in the safe cocoon she provides. We make plans. Tonight we'll have dinner at the Toro bar. Tomorrow we'll get up early to see the running of the bulls in Pamplona. We watch the same commercials over and over again. I'm usually only annoyed by the ones for detergent, or where there's talking instead of music. It's the same for Grandma. When a bad commercial comes on we close our eyes in frustration so we can't see it. I get fixated on those dull speeches and think about the presenters talking in front of their microphones. But when a new commercial comes on, I give it my full attention. It's relevant to me, I'll be seeing it often, so I might as well find out if it's any good. My favorites are usually the ones for jeans. I wonder how the models must feel, with everyone desperate to be as perfect as them, knowing the pants are made in exactly their size, because their size is the one people think is best.

I try not to look at the clock because I have a feeling that the more I stare at it the less its hands move. We change channels. We do a puzzle. The heat dies down. We watch *Baywatch*. That night we go to bed at eleven. We have to get up early for the running of the bulls. We don't put the TV or radio on and instead sing the first lines of the "Escalera de San Fermín" five or six times in a row while whacking the mattress. After the last round, Grandma slips in a perfect fart to finish the song. Then she tells me "Little Red Riding Hood", "Snow White", "The Wolf and the Seven Young Goats", "The Half Chicken", "Patufet", and "Puss in Boots". I ask for them in this sequence, like I'm ordering appetizers first and then the main courses, depending on how well each will go down.

It's not even light yet, and the TV is already on at full blast. The running of the bulls is just another chaotic fiesta where a bunch of animals have to suffer just for the perverse entertainment of a few thousand drunks. This is the year when I come to loathe that kind of celebration. The fair, the Rocío procession, it's all the same to me. I don't want to go back to the Holy Week festival either. Kids clamor around the penitents, begging for drops of wax. At what age do they start getting excited about it? Is it a classic contest to see who can make the biggest ball? Do they keep them as souvenirs? Do the balls have some kind of religious meaning? One day, on Calle Imagen, I was dying of thirst, when a penitent insisted on handing me a piece of wax. A pack of four demon children were already pestering him, so maybe he was trying to teach them a lesson. He pointed to show that he was choosing me, like he was saying, "My wax is only for good little girls." I felt bad, but I didn't get up from where I was sitting. Why would he do that? How could it seem like a good idea to burn my hand with that stuff? Which isn't to say I'm not touched by this huge celebration of suffering, that it has no effect on me. Who knows, maybe it would be good to have more contact with pain. But I feel like I've already got plenty of processions wailing inside me.

"How long?" I ask.

"Any minute now!"

It's a long and boring wait. Nothing's happening on TV. Grandma's jumpy and nervous, pressing her long, brittle nails against the round, glass, cloth-covered tabletop. At last the bulls are released and the frenzy begins. Grandma is deeply engrossed, crying at the bulls to watch out, and at the runners with their red kerchiefs to watch out too. Her voice is urgent and piercing, she holds on to her seat with both hands, her butt hovering there like she's about to shoot out of the chair and run off. The running lasts only a minute but I can't stand it and go back to bed. I hear her shout a bit more and then laugh her head off.

"Marina! Have you gone back to bed?"

"Yeah."

"I'm going to get churros at ten. Want me to wake you up?"

"Yes!"

"What kind do you want me to get?"

"Both kinds!"

I don't fall fully asleep but doze like an angel, listening to her watch TV while the sun comes up. Soon she comes into the bedroom and gets dressed. She smells of Gloria Vanderbilt. I close my eyes. Then the delicious aroma of something just fried wakes me up. I leap out of bed. She always brings back too many churros, but we finish them anyway.

"I saw Reyes, she said Lucía might come this afternoon."

This is first-class information. My heart does a somersault. I start devising a welcome note to tell her I'm here. Domingo brought a pack of Post-its home from work a while back, and it made me mad that I had no excuse to stick one up anywhere. I'm thrilled to finally have a message for someone. Here's what I write:

> "HI LUCÍA, I'M AT MY GRANDMA'S
> ALL SUMMER. CALL ME."

I waste three Post-its trying to get it right, then figure I won't go to hell for not getting the words properly centered. I have the handwriting of a retard, it's not going to happen. What

I can do, though, is draw a bow and a flower in the top corners, and a sun and a double ice cream cone in the bottom ones. I sign my name and draw an arrow too. I leave the house, not closing the door, and cross the scorching ten meters between the two entryways. I stand on tiptoe and stick the note on the part of the aluminum intercom without the buttons. Now the arrow I drew points to Grandma's house. I blow on the Post-it to make sure it can withstand the breeze, then go back to the living room to keep an eye on the entryway from the window. Five minutes later, the son of a neighbor on the third floor of Lucía's block shows up looking cranky, a helmet hanging from one of his arms. He stops in front of the yellow note, unsticks it, makes a disgusted face, crumples it up, and throws it onto the ground. How old is this monster with sunglasses and slicked-back hair? You've known me and Lucía since we were babies. Why look down on us? Why be so mean? He opens the door and goes inside. His greasy head pops up three times in the staircase windows before he gets to the third floor. He crosses the living room, reaches his bedroom and closes the blind. Where are you coming from in such a shitty mood? Work? A party? What do you have against little girls writing notes and sending each other flowers and bows?

I go out right away and pick up the crumpled Post-it, write another that turns out better, and stick it in the same place. I'd better not keep watching or my feelings will end up getting hurt. Grandma is in the kitchen. On the TV, there's one summer toy commercial after another. Fifteen minutes go by. I decided not to look out of the window for half an hour, but now I can't help it. I can't see the bit of paper stuck to the intercom or on the ground from where I am. I go out to inspect. I find it crumpled up in a ball in a half-empty trash can. Who was it this time? Why can't anyone deal with a friendly note stuck to a wall? I've made the same old mistake of being too eager and sending a shoddy message. Now I look dumb. There's always a fuss around Lucía whenever she comes, it's hard not to notice. After four o'clock I figure the afternoon is well underway and loiter constantly by the window. I've often heard that Lucía is coming but then she hasn't shown up. Then again, there was one afternoon I got her all to myself. First, her mom took us to the movies and waited for us in a bar while we saw *Home Alone 2*. Lucía laughed so hard she kept whacking me on the legs. It stopped being funny pretty fast and she did it the entire movie. I couldn't wait to get out of there. Then we went to her house and I realized lots of the things she'd told me were lies, but that she did have the *Beverly Hills, 90210* theme song on cassette. A bittersweet winter afternoon.

At around seven, when I've had enough of trying to make conversation with Felipe and Canica, Mom calls to say she's feeling stronger today and she misses me. Hearing her tired but playful voice is the best way to pass the time. She just wants to chat. We can talk about anything, but she won't let me get away with sass. Usually, she doesn't need to say a word: just a sharp look from her puts me on alert. Her patience wears thin. She's my mom, but she's other people too. I don't know who they all are, but they've been showing up more and more in the dark flick of makeup she wears on her eyelids. I like thinking about those other people's faces. The virgin with bobbed hair, the gypsy, the punk rocker, the

Terminator who'll end this vacation, frowning in sunglasses. Today is a Schwarzenegger day for her. I can't see her over the phone, but I can tell what kind of mood she's in just by the sound of her breath. Her face is swollen, it's the same face as when she gives herself injections on the couch while I'm watching cartoons, when she stuffs herself with pills before dinner, slamming her fist on the table as she gulps them down. When this face prays, it doesn't plead for kindness from fate. The prayer goes something like this: "Goddamn you to hell, Future, don't you dare fuck with us." There's no begging. Threats and demands are more her style. I wish I could spend more time with her. Sometimes she runs into people who seem to be judging her. It's not that they're seeing in her a person who I don't know, they're seeing someone I don't think exists. That kind of attitude makes me mad, makes me want to sass. But today we chat about harmless stuff. Clothes, cartoons, and food. The armchair is the perfect place to wait for news while I entertain Mom on the phone. I have my snack here like I'm at the movies, waiting till Lucía and her mom to come into the frame. When they show up, I devour them with my eyes. Now I'm glad I didn't manage to stick up my little note. They would've thought it was weird and I would've had to see them laughing at me.

I go out into the street. The atmosphere in the plaza is maybe a bit too lively for me, there are lots of grown-ups in the mix. Luisa, the official neighborhood drunk, is out and about and in the mood to party. That explains it. This has been happening every so often for years. It's awkward. We kids are told to ignore it if she bothers us, but it's not always that easy to shake her off. I hate having to snub her. She's nice when she's not too soused, but more often she staggers around at all hours, her chubby cheeks in a flush. She has a hunchback and saggy tits. She gets the urge every now and then to sing and shriek. Her husband drinks too, but usually at the bar. Their four kids figured out how to make a living at the speed of light and now they've all flown the nest. When they visit, they sit on the bench outside before going into the house and after coming out. They spend a few minutes smoking and taking deep breaths. They're sweet to us, like they feel bad about the trouble caused by their mom. The older daughter is the one who comes most often. She has brown skin, a big nose like Lola Flores, and a graceful walk. I'd say she's the one who carries most weight in the family, she seems most aware of all the ins and outs of the situation. She wanted to be a hair stylist, but it didn't work out. Now she's a waitress, though once in a while she brings a hairdryer and some round brushes and makes a little cash doing the neighborhood ladies' hair. I've seen her smoke a lot of cigarettes, collapsed in a heap on different benches.

It's impossible to focus today. I'm keeping still as a mouse in my hideout by the water tank, trying not to be noticed. If Luisa corners you it's exhausting to say the least. She talks about filthy stuff, but then big fat tears start rolling down her cheeks with their spidery veins, she gets up in your face and tells you that you're drunk too, she breathes all over you, and if she catches on to the fact that you're scared she looks up at the sky and screams. Dealing with her is a pain in the ass, but no one gets mad. We feel bad for her, all of us do. Mom says she's had a rough time and when you've had a rough time it's easy to give in to vice. She must get up feeling really sad, with a splitting headache, and since everything around her's a mess, all she can think to do is start drinking again. Alcohol freaks me out. I've never even wanted to try champagne on New Year's Eve. Luisa's closest neighbors take her inside. You can hear them trying to calm her down through the open window.

It's almost time to go inside. The few of us that are left sit down quietly while the rest of the neighbor ladies talk about what happened. Macarena, her little brother, Lucía, and I make a small circle. In summer, it only makes sense to be out on the street at night. I wish we could stay here till dawn. We've barely made use of the time.

"Do you like the name Luisa?" Lucía asks.

"It depends," Macarena answers. "For a young woman, no, for an old one, yes."

We agree.

"And Antonia?"

We laugh. Antonia sounds awful to us. Lucía, Macarena, and Ignacio are OK. Though there are some doubts as to how well Macarena will age.

"When we have kids we need to make sure we think of names that'll work all their lives. For example, not Daniel. It's a good name for a kid, but then what?"

"Well, I like Daniel as a name for a dad and a grandpa," Ignacio replies.

"You're just a little kid and you don't get it," Lucía says. It's hard to argue with her about anything. She crushes you the first chance she gets. I wonder if she ever feels crushed herself when she's with the grown-ups. How many times have I have trampled on the littlest kids without realizing, but kept on thinking I'm so nice to other people? Lucía's uncle has just shown up on the street, with his greasy, gray little curls at the back of his neck and a cigarette in his hand. There's a certain kind of man that shows deep disdain for socializing with women and children, like they think we're the biggest pain in the ass of all time, the antithesis of everything interesting and fun in the world. These men would rather play slot machines in seedy bars than sit down for a while with the women and children in their lives. They loathe us. We're a terrible burden, the epitome of boredom and oppression. It's no problem, the feeling's mutual. I see men like this in all neighborhoods and do my best to avoid them. Lucía's uncle is one of the worst. He slouches and has a bitter, overbearing expression. He avoids looking at us. He won't say hello. He never does. Nana Reyes follows several meters behind him. He opens the door, goes through, and closes it, not waiting for her. She has bad legs and is a slow walker. I can't fully grasp the horror of the situation, but I know enough to see that this jerk is humiliating her and wishes he could brush her off somehow. By acting like she doesn't exist, I guess. What could hurt more than that?

"Good evening," Reyes says meekly. She nods at Lucía, her way of telling her to hurry up. There's tension in the air and all the neighbors evaporate. Grandma isn't remotely amused. She starts ranting in a low voice as soon as we get inside.

"Did you see how Uncle Shithead showed up and left her on the doorstep like he'd never seen her before?"

"Yeah."

"She walked down the whole street alone. He's always so rude, always giving his wife the cold shoulder. What's the matter with him, why's he so arrogant? The woman has bad legs and can't walk as fast. Is it so hard to wait? Or they had a fight in a bar. Can't they patch it up? Jesus Christ, I can't stand him."

"He's dumb, he never says hello and he gives us dirty looks."

"There's no excuse. I can't stand him. What time is it?"

"Twelve thirty."

"Let's go to bed, remember the alarm's going to go off tomorrow."

Maybe tomorrow I can get up early and go see Lucía for a while. I say this sixteen times over before falling asleep, with Grandma still awake and the radio on.

It's eleven and I'm still in bed. I wonder if Lucía's around. For her sake I'm willing to get up and get dressed. I go outside and cross the gap between her building and mine. I hate calling at people's houses, it makes me nervous. No one answers. I sit on a bench and soak up the morning sun, the light that doesn't yet burn. Lucía pops out onto the balcony. I can't see her clearly, but I know she's looking at me. She waves me up. She's wearing summer pajamas and her hair is straight, thick, and disheveled. I focus on the image, chewing it over as I walk to the door again. She opens from upstairs and I start the climb. This concrete staircase is one of my favorite things in the world. It's been months. Plaster handrail, narrow passage, here and there a picture of Jesus. I focus on who has a doormat, on the layers of color peeled off a thousand times and spattered with flecks of dried paint. The door to the apartment is dark brown and standing open. There's no one in the living room.

"Are you on your own?"

"Yes!" Lucía answers from the bathroom.

"Where are you?"

"Come here!"

There's a loud tinkling sound.

"Are you peeing?"

"Yes, come on in."

I find her sitting on the toilet, her knees pressed together. Her pajama pants and underwear are crumpled around her ankles. I think she has fewer hairs on her coochie than me, and this is somehow surprising. She still hasn't looked at me. She keeps her eyes fixed on the bathtub.

"I got my period the other day."

I don't know how to react to this announcement. She's a liar, but I can't risk disappointing her just in case it's for real this time. That would hurt her feelings. Lucía knows how to manipulate these factors to get attention. I crouch down and rest my hands on her knees.

"Seriously? Already?"

"Yeah."

"When?"

"In the bath at my house."

"But when?"

"Last week."

"And what was it like? Did it hurt?"

"Yeah, my tummy really hurt, like I was having a baby."

I blink in alarm, inviting her to go on.

"I was in the bath at my house with a ton of soap, making bubbles and putting foam wigs on my head."

"Well, and what happened?"

"Well, when the foam started to disappear, the water was all red and the tub was about to overflow."

"What?"

"I mean the bath nearly overflowed because of the blood gushing out of me."

"I don't know if that's possible."

"What do you mean it's not possible, it happened to me last week."

"I don't think it works like that, Lucía, I don't think you bleed that much."

She averts her eyes from the bathtub and turns to look down at me for the first time. She snatches my glasses away and dangles them in her hand.

"Hey, don't break them!"

"Stick your tongue out."

"What?"

"I said stick your tongue out."

I stick it out.

"Now look at me."

I can't. I don't answer. I stay stiff with my eyelids lowered.

"Look at me, Marina."

"I can't look at you."

"Why not?"

"Because I can't."

She opens her mouth and leans in until her tongue touches mine. I'm rooted to the spot and shaking. It's like I'm in a car teetering on the edge of a cliff and I can't stop wondering if I'm going to make it out in one piece. The answer is no. I tear my glasses out of her hand and run through several doors and down several flights of stairs until I get to Grandma's back patio. I breathe deeply, lean on a chair, take up the exact position I was in a minute ago in front of an invisible Lucía, and I kiss her. I suck on her mouth, her face, her teeth, her jaw, and I stroke her hair. It seems I can only get along with ghosts. I sit in the chair and press my face into my thighs. It's like I need someone to break open a lock. What's wrong with me, Lord? And what's the cure? Why was my dream cut short? You know I've been waiting years for a chance to mix my fluids with hers, but at the moment of truth, just when I least expect it, I get hit with a rock-hard, unbreakable mental block. If a person gets too close, I'm suddenly an invalid. All the synapses in my brain are cut off, my limbs stop working, and all I can think of is getting away as quick as I can. I just took a quiz and they gave me a big fat fucking zero. I turned my paper in blank and took off. It sucks to be such a chicken when I've spent my whole life preparing for this. I could've had it all, could've joined the carnal pleasure club, gained her trust, seen my face grow sharper in the mirror, proved to everyone that I wasn't scared anymore. It didn't happen. I missed my chance yet again. I wanted it with all my heart and I couldn't do it. She won't give it another shot, and I'll never be brave enough either, because I'm never brave enough for anything. It'll be like none of this ever happened. Freddy Krueger and Don Pimpón, my cruel patio friends, envelop me in their warmth. This must be more or less what happens to all scaredy-cat kids, none of us feel like we're part of the game. Is it really as impossible to control as it feels? Is that why I get the sense that it isn't really my fault? Does that make me sort of crazy? The fact that I can't control my thoughts, my actions? I'm tired of feeling cheated just for having been born. I long for the cool darkness of nonexistence. Maybe they should've aborted me. There must be others who felt the same way before me, before they called it quits. I can follow the dotted line that drove them to break the contract and send it to hell. I see the idea rush at me from the cradle like a train, and I can't remember a single Supremes hit to keep me safe. At first the train of terror was a friendly cartoon. By now it has the look of a demonic toy. Maybe one day it'll turn into a real train and mow me down. I calmly swallow this thought. I look at my shaking hands and see my grandpa's bones showing through my translucent flesh. My grandpa, leaving his childhood behind on some other back patio, starting to figure out how the world works, catching glimpses of what goes on in dark corners. Where are you now, Grandpa? Are you right here, pulsing inside me? Do you understand why I freeze when I do? We've never spoken. We never will. But I feel like I know you, like my blood and insides and gestures know you. My hands know you, and my thin fingers and nails do too. Is there something wrong with my head? Can it be cured? Will my family suffer because of it? What will become of me, Grandpa? I stay on the back patio until night falls, sweating fear and shame alongside my friends on the train of terror, who today seem to understand me better than ever. There isn't enough fried chicken in all of Andalusía to fix me, but I can almost feel a big, gentle hand resting on my head, a hand that writes graceful letters full of feeling, the one I've been dreaming about ever since I asked my first question.

While I sink into a state of mental anguish that keeps me awake at night, Grandma gets up at dawn to see the running of the bulls each day. In the mornings, exhausted, I toss and turn in bed until ten, doing my best to tune out her cheers and yelling. Then I get dressed and we go out for churros, a mission I find deeply comforting. This routine helps get the mornings off to an upbeat start, and for a few days it keeps us in a good mood. But as soon as the running of the bulls is over, I lose the habit. That one and all the others.

I'm sprawled on the couch in a T-shirt and panties, keeping one eye on a coloring book. I'm only five, so I'm still not very good at arts and crafts, and my lack of precision is quite frustrating. I've tried to give a satin finish to the trimmings on a pink dress by rubbing lip balm on the page, and the result isn't quite what I'd hoped for. I try to undo the damage by coloring over it with a wax crayon, but now the rest of the colors are slippery and there's nothing I can do. Oh well, I had to try.

Mom has dolled herself up this afternoon and she seems on edge. Grandma sits at her sewing machine, ear turned toward the TV. Sometimes she stretches out, groans at the pain in her back, peers at the TV and remarks with surprise at what's onscreen, since she pictured it differently.

"Would you look at the fabulous hair on that girl! I thought she'd be an ugly little thing from her voice!"

I drop the coloring book and watch Mom pacing between the bathroom and the window onto the street, retouching her hair and her lips, painted purple to match her blouse. When she comes over, she speaks almost without seeing me.

"Marina."

"What?"

"Get dressed, someone's coming to visit."

"Who?"

"Remember I told you about Domingo?"

She's been seeing him for a few months. She's told me that he's funny and clumsy, that he knows about lots of things and he makes her laugh. She never introduces a boyfriend unless things are serious, and more and more time has passed lately between one and the next. I guess he's coming to meet me this afternoon. I realize now that she's tense, my opinion matters to her, the relationship's future depends largely on what I think.

"Yeah, I remember."

"Well he's coming over in a while to say hi, if that's all right with you."

"Yeah, why not."

I sit up straight on the couch and look nervously out of the window too. I wonder what kind of guy is about to show up. I go to my room and open the closet.

"Mom! What should I wear?"

"Hold on, I'll help you. Sometimes I forget how little you are, you know?"

"Yeah."

"Look, put this pinafore over your T-shirt and you'll be presentable."

She takes it off the hanger, I hold up my arms, and she pulls it over my head. I turn my back so she can fasten the buttons.

"How's my hair?" I ask.

"Oof, crazy. Come to the bathroom. Have you brushed your teeth today?"

"This morning."

"That was a long time ago."

She redoes my ponytail while I brush my teeth. I spit and she studies me again.

"Now you look like you're from a good family. Come on, go back to what you were doing. Good girl."

"OK."

I go back to the couch and color in a giant rabbit without paying much attention, choosing the crayons on autopilot. I'm soothed by the sound of the sewing machine until the doorbell rings. I was so absorbed in the rabbit I missed Domingo passing the window. Now I'll be completely surprised by what he looks like. "He's here!" Mom says under her breath.

He tells her how pretty she looks, gives her a kiss on the cheek, and strides in with a nervous smile. He's red in the face and has a big head. Grandma gets up and goes over. She looks like she wants to interrogate him. Domingo goes up and holds out his hand to greet her.

"How are you, ma'am?"

"Very well, thank you, dear, but my back is killing me from so much sewing."

"I'm sorry to hear that," he says in a high and quaking voice. He got stuck on the letter S for a few seconds. He's the first person I've met with a stutter. I wasn't remotely expecting it. He turns to me and pretends to be surprised.

"Ah, and you must be Marina!"

"Yes."

He holds out his hand and we shake. It's a bit hard to understand what he says, but he's nice.

"I'm Domingo, nice to meet you."

"You too."

"Look, I brought you this."

He takes a kind of hollow ball out of his pocket. It's multicolored and has a rattle inside. I'm pretty sure it's a cat toy, and it looks very second-hand.

"I found it on the ground on my way here and thought you might like it."

I take the ball and rattle it. I appreciate his honesty. It isn't a flashy gift, in fact it's a really shitty one, but the colors are pretty, and by telling me where it came from he's also admitting that I was on his mind and he was concerned about whether I'd like him, but that he doesn't really give a damn what I think. I look up at him, smile, and deliver my verdict.

"Yes, I like it. It's nice."

PART THREE

10

I haven't lived through enough of the twentieth century for it to mean much to me. The first half of it isn't even in color, and the beginning might as well be prehistoric, so dark it's a little bit blue. Before 1900, all I can get a sense of is a lump of Play-Doh carelessly mixed together, all brown and dirty. We come from the shadows. The millennium will end in a shade of burnt orange, warm and gloomy. The nineties are all that stands between us and what's next. People act like it's some kind of triumph, like they've won some epic battle with a horrible monster. The grown-ups all seem burdened by a past full of suffering. They talk down to us, saying kids have it easy these days, like everything's a piece of cake. Things aren't as simple for us as they think, but we like to let them believe it'll all be fine, that if they die soon, they can die in peace and feel like the story had a happy ending. But we know we won't be that lucky. According to my calculations, we'll all start dying around 2040. We won't even be halfway through the story. We'll be there to witness the upheaval. What will change the course of the future? Domingo says it's always something. And eventually we'll be the last ones still holding the torch of these times, when that something has gobbled everything up. Will it be aliens? Time travel?

Teleportation? Immortality? Mom's been talking for a while and I haven't been listening. I hold the phone to my ear again and try to follow the conversation.

"If you think about it, two thousand years isn't that long."

"For God's sake, Mom."

"What."

"Two thousand years is *ages*."

"Look, do the math. Two thousand years is eighty lifespans, more or less."

"Eighty lives?"

"Yeah, right?"

"You did the math wrong."

"No, hang on, it's forty."

"What?"

"It's forty lives, sweetie."

"It can't be, that isn't enough."

"If you say so."

For some reason this number makes us both sad. We talk on the phone a lot and don't always have much to say, so we spend the time on chitchat. I'm not usually brave enough to bring up anything naughty, and she seems to prefer light, relaxed conversation anyway. I break the silence by asking to talk to Domingo. Mom passes him the phone.

"Dom."

"What's up, Partner."

"I'm gonna ask you something, OK?"

"Fire away."

"Do you think the future will be OK?"

"OK in what sense?"

"In the sense of will it be really weird."

"I think I need more information."

"Let's see . . . Like, why are movies about the future so scary?"

"They're not all scary."

"Tell me one that isn't."

His throat makes an odd sound when he concentrates or does anything complex, like something's creaking inside him. Here it is, right on cue.

"*Total Recall* isn't scary at all," he says.

"What the hell do you mean it isn't scary? Don't remind me!"

"But it's really fun."

"Why can't it be both?"

"Look, Partner. Humans have always imagined a pretty dark future, but these days it seems like things are getting better, not worse."

"Seriously?"

"Looks like it for now."

"I don't know, it's like, it's always dark in the movies."

"Because it's cheaper that way."

"And because it scares the shit out of people."

"Come on, Partner, you love horror movies."

"Some are good but they still freak me out."

"But you're in love with Freddy Krueger."

"Don't you dare talk to me about Freddy. Why did you guys let me see that movie?"

"What do you mean, why did we let you see it? We told you how scary it'd be and you snuck in anyway."

"And you guys noticed and didn't say anything!"

"Well there's nothing wrong with a bit of fear, and anyway you seemed determined."

"Well, I regret it."

"Why would you regret it? Freddy's a really nice guy, you two make a great couple."

"Don't say that! Anyway, I wasn't even talking about horror movies, I said movies about the future."

"Well, I'll bet you really like *RoboCop*."

"*RoboCop* totally sucks!"

"You're such a drama queen."

"Drama queen? You show me movies that make me crazy, way more than I am right now."

"Crazy how?"

"Well sometimes the weird stuff I've seen piles up in my head and I can't get it out."

"I understand. Don't be scared though, that weird stuff's harmless."

"How do you know?"

"Because it's weird, plain and simple. It's no creepier than life, which is very weird indeed."

"OK."

"But those sappy little movies of yours are more dangerous, even if you don't think so."

"How? *The Little Mermaid* never gave me any bad thoughts."

"But they brainwash you. Plant toxic messages in your head."

"I don't know about that. But if everything's weird or evil, is there any way out? Between one thing and another I feel like I'm screwed."

"Hey, d'you really think you're crazy?"

"I don't know. Sometimes I don't and sometimes I do. Like, a lot."

"Well you know what I say?"

"What?"

"That's a good sign."

"What?"

"That you say you think you're crazy. The real crazies are always saying, 'I'm not crazy, I'm not crazy, let me go!' That's what's really scary – people who say they're perfectly fine, totally normal, that everything's under control. Don't trust those people as far as you can spit."

"But in that case, what's the deal? Everyone's a bit crazy?"

"Pretty much, and anyone who says they aren't is an idiot, a con artist, or a sicko."

"But I'm really scared of being crazy."

"That's normal. The mind is a very complicated thing. Just look at your mother, always claiming she's nuts when she's the most rational woman I've ever met."

I think for a moment, but then one of my favorite theme songs pipes into the living room. I've got to hang up right away.

"Gotta go, Domingo, *Baywatch* is starting."

"Ugh, for the love of God, and that shit doesn't scare you?"

"I don't care, I want to see the bikinis. Bye!"

"You're such a sucker for good looks, sweetheart."

"Yeah, yeah, yeah, yeah. See you!"

"All right, see you."

I don't like missing the opening credits. You never know what'll happen in an episode, some have more naked flesh than others, but the opening credits are always bursting with it. Luckily at my house they're pretty permissive, but it's funny how many grown-ups enjoy horror and let us watch violence, whether it's real or pretend, when they're radically opposed to letting us see anything sexy. I have nothing against either, I'm drawn to both, but I've noticed sex suits me better and it makes me mad that people think it's somehow worse than gore. Grandma is a fairer judge than most; anything can interest her. In fact, if there's blood and guts on one channel and tits on the other, she prefers the tits whether I'm there or not, whereas Domingo would opt for the blood and guts without thinking twice. *Baywatch* is pretty terrible, but Grandma loves it as much as I do. We both have our reasons.

"Bring the pistachios, honey."

"You bought pistachios?"

"Yes, this afternoon. Hurry, Mitch Buchannon's on, look how handsome he is."

"I don't like him."

"You don't?"

"No."

"So who do you like?"

"I don't like any of the men. I like the women."

"Ah, and do you like them all or just one?"

"Shauni's my favorite."

"Ah, the little blonde with the square face."

"Yeah."

"Very pretty girl."

This afternoon's conversation was good. Mom's out of the hospital and was calling from home. I picture her napping all day on the couch, while her wounds heal. Hospitals are nice, I adore doctors, and I wish they'd let me visit, but they freak Mom out so it's great news that she's out of there. I'm feeling better. We start in on the nuts and don't stop. During the commercial break, Macarena's little brother shows up at the living-room window. He asks if I'm going out. It seems like a real effort. I'd rather stay here and draw my favorite swimsuits when the episode's over. In the end I get pretty excited and draw a beach packed full of women, all friends with each other. What will my body be like when it's fully developed? Will I be tall? What kind of tits will I have? It makes me madder and madder that I wasn't born in a boy's body. I wonder if it's as weird for them? I don't know, but I don't think so. It must be embarrassing to have your voice change and then lose your hair when you get older, but this is weirdness on a whole other level. I don't want to get pregnant or give birth, I don't want to be thought of as weak for suffering more, when really the opposite's true. I've always liked dresses and bows, but the more unhappy I am the more I want, deep down inside, to somehow turn into a boy. I don't feel fully like a girl, and I doubt I'd feel fully like a boy. I'm neither one nor the other. But if I had to choose, maybe sometimes I'd rather act like a guy.

I complain, but the truth is I don't know what I'm talking about. I barely know any men. I wish I was more familiar with them. I'm curious about how Domingo shaves, how he's going bald. When I'm near my cousins I devour them with my eyes, but I don't get the chance too often. One time, when I was three, I was sitting in the street with Mom and we heard the knife-sharpener go by. I'd never heard him before. She explained what he does, and the superstition – how if you hear the knife-sharpener go by blowing his whistle, you have to put a white cloth on your head and make a wish. That day,

I was wearing a little white apron Grandma had sewn me, part of a costume I'd put on over my skirt, and we draped it over our heads, closed our eyes, and each quietly made a wish.

"I want to be a princess," I thought. I regretted it right away. At the time I had no idea what princesses really did. I've never cared for their style, and at this point it seems like a hard and boring job. I asked fate to let me correct my wish and tried again: "I want a dad, a grandpa, or a brother." They were all as good as each other, and if I could have all at once, even better. I've been told stories of absent dads and dead grandpas, but stories don't have a smell or a voice, you can't see the ageing skin on their fingers up close. How I longed to feel total trust in one of those larger, coarser creatures called men, the same trust I have in some of the women in my life. I want to know what men are like inside, but if you get even a tiny bit close, you risk being labeled a slut or a tomboy. Which is especially awkward since I don't see what's wrong with being a slut or a tomboy. "Boys on one side and girls on the other." People go on and on about this, pretending to hate the other team and acting kind of disgusted by them. But it's boring when we don't mix. It's not like I haven't noticed how they stare at our dolls and want to get closer. But their fear of being bullied is stronger so they sabotage their weakness for pink. I get it. I feel bad for them. A lot of them are so scared but want to get to know us so badly that all they can do is come over and annoy us. Lift up our skirts, ruin our dolls. The skirt thing can suck or it can be funny. I usually find it funny since I have a one-track mind and want to be touched any way I can, but still, it bothers me that it has to be this way. Boycotting our games is a cheap kind of terrorism. "Fighting and fucking go together," I once heard someone say. That theory makes more sense, but I don't agree with it either. We're so far removed from each other that all they can do is pull our hair. I refuse to accept getting annoyed as a form of courtship. I'm not very sociable anyway, but if you ask me, I have a whole lot of compelling reasons to reject this state of affairs.

I don't quite know what to make of Domingo. For example, he claims that men don't cry, and goes out of his way to make fun of the idea if it comes up for any reason. He has the laugh of a bad little boy. Fake, cruel, affected. I can't be expected to trust a bad little boy.

Making friends with a boy would be enough to satisfy my curiosity. Sitting next to Juan Carlos in class was really a stroke of luck. We got along pretty well, but it takes a while to build a solid friendship when you're starting out from such different places, and right when I was about to manage it they carted me off somewhere else. I don't want to start over again. I'm tired. I'm tormented by that last scene with Lucía. I lost all the points I had left. All I want to do is stay in bed and hold on to my favorite things. Little things are easier to control. I'm feeling more and more attached to my toys, my cartoons, my felt-tip pens, my *Dragon Ball* cards.

Maybe the rule is that you can't like anything in this world completely, and especially not all the time. Simple pleasures are what give stability. The basics never let you down. A dish of breaded chicken fillets, a lemon ice-cream, a doll with a nice hairdo, someone showing you their duplicate card collection and finding one you were missing in the middle of the stack. I'm dead serious about these things, since they're the only loves that wouldn't be taken away from me if everything went to shit. Just how badly would things have to go for me not to get a popsicle once in a while?

"Grandma."

"What?" she answers, without lifting her eyes from the white square she's crocheting.

"Do they serve breaded fillets at convent schools?"

"Oh, honey, I don't know."

"What about grilled?"

"For sure."

"I like them grilled too."

She looks at me over the rim of her spectacles and keeps crocheting.

"You want them for dinner? With a bit of lemon?"

"Oh, yes."

"With fried eggplant?"

"Yes, yes, yes."

I go into the kitchen with Grandma and watch how she peels the eggplants and sets them to drain. She lights a cigarette and we go out to the patio to water the plants. When we go back inside, I ask if I can put the flour on them myself.

"All right, but you have to shake the eggplant to the rhythm of a baión, that's how you make them crunchy."

"OK."

We drain them and put them in a lidded container with the special flour for frying. I hold it and wait for the signal.

"Ready?"

"Yes."

"All right then."

She starts singing while I shake the eggplants, mixing them with the flour.

I wanna dance the new beat
When they see me go by they say
Girl, where you going?
I'm gonna dance the baión!

Here comes the black zumbón
Dancing the baión like crazy
He's playing the zambomba
And calling out for the lady.

She repeats both verses, snapping her fingers, and the egg-plant is ready for frying. Grandma's no good at solving big problems and serious difficulties stress her out, but the small ones are her specialty. She won't save your ass, in other words, but she'll rub the best ointment on it. That helps too, it's important. Mom, on the other hand, is the kind of warrior who charges into the front lines screaming, who gets punched in the face and keeps going until she's completely spent, who's capable of using her last breath to stab the enemy, never stopping to wonder if her butt is sore from shitting herself in the trenches. Here we are, a little girl and an old lady, setting the table carefully while she's out there doing battle. Sometimes I think Grandma's greatest virtue is being a masterful actress, the kind good enough to pretend that she's actually bad at it, so everyone will trust her since they all think she couldn't possibly lie. She knows exactly what's going on, but she focuses fully on the present, on the basic joy of continuing to exist.

"Grandma," I ask, once the food's on the table.
"What?"

"Would you know how to make clothes for my dolls?"

"I sure would."

"Really?"

"Of course. What do you want me to make you?"

"Lots of things, but first a nurse's outfit and one for a lady surgeon too."

"One green and one white, right?"

"That's right."

"And you don't want one for a princess? I can make you that too."

I think of the Chabel Cinderella catalog. The outfits I like are clearly for the poor version, before the fairy godmother shows up.

"Yeah, well, one might be nice, but I'd prefer a peasant doll first."

"Well, look, as soon as we finish this, go to the closet and check in the bag of scraps, there must be something. Bring me some snaps as well, and we'll see what we can do."

I finish the dish of eggplant with gusto and run to dive into the mound of bits of fabric. The warmth of hope flares in my chest. If you feel like you're running out of steam, forget about the war, Mom. Use your last breath to come and see me, no matter how ashamed you are of your wounds.

The hours drag on through our half-hearted activities. Pick jasmine. Watch the flowers open. Smell them. Water the plants. Make croquetas. Draw. Sew. Change my dolls' clothes. Do their hair. Draw wounds on them so I can make them better again. Watch TV. Listen to the radio. Go to the supermarket. Say hi to the butcher. Talk on the phone. Slowly flip

218

through the pages of twenty- and thirty-year-old magazine patterns that Grandma keeps on the shelf. Mark with an X all the little girls' dresses I'd like to own, even though I know that between the fact that I'm growing up and the fact that I hardly go outside I'll never have time to wear them. Macarena and her brother in the living-room window. Me signaling "no" to them with my finger. No, and no again.

Summer is a hot pond four months deep, but from July 20 to August 10 the immersion gets more intense, like the sun's shining so brightly that the pond-dwelling critters dig down into the mud at the bottom, looking for shelter. Houses turn into dark caves. If I go outside, it's usually in company, or at four in the afternoon when no one's around, and I skulk about near Amor's motorcycle and the windows I think are the creepiest ones. In some of the first- and second-floor apartments, the residents never raise the blinds. I guess they want to hold on to their privacy at all costs. Some of them are elderly hermits. Others just antisocial adults. I picture them fucking all day with their homes dimly lit and hope to see something, maybe a shoe lifted in the air, through an unexpected crack.

Grandma put an air-conditioning unit in the small living room last year that blasts air right into our faces when we watch TV. Our quality of life has improved a lot, in other words. In the apartment Mom and I share with Domingo it's much worse. Being there often makes me feel like I'm floating in acid. But here, on the ground floor, the room dark and barricaded until eight thirty at night, I feel more like I'm inside a big, calm belly. When I'm nervous, my tummy hurts. To avoid this, I try to keep it entertained with plenty of food, and topics of conversation heavy enough to distract from the burning that speaks from inside my chest. I draw ferocious battles between hellish beasts. I try to make it obvious that they're gigantic and press really hard with the red crayon. There have to be claws, blood, enormous fangs on display. The bigger and more gruesome the better. I get pretty worked up. I twist limb against limb to the point of absurdity, and then, once my technical failings put an end to that, I take out a lined Renault Clio notebook and, stabbing my pencil into the page, start to outline my own death in the jaws of a great white shark. I would see it coming, see it cutting a path through the crystal-clear water, feel the ripples a fair few seconds before it sank its teeth into my leg, turning everything red, just like in Lucía's bathtub. Why did I have to argue when she told me about getting her period? It was a good story. Why couldn't I let her suck on my tongue a bit? There was nothing wrong with that. Will I always stand in my own way when I want something so badly?

"Grandma, are there sharks in Marbella?"

"Well, I don't know. I think so."

"For real?"

"There must be. Don't you know how deep the sea is?"

Her logic is so ironclad that I take it as fact. This means I've been in the water with them. I imagine them swimming beneath my feet, surrounding me like a bunch of suitors around a window with iron bars. I could give myself to them easily, since there'd be no escape anyway. It's midnight now. Our favorite show this summer is on, a mysterious one called *The Twilight Zone*. The usual happens: I wouldn't miss it for all the world, but then I have a few terrible nights after watching it. It's not that it's all that scary, there are even some funny moments, but the tone makes me question everything I think I understand. Lots of people come on, talking seriously about things that seem like they can't really exist. What's up with that? Grandma believes in the paranormal and claims she's had two encounters with UFOs. Not one, two. She's told these stories over and over again. The first time was right here, from the same window I'm looking out of now. In the middle of the night, the sky began changing color. Puzzled, Grandma went out into the plaza, and saw, beneath a purplish glow, a kind of gigantic Cruzcampo beer bottle sailing silently across the sky like an airship. The next time, she was driving around the countryside with Manuel, her second husband, when they were blinded by a dazzling light heading toward them at breakneck speed. When it was about to hit them and they tried to shield themselves from the blow, the light took off and vanished into thin air. For her, these stories are as true as the air she breathes is real, and she gets deeply offended if anyone dares to dispute them. Whenever we visit anywhere new, we're always on the lookout for possible UFOs, and there are always a bunch of false alarms. I don't know if she's losing her marbles or trying to drive me nuts, or both. I try, but I can't believe in aliens. It would help me a lot, I think, but I can't make myself believe in anything.

How many possible versions of reality are there? Why is the official one so sketchy? Why are none of them convincing? When the fuck will I get to see my mom?

It's time to go and buy the annual bottle of Gloria Vanderbilt. It's already August, the city is deserted and burned to a crisp. Grandma gives me a tight, wet, dirty ponytail, we smear sunscreen on our noses and shoulders, and then we go out. She's wearing pink lipstick, a lilac, Japanese-style dress, and gold earrings. We set out at around six in the evening. The heat doesn't bother us too much, but sometimes we get an attack of thirst and almost come to blows over the water bottle she keeps in her bag. What does worry me is taking the bus with her. She loves to chat with the other passengers, but I'd usually rather have nothing to do with people. It's too bad, really, since the trips could be nice, but they always get ruined. Today I'm in luck, there's no one in this hot rattletrap apart from us, and the driver is clearly hostile to friendly advances, so the only sound on the ride is her voice reading off the signs as they catch her eye. She points out the houses she thinks are pretty, and the gardens and animals.

"Tixe ot orrocos," she suddenly says. It's "exit to Socorro" with the words read backward, just as it appears written in the window in front of us. We laugh listlessly. I wanted to wear my jelly sandals to keep me cool, but the soles are so drenched in sweat I'm afraid I'll slip in my own shoes. When we reach the last stop and stand up, I realize the true enemy is the hellish blisters on my heels. It's amazing how easily kids' skin can break. I guess this means if I got cooked I'd be nice and juicy. I've seen a bunch of comic strips with babies getting roasted like suckling pigs, usually served up at banquets full of guys in suits. Those cartoons don't make the prospect especially appetizing. What they tell me, in their inimitable style, is that guys in suits are not to be trusted.

When we get to the department store, I see that it's true, that where there are lots of suits the mood is anything but relaxed. The perfume section is overwhelming. They produce the swan-shaped bottle in a matter of seconds. I try to spot Mom's perfume behind the glass counters but it isn't as common and I can't find it. While Grandma pays, I go over to another assistant and quickly ask if they carry the brand. She gives me a funny look.

"And who are you with?"

"I'm with my grandma," I answer, pointing at her. Grandma is at the register, laughing and talking about recipes for split-pea soup. How does she steer so many conversations onto the subject of soup?

"All right, come with me."

The uniformed assistant leads me to a separate counter and takes a rectangular box out of a drawer. I read the label.

"Yes, yes, this is it! Can I smell it?"

"Well, I don't have any samples, but you can put your nose up to the bottle if you like."

"Yes please."

A free sample of this smell would solve some of my problems in the short term, but this is better than nothing. I take a long, deep sniff at the gold spray pump. Grandma grabs me by the arm.

"Don't wander off without telling me, honey, you have no idea how much it scares me."

"It's OK, I didn't go far."

The assistant smiles to show that she was on top of things.

"What are you doing, smelling your mother's perfume?"

"Yes."

"Oh Jesus, Lord have mercy."

Grandma sighs sympathetically without pursuing the matter and says goodbye to the girls from the beauty department. Our next mission is my favorite: picking out a small treat for each of us. In the decor section, she finds a pair of ceramic brown owls, one dancing and the other singing, and pictures them on the TV stand at home. I adjust mentally to my limited budget of a thousand pesetas, give up the idea of the perfume bottle, and melt at the sight of a pink Hello Kitty pencil case with an eraser and pencil sharpener that pop out at the press of a button.

As we wait for the bus home, I peek inside the green-black-and-white plastic bag and look over what's inside.

"Hey, Grandma."

"What."

"Where are the owls?"

"Oh, fuck!"

She opens her purse and takes them out. She stowed them there on her way to the stationery department because she was tired and thought she might drop them. She asked me to remind her before we went up to pay, but I forgot.

"Does that mean we stole them?"

"Well, it was an accident, but yes."

"How much were they?"

I take one and look at the price tag under its claws. Five hundred and ninety-five pesetas. For two. We piss ourselves laughing on the bus, which is just as empty as the last one. August has its consolations. The neighborhood is quiet until night falls. I water the patio plants while all kinds of land and sea creatures stalk me, and inspect my Hello Kitty pencil case at the table, marveling at the beauty of all its details. The jasmine has opened on the two nightstands. We've just had dinner. We're getting undressed in the bedroom. While she puts on her white polka-dot nightie, I run to the little TV and flip through the channels, looking for something new and interesting.

"There's a good movie on at eleven."

We don't usually agree on what makes a good movie good, but sometimes one comes along whose qualities are obvious to us both. Here it is. It's from a decade that usually sucks, but in this case everything's beautiful, magical, and profoundly disturbing. We take the plot very seriously. The main character is a girl called Carrie and her nun-like beauty gives me a knot in my stomach that won't stop twisting. Everyone shuns this poor angelic girl, and she ends up dead. I don't want to be the neighborhood Carrie. Grandma is outraged by how she's treated, since she's just as pretty as the other girls and knows how to make her own clothes. I have a distressing realization that even the fantasy part of this story is more realistic than *Saved by the Bell*. *Saved by the Bell* is the future I want for myself. I'd like to be something like Jessie. Though it's also distressing not to have telekinetic powers. It would be so handy to be able to move things just by thinking about them. At least then I'd be brave enough to sing and dance in public. Grandma and I laugh and shriek at the scary ending, and it's like the tension around us has all dissolved. Grandma goes to sleep. I get up and tiptoe into the living room. I look at the cabinets, both full of exotic glasses. My favorites are the brightly colored highball glasses. I try to move them with my stare. Nothing happens. I wish

I could've used them, for some birthday party maybe, but Grandma never lets anyone touch them, she cherishes them and doesn't want them to get broken. I guess for her it means keeping the good times with her, the times she spent with her second husband, who she apparently never fought with. Mom, on the other hand, does remember a few fights, and she mentions them with the same rage in her voice as she does those cops in gray uniforms – the really old-school, dangerous ones who gave her a beating once at a protest she'd joined to call for a world that was more fun and less of a total drag. I go to the bathroom, open the cabinet doors, take out all the cosmetics, and scatter them around the sink. I mix them all up in the lid of the never-ending conditioner tub, trying to formulate a particular recipe, but all I know about chemistry is that scientists always look really focused. I put on an earnest face with this in mind and blend some nail polish remover with a smear of Manuel's ancient hair-growth treatment, adding a few drops of baby cologne and a few more of Gloria Vanderbilt. I hold the concoction up to my nose, hoping to get a whiff of Mom's distant essence, but I'm disappointed. A loud snore takes me by surprise, and I imagine Carrie melting the bars on the window and floating effortlessly into the living room. I pick up the debris from my failed experiment and go back to bed scared stiff. I cuddle up to the polka-dot nightie.

I've got plenty of other credentials, but no gift whatsoever for telekinesis. Still, please, Lord, don't let me end up like Carrie.

I wake up the next morning alone in the double bed. There's no one at home. I turn on the TV. I'm pretty depressed it's so late – I've missed all the cartoons. They're repeating last night's variety show, because it's Sunday. Rocío Jurado and Raphael are belting out "Como yo te amo" at the top of their lungs. I'm bawling in no time at all. I stay glued to the screen, tears streaming down my cheeks, until Grandma walks by the window and I wipe my face with my arms, stifling a sob.

"Goodness, we've got a loony in pajamas on our hands!" she cries.

"Hi!"

"A little bird told me you're going to stuff yourself with chicken wings for breakfast."

"Ooh, lucky me."

I lean back in the chair and let out a sigh I didn't know I had pent up inside me. Grandma to the rescue once again. She rushes over to the TV, butcher's bag in one hand, and raises a finger to stab at the screen:

"See how pretty Rocío Jurado is with those nice boobs."

"Yeah."

"She's a looker, that hairdo is really something. Did she sing 'Señora'?"

"Not as far as I know."

"'Señora' is my favorite, but I like this one too. Look, it gives me goosebumps."

"Me too."

"Really? I thought you were more like your mother, a rock 'n' roll girl."

"Mom likes lots of things. She likes Rocío Jurado too. And Marifé de Triana."

"How should I know what your mother likes, she hasn't got an ounce of shame."

227

"What's that got to do with anything?"

"Nothing, honey, it's OK, your mother is very good at lots of things and she's crazy about you. Let's see if she calls."

She gives me a kiss on the head. The hole in my chest opens up again but I fill it with chicken wings. After we eat the phone rings. Grandma looks at me, raising her eyebrows in hope, letting me know it must be for me. I pick up. It's Mom.

"Marina!"

"Hi Mom, how are you today?"

"I have good news!"

"What?"

"I just picked up some test results from the hospital and they say I'm better."

"For real?"

"Yes, sweetie. Hats off to my doctor, that clever bastard, and his fucking mother too."

"Hats off!"

"And we're moving to a new neighborhood."

"What?"

"That's right."

"Which neighborhood?"

"One with lots of swimming pools."

"For real? Are we going to have a pool?"

"Yes."

"And then what? Where am I going to school?"

"There's one nearby, I just called and they told me when to send the forms."

"Ah."

"I'll pick you up tomorrow and take you to see it, sound good?"

228

"Of course! But Mom?"

"What."

"I don't know, tell me more."

"What do you want me to tell you?"

"I don't know, more. Like what's going to happen and stuff."

"But I'm telling you everything as soon as I find it out."

"But I'm talking about if the treatment's going to make you better."

"Oh, sweetie, there's no cure for what I have, but as long as my body doesn't give out we're going to move somewhere with a communal pool, what do you say?"

My laugh holds so many feelings that it's more like a stammering croak.

"Communal like the ones in hotels?"

"Yes, the residents get in with a card."

"And will we have cards?"

"Of course."

"With photos?"

"Yes."

"We'll probably never get around to putting the photos on them. But I'd rather you die somewhere with a pool."

Now she's the one laughing with a kind of grunt – dark, bitter, joyful.

"What about the nuns?"

"Don't worry, they told me you can do your communion along the way if you need to."

"OK, all right. But couldn't I have gotten baptized along the way too?"

"You don't understand what a big deal baptism is for those people."

"It sucked, I was so embarrassed."

"But it only took a minute."

"Mom, I don't want to do communion, OK?"

"I know, I know."

"They make kids drink wine, Mom."

"You're so scared of wine, it's really something."

"So, are you coming tomorrow?"

"Yes."

"Around what time?"

"I don't know, I'll be in touch."

I say goodbye, bewildered but happy, and replace the receiver. Don't the grown-ups realize what they're doing to their kids when they hit us with these sudden twists and turns, like it's no big deal? I let myself fall butt first over the arm of the old green chair and land in the seat. I pick up Canica and we lounge in the afternoon sun. Felipe is sprawled out near the phone watching the canary, which won't stop chirping. Grandma hangs the cage closer to the ceiling every day. I look over at Cristina's grandma's balcony. This is where the gifts were when my dad came in dressed up as Balthazar with his friends. Mom looked like a little girl back then. She calls again at ten in the evening. She says she'll come for me tomorrow at noon. I'd rather not get used to the idea, just in case. I'd rather go to sleep without counting on it.

Mom is supposedly on her way, and I want to savor the realness of her arrival, revel in every step she takes across the distance between us, so I sit in the entryway. I wanted to put on my Minnie Mouse pinafore but there's still a patch of runny poop on it, so I'm taking another chance on the palm-tree skirt, and a T-shirt with Goku and Vegeta posing on another planet. I've brushed my teeth and washed my face. I've been sitting alone in the entryway quite a while, leaning on the aluminum railings, opening and closing the gate that leads to the faucet across from the steps. I used to hide things in this dark and greasy hole when I was little. Some of them I forgot about, and they got lost. Others got dirty, which made me sad. Back then I could lift the gate with my finger, but now I have to use a little stick. The heat starts pressing in again. Something moving across the street catches my attention. It's Mom, walking alone in the dazzling orange light. She's wearing a black miniskirt, a floral vest, flat shoes, sunglasses, and carrying a purse. She takes off the glasses once she's closer. I get up, holding inside the tangle of feelings assaulting me all at once, and give her a hug. I don't know what to say, and what comes out is cold and shallow.

"Hi Mom, you look really pretty."

"Hi, Marina! So do you. Is Grandma here?"

"Yeah, in the kitchen."

"I'll say hi and then we can go on our outing, all right?"

"OK."

We head to the car hand in hand. Now we're waiting for the traffic light to change.

"It's been a long time since I've fought with anyone," she says, out of nowhere.

"Well, if you do, make sure it's when I'm not around."

"No, silly, I just said I haven't done it in a long time."

"Yeah, right."

She laughs and shoots a defiant look at the next driver over. It makes me kind of happy since it means she's getting her strength back, but the last thing I feel like today is dragging a stranger into a scuffle.

"Mom, so, about you being sick, what's going on? Tell me more."

"What's going on?"

"That's what I'm asking."

"Well, I've got more problems than a math textbook, as usual. But listen. As long as I last, we'll try and live a normal life, all right?"

"OK."

"I mean, what else should we do?"

"How should I know? That, I guess. What you just said."

"Well, of course. And things could be worse, right?"

"Yeah, I guess so."

"Don't worry, if it gets any worse I'll tell you."

"But you have to tell me, OK?"

"Yes."

Bringing up these worries has stamped out her appetite for trouble, at least for a while. We've managed to avoid the usual scene where she ends up yelling at someone that they're an asshole and can go fuck themselves while I hang around sighing and trying to look polite. I understand that this is her way of letting off steam, whereas mine is to stay stock-still and weather the storm. In any case I don't think she'd want to upset me like that, no matter how nervous she is today. We take a wide, dry road that I've never seen before. Mom talks about the virtues of the new place, trying to convince me, so I don't worry and even get excited about it. We drive by without getting out of the car. It's scorched, flat, and colorful, an oasis of yellow and orange in the middle of a desert of empty lots. It doesn't look bad. Mom points at a dumpster.

"Hey, sweetie, look at that great little coffee table."

I agree. We pick it up together, put it in the car, and go back to eat stuffed peppers with Grandma. I admit that I love hauling things out of the trash with Mom. At the traffic lights she beams at me from behind the wheel. Are we really going to live in that place? I'm so happy that I wonder if it's all just a ploy to get me on board with moving. I've gotten much gloomier from being so tense for so long, and now I'm almost mad that it was all for nothing – at least an unhappy ending would've made this dismal summer seem like it had more of a point. But I don't want to get my hopes up either. Happy endings are never permanent around here. I never know how long any situation's going to last, and I learned when we went to live with Domingo that what you expect isn't necessarily what's going to happen. I was only six. I'd gotten used to the idea of Domingo being Mom's boyfriend, but I thought it was just me and Mom, just the two of us, who were going to live together. I don't know, I guess I just got confused, you never really know what's going on at that age, and when we got to the new apartment and there he was, waiting for us, it was like finding a meal you don't really like when you get home from school. I understood late, and all at once, and I couldn't even make it feel bad or unfair. It was better for Mom, so it would be better for both of us. And he's definitely my favorite of all of the men of hers that I've met. There were better-looking, richer ones, including my dad. But what makes Domingo so special is that he's the only one who's treated me like a person. He knows me. He likes me. It's such a relief.

"You're not like other kids, Marina. People say you're uptight and fussy, but you're also pretty delightful."

"Mom!"

"Don't get all worked up. Listen, OK? I'm telling you something good."

I listen.

"What I want you to know is, I realize I'm always getting you into sticky situations, and then I try to protect you from the fallout, but it's impossible."

"Yeah."

"I can't tell you everything. I wish I could, but it's just not going to happen."

"Yeah, I figured."

"It's tough hiding things from you, sweetie. You've got no idea how careful I have to be. Especially when you pay so much attention to everything."

"Sure. I get it."

"For example, you understand that it's better for Grandma not to know she has a nephew in prison, right?"

"Of course."

"And I trust you because I know you'd never snitch. There'd be no point anyway, we'd only upset the poor woman. Not everyone is ready for prison stories. You? You're good with prison stories, but disease stuff, maybe not yet. But Grandma's great at disease stories. I'll bet Grandma hasn't gotten you worried at all over the summer, has she?"

"No."

"See? So, enough of that. Tell me, what have you been up to?"

"But we've talked a million times, Mom. Don't make me tell you again."

"Have you been going to bed really late?"

"No."

"I'll bet you stayed up watching TV until three a bunch of times."

"No way! Two at the latest."

It was an effective speech. I can't really argue with her. For my part, I know she has nothing to gain from hearing how many nights I've been up till five in the morning – how many times I've watched the sun rise this summer, my heart in my mouth. Not everyone can process just any kind of information. You have to feed it in bit by bit, so the machine won't get jammed.

As we eat dinner and I try to take in the new plan, Mary Santpere appears on TV. She fell asleep on a plane last year and never woke up. Grandma says she thinks that's a wonderful way to die. Domingo often tells the story of how his grandma had a good death, watching TV in an armchair. I wonder what that would be like. You fall asleep and it's all over. From one darkness to another. So calm, so dignified, so peaceful.

11

The new apartment is on the second floor and there's a streetlamp outside my window that shines all night. On the other side of the light there's a road, a few pine trees, a train track, and a big vacant lot that allows for a view of a large patch of sky. The small living-room balcony looks onto a strip of lawn and a brick building. The mixture of green and dark red is warm and refreshing at the same time. There isn't much left of summer, the days are getting shorter, and I like the way the colors darken at dusk. It's like living in a small city where it's vacation time all year round. I guess it just feels that way because it's summer, it's hot, and I still don't have to go to school. It'll be different when winter comes.

I like the idea of sleeping close to the train tracks. I have an urge to figure out how often the train goes by. I wait. The horizon is flat, wide open, dry. During the day it looks really dusty, but by night it's seedy, dark, and alluring. Mom will kill me if she ever finds out I've crossed the tracks, so I've got to find a roundabout way of getting to the other side. I want to go see if there are any used condoms on the ground. I'm convinced people must be fucking over there at night. I wonder where. I think from now on I'd rather spend weekends here. I can't pass up the chance to spy on the clump of pine trees on Fridays and Saturdays. I'll stay awake at least until three. I'm sure I'll catch some teenagers getting it on, at least. I'd like to go over there, even though I know I'm too young, but I'm still not strong enough to make a good plaything. I wish the world would present me with the perfect opportunity to get lost in the forest and be attacked by the wolf. I don't want him to force me to do things anymore, I want him to eat me. I'd make an excellent snack. Then, when he falls asleep, I'd slit his belly from the inside, fill it with stones, then stitch him up and take off. That's my specialty – doing things late and badly. Sigh. I know it isn't so easy, I know I'm no good at things. If I can't even kiss a girl sitting on a toilet, how am I ever going to escape from home?

I think I hear the train coming. I jump out of bed, put on my glasses, and run to peek out of the window on tiptoe. The stop light is green now. Does that mean it's coming? Here it comes. It doesn't have passengers, only cargo. What could be in those freight cars? There's a whole bunch of them. Old, reddish, green. My new roommate snakes away into the distance.

The next morning I'm tidying my room when Mom hollers at me.

"Marina, come here! Quick!"

"What's the matter?"

"Diana Ross is on TV!"

I dash to the living room and find Mom dancing in front of the TV. I've spent the last few months thinking I'd never see her dance again.

"I would've loved to be a backup singer!" she exclaims, spinning around on tiptoe. I get so close to the screen I'm almost touching it, and devour the picture of this happy, sensitive, playful woman, reveling in her own existence in a siren-red dress, white gloves, and a Cleopatra wig, and singing a hypnotic tune whose words I don't need to understand at all. I know who Diana Ross is because a few years ago Mom called me in just like today, on a Saturday morning, so I could see her. It was urgent, I couldn't miss it, she knew I was going to love it. It was true, I love her so much that something aches deep inside me. I want to be part of her magical world full of light, but no. My life is nothing like hers.

"How can she be like that, Mom?"

"Like what?"

"So graceful, so pretty, so good at everything and not afraid."

"But sweetie, you just have to want to. If you're not afraid of anyone laughing at you, no one will dare. Anyone can be a queen, it doesn't matter if you're fat or thin or white or black. If that's how you feel, no one can take it away from you. When this chick started out she was just a regular girl."

"Is that how you feel?"

"Me? Yeah, ever since I was little."

"Oh. I don't. But it must be really nice."

The video ends and another comes on, by Alejandro Sanz, which I don't care for at all. I bolt to my room to hold on to the Diana Ross energy, and, thinking anyone can be a star if that's what they decide, I leave the house feeling more than ready. In the excitement of the moment, I put on my baptism shirt with a pair of white shorts. I think I'm dressed like a tennis player, which got me excited in front of the mirror, but I feel ridiculous as soon as I step outside. It's too late to change my mind. The six teenagers sitting in a circle on the ground have already seen me and can't stop laughing. I want to go home but it would be even more embarrassing if I ran back to change and tried again with a cooler outfit, so all I can do is keep walking and wait for the shit to hit the fan. There's no magic glitter running through my veins, it's more like dirty, brackish water, like I died of thirst in a puddle and they resuscitated me right there in the sludge, at the end of the driest August in history. I'm no good at anything, I can't keep eye contact with a friend who has her panties down, I can't dance with Mom and tell her how much I admire her, how much I love her. I steer clear of the evil young legs until one kid pretends he's going to trip me. It's a typical nasty trick and the dumbass takes his foot away in time, but he's managed to throw me off-balance and the gang double over with laughter as they watch me try to get a grip. I have an intense and unpleasant history with these kinds of jerks, clearly there's something about me that attracts them. I wonder if one would have it in him to force me to do something nice. If they weren't so stupid I think we could come to a healthy agreement. The clapping and sniggering fade as I turn the corner and look for the road to sin. This summer I've figured out that social success isn't my domain. My domain is lonely ponds filled with monsters that sneak out and gobble you up. Near a barren traffic circle, I spot two condoms and a syringe. My heart does a somersault. I stare danger in the face. I have no trouble talking to objects. I wouldn't crouch down and touch this shit for anything in the world, but head over and check it out? Absolutely. I'm up to the task. And I've never wanted to explore a neighborhood so badly. It's like getting to live at a Workers' Resort. Just what I wanted. So why am I still so sad? Why am I sad all the time? Why am I so scared? Where are my warm, fuzzy feelings? I mean, I'm tough when it comes to some things. Being an orphan, for example. That I could handle. Life's challenges don't scare me as much as people do. Kids, teenagers, grown-ups, the rowdy table-soccer players always crowding around swimming pools. Maybe old folks are less dangerous, like it's not worth it for them to keep up the fight anymore. You can tell a lot of old guys were assholes in their time, but I'm sure it's never too late for them to learn how to braid someone's hair.

My bedroom looks creepy from out here, small and dark in the middle of that enormous, smooth wall. This side of the building isn't as inviting as the rest. It doesn't face onto anything. It's been a while since I left the apartment and I'm thirsty. I retrace my steps and make sure that the entryway is clear from the nearest corner before making my suicidal appearance. There's no one around. The sun bears down on me. I run over to the intercom and they open the door. I have to stop and squeeze my legs together a few times on my way up the stairs. The closer I get to home, the closer I am to wetting myself. The first drops seep out as I step through the door, and there's a weak but persistent dribble all the way to the bathroom.

"Mom, I've wet my panties!"

"Well, change them, then. But hurry up, I'm about to serve lunch!"

"But I've wet them a lot!"

"Clean up and come to the table, for fuck's sake."

"OK, OK!"

I take off my wet clothes, wash them quickly in the bidet, and put on some clean panties in the hallway. Once my hands come into contact with soap and water, they produce a surprising amount of liquid dirt. They feel softer now. I stroke my butt cheeks. There's rice on the table, with just a few green bits in it.

"I have something for you," Mom says, out of nowhere.

"Oh really?"

"Yeah, I was keeping it for when we moved and I just found it in a box."

"What is it?"

"It's a cassette."

"Really? Is it Michael Jackson?"

"No, it's James Brown."

"Oh. Who's that?"

"Just put it on, you'll like it. I left it in your room."

When lunch is over she falls asleep and I dash to my room to play the tape. It's true, I like it, and I recognize some of the songs from TV commercials. It's fun. It makes me feel almost purged of the strange spirits that took hold of me on my morning walk. I wander around the house over and over, basking in hope. I go into the rooms, memorize how things are arranged, take a detailed inventory, then put them back where they were. Where are they keeping the comics in this place?

Domingo gets home from work and the three of us go to the pool. There's a bar with a straw roof, and a totally cute blond lifeguard in red swimming trunks in the shade under-neath it. That's pretty much how I picture James Brown. We have temporary passes without photos. We're the new kids once again. Mom asking everyone's name again, scrambling to catch up, to adjust to the way things are done. Domingo looking like a nerdy pimp, attracting funny stares again, so hard to classify, stuttering more than ever, nervous at having to face new people, one of his balls always about to slip out of his swimsuit. Me not talking to anyone again. But now with a swimming pool.

We settle in beneath an umbrella. It's really noisy. I get in the water just to do something, in the shallow end, the area for little kids. It's too bad I'm almost past the respectable age for using a floatie. A couple of pairs of teenagers are necking in the deep end and the lifeguard tells them off. From the water I see a ring of kids pointing at the book Domingo brought with him. Hardly surprising. There's a picture of a naked redhead on the cover, and on top of that when you get closer you realize the title's *The Fuck Machine*. I don't know what to think, if Domingo is being inappropriate or if those kids are just half-wits. Just in case, I glance at the book then head back to the apartment to avoid being seen in public for too long doing nothing. Once I'm there, my curiosity about the new surroundings wins out. I put some shorts on over my still damp swimsuit and go back out in search of adventure. I choose a direction I haven't tried and head toward the stores, where I pore over the products on offer in the neighborhood. There are family-friendly bars covered with tiles and aluminum where they're bound to have great food, a couple of candy stores, and a preschool with a gigantic Snow White mural, where nearly all the neighborhood kids must have gone. I picture the kids I don't yet know coming here, still innocent, getting less and less sweet as they get bigger, just like always. Preschools are usually creative with their decor, and Snow White isn't just surrounded by dwarves but also a bunch of Smurfs and a few characters from *Bambi*. I look at Thumper the rabbit, and suddenly feel teary-eyed and flee the scene. Hightailing it when your heart is breaking is a fail-safe strategy that adults can no longer resort to. Poor things, it's obvious most of them want to cut and run, and I wonder what's stopping them. Being out of shape or embarrassed, uncomfortable shoes, not wanting to mess up their hair or get their shirts sweaty? A windowless hole in the wall grabs my attention and I slow down. Inside a bunch of kids are playing videogames and table soccer in the dark. A few grown-ups are playing pool and acting superior. There's a bunch of people gathered tensely around an arcade machine, following the game of a little kid hooked on *Buster Bros.* who's about to break the record. I go over and stand by the machine, admiring his skill in silence.

"Get her away from there, she's distracting me!" the player yells, punching viciously at the buttons. I walk away in a huff, wondering when they forsook Snow White and became consumed by such violent urges. They must've all had their first communion, or they're at least going to catechism. Do their parents really think those classes will teach them to be good? I guess the kids just pretend, maybe even believe all that stuff for a minute, but as soon as they're back in the street they turn themselves over to the laws of Satan. The Devil is sort of a friend of mine in theory, but once I leave the house it isn't so easy. The trick is to be officially Christian and be naughty behind the scenes. Then you confess and you're good to go. I feel like I walk hand in hand with evil, but my behavior's impeccable on the outside. But I still

243

end up just feeling weighed down with guilt. I'm doing it all back to front.

I look around. A bakery, a branch of the San Fernando Bank, a sign for a podiatrist, one for a dentist, a video store. So there's a video store. I feel drunk with possibility and take slow and deliberate steps, savoring my approach, aware of the delights awaiting a girl like me in a place like this. I pass through the entrance plastered in action and horror posters with religious calm. Inside, there's a young couple looking around indecisively and a gang of kids my age loitering around the porn section. The dirty movies are half hidden next to the counter, all of them edgewise, the images covered with stickers, the kind you can scratch off a bit. The guy behind the counter loses his patience, gets up and tells them they can't do that all afternoon, do they think he's stupid, any day now he's going to snitch on them to their parents. The gang leaves and the guy shakes his head kindly. He'll never snitch. He's young, flabby, gentle, and besides, he works at a video store. He gets what's going on, he remembers what it was like. I give him a little smile and a wave. He sits back down to relax, picks up a magazine, and starts reading where he left off. I look through the cartoons on offer until the couple decides on a lame-looking romantic comedy. While they're renting their movie, I drift over toward the porn and wait for the right moment to caress the few tiny cover photos that have escaped the censorship of the stickers. Sometimes I don't need to see as much as to touch. I raise a hand, run my fingers over a two-millimeter pussy between some splayed legs, then vanish into another section before anyone can catch me, the spark still in my fingers and rising all the way up my arm. The horror movies are in the opposite corner. Some of the pictures on the cases are really disturbing, but it's pretty much legal for me to be there. The couple leaves. The clerk fixes his eyes on me briefly, sizes me up, and decides not to interrupt my browsing. I head into a less risky section just in case. I don't want to make an enemy of him, I want him to stay calm and trusting. Suddenly, a video on an improbable floor-level shelf, all on its own, makes me lose control of my limbs. I move toward it, hypnotized. I can't believe it. This one has it all. It's horror, it's porn, and it's terrifying – a genuine unmasking of human depravity. I realize the relief and distraction from worry I find in violence is an addiction. It's magnetic. Sex has an even better effect, but that stuff's more tightly controlled, and anyway the two get confused, both in fiction and in my head. I rub my thighs together. My wet swimsuit tugs at my flesh, which is also wet. I keep staring at the bleeding body of this woman impaled on a stick in a primitive village. The title is *Cannibal Holocaust* and they try to sell it by claiming that human eyes have never before seen so much horror. From this angle, no one can see what I'm up to. I hold the case in my little hands and turn it over. It looks truly depraved, like it'll really live up to its promise. I don't actually want to watch it, but the images are electrifying. I can't let go. So it's true, people really do get impaled on sticks. They shove the stick up your ass and push until it comes out of your mouth. You're still screaming when they start, but by the time they're done pushing you're dead. Then they roast you over a fire like a wild boar, or drive the stake into the ground so that the nearby villages

245

can see what the people who hunted you down are made of. It's no exaggeration, it's been done a whole bunch of times. I'll bet someone split their sides laughing when they saw it happen in their neighborhood. I've never understood why people laugh at victims and I never will. I guess they must get a kick out of feeling superior, or get some kind of relief from such immediate, casual cruelty?

In the evening, Domingo's little brother Pablo comes over for dinner. His visits are usually some of the best days of the year. He's young, sweet, affectionate, and always in a good mood. He shows me and Mom a lot of respect while still being really approachable. Once, when he came to lunch, he spent the whole time picking the saffron threads off my plate. While he went to that unnecessary trouble on my behalf, I had an intense tingling feeling on the back of my neck. When we finished lunch, I climbed into his lap without saying a word and took a total rest from all my fears for over five minutes. Tonight we have roast chicken for dinner, and after dessert the brothers get a fit of the giggles.

"All right, we're going out onto the balcony for a quick smoke," says Domingo, getting stuck on the G and the B.

"But you always smoke in here."

"That's right, Partner, but we have imported goods today, some of that strong-smelling Dutch tobacco I like."

He's happy. He loves giving me that spiel every time he goes off to smoke a joint. I think it's funny too. They go out to the balcony and close the door from outside, still laughing. They're celebrating the fact that the days of military service are numbered. The mili, haha, the fucking mili, to hell with it, haha. They're just like Beavis and Butt-Head.

"Pair of overgrown boys," Mom remarks, offering me another slice of watermelon. They come back in ten minutes later, rubbing their hands.

"There was some chocolate around, right?"

"Yeah, go ahead and bring it over."

They've rented *Conan the Barbarian*, a movie we all like a lot. We eat the whole bar while we watch it. When it's over, Domingo goes out to take Pablo back to his neighborhood and we're left alone. Mom looks at me.

"You haven't said anything about James Brown, but I've heard you listen to him a few times."

"Yeah, I love it!"

"See? I know you."

"Yeah, yeah. I bet he's really handsome."

"You think? What do you think he looks like?"

"I don't know, tall and blond."

"Tall and blond, huh?"

Mom laughs.

"Why are you laughing? What's he really like?"

"He's short and black, sweetie."

"Seriously?"

"Seriously."

"You're not making fun of me?"

"Of course not. Why would I lie to you?"

"That seems weird."

"He's black and he's an amazing dancer. He's got incredible style. Maybe he'll be on TV some time and you can see him."

"And is he young or old?"

"He's on the older side, maybe sixty."

"That's so weird, I figured he was thirty at the most."

I stare at the wall, eyes popping out of my head while Mom stifles a giggle. I absorb the news slowly. I can't imagine him, and the chance of seeing him on TV seems remote. What's he like? Sometimes the way you picture things is nothing like how they really are. First Bud Spencer hasn't won any Oscars. Now James Brown is black. And Diana Ross, is she black or not? Because I've seen her but I still have my doubts. Maybe she's mixed-race? And Whitney Houston? What difference does it make. I love Whitney, but I don't plan on telling anyone. She's too sappy. I don't want anyone to suspect I'm even a teeny bit romantic. If you're romantic, you're weak, or so Domingo keeps saying, and I plan to be a genuine John Wayne for whatever's left of my childhood. A stone-faced look, a heart eaten away by anguish. I hate John Wayne, he's super boring, but something tells me Domingo's right, that if I let myself get carried away like Whitney, and Mom caught me getting all soft around the edges, the morale in this household would plummet.

Domingo swaggers in like a cowboy and we go to bed. I stay awake, playing with my dolls in the dark until I hear two simultaneous snores. Then I put on my glasses, get up, and creep to Domingo's nightstand. I snatch the book with the dirty cover and take it back to my room. The orange light shines in from the street, so I don't need to turn on my lamp. I crack it open at a random page and start reading. There's nothing about a fuck machine. I look at the contents page. There are lots of stories, the last has the same title as the book. I start paying attention when I come across a girl's name. She's called Tanya and her arm is stuffed full of wires. The train has just gone by. It must be after four. I put the book back in its place and pick up a few dolls from the floor before getting in bed. I arrange them in a row tucked under the sheets and drift off to sleep, sighing for sweet, ill-fated Tanya. There aren't enough violent dolls on the market, with pastel-colored rifles, dressed for combat, like in video games. Articulated, gorgeous, and tough. From now on my dolls are going to learn how to fight. Action Men don't cut it. They look like a bunch of knuckleheads.

In the morning, the sun shines on the pool and everything's calmer and more innocent. Grandma is visiting and you can feel her enthusiasm in the air. She praises the lawn, the umbrellas, the water, the bar, the sky, the hedge, the showers, the mothers, the babies, the kids, the beer she's about to order, the ice cream she's going to buy me, the wonderful place we've rented, and the handsome lifeguard, who turns out to look nothing like James Brown. We start with a game of cards. Mom and Grandma smoke cigarettes and make conversation with other women of different ages. Mom takes a quick dip and goes home. Grandma and I are left alone in the shallow end. A few meters away, a quiet little girl in a green swimsuit is cooling off. She makes eye contact and starts swimming toward us, splashing around in a clumsy, childish way.

"Look at that lovely girl, Marina. She looks about your age, maybe just a bit older."

The girl smiles and stands up. She doesn't know I need glasses yet. I'm wearing my good swimsuit. She inspects and approves it. I like giving this fake first impression of total normality, and she accepts it in good faith. Her name is Prado, she's ten, she lives in Block 8, and you can see her balcony from here in the water. It's almost two. The pool is warm and quiet. For the fifteen minutes we spend together before going to lunch, she teaches me to dive down and swim between her legs, something I'd never have dared to do without some cheerful command. After twenty minutes of friendship, we say goodbye on the lawn.

"Coming down later?" I ask anxiously.

"Yeah, but I have visitors. I can come down after eight."

"OK. Are you going to wear a dress?"

"What?"

"I said are you going to wear a dress later?"

"I don't know, why are you asking?"

"Because I'm going to wear one."

Prado gives me a weird look. I'm acting weird. Kids can tell you're different in the blink of an eye. I guess it's a survival strategy, a way to avoid ever feeling exposed, outside the comfort of the mainstream.

"Marina, almost no one our age wears dresses."

"Yeah, that's true."

"Well, I have one that's getting too small, if you want I'll wear it for the last time today to see my grandma and grandpa, then I'll come down."

"OK."

I've bargained with her in a civilized way, but now I'm a little bit worried. She's made it clear she's making this allowance to welcome me, but it's the last time she'll go out dressed as a little girl by choice. She's doing it as a favor, and only because she can use it as a chance to please her family. I'm quite a bit shorter and punier than her. She must weigh over thirty kilos. She's the first person I've spoken to in this new dimension and I'm drawn to her. It's a miracle. I'm not usually this lucky. She's pretty, but I can't help finding all my friends pretty. The main difference is that she seems unique, quicker and more interesting. She's got a proud streak, which must have swelled when she noticed my weakness as we said goodbye.

I spend most of the afternoon trying to pick the right dress, knowing my time for dresses is almost up. I can't think of a single respectable way to keep wearing them. I saw it coming when I stopped wanting to wear a flamenco dress. Maybe when I've grown and my body develops I'll go back to knowing how to deal with the issue. But for now, I think the time has come for me to turn into a boy. Being a girl is a minefield. I wish people would understand that I want to get hurt and also have bows in my hair, but I guess I can't blame everything on other people. I've got to experience physical contact with other humans, get rid of my fear of pain. I've got to take the doll out of the box, no matter how hard that is. Get her dirty, mess up her hair. I'm starting to understand that this is a pretty rough neighborhood, and what I really want is to get my knees torn up.

Mom's just come back from giving Grandma a ride home and she's lying on the new second-hand couch. While she naps, I lean on the table we dragged out of the trash, with my first Chabel doll and the kitchen scissors. The doll has long blonde hair. That's about to change. Without measuring, carelessly, I chop the hair off at her neck. I turn her over to see the results of my work. Her hair looks wild and twisted. There's no way to make it even except by shearing a bit more off, and she ends up with a jaw-length bob. Is she still the same doll, or has she turned into a different one? I'm still holding the scissors in my shaking hand. I notice Mom watching me, saying nothing, her face resting on one arm. I ask her the name of the school I'll be going to. She answers and doesn't mention the massacre I've perpetrated, but I can tell from the look in her eyes that she approves. She likes it when my hair gets messy and I get dirty. Time for me to join her side. I pick out a white dress with a purple pattern and go downstairs. Prado is wearing an orange dress, so she's easy to find. I'm relieved as soon as I see her on the lawn with some other girls. There's a pale-faced Tanya with crooked teeth and green eyes. Three of them are my age. We're going to be at the same school, in the same class. It's the first time I'll ever start a new school already knowing people. And on top of that, we're neighbors. I'll walk to school in the mornings, wearing my backpack. They show me the vacant lot you have to cross. I memorize their addresses and birthdays. They all went to the Snow White preschool.

"Do you know who you're going to sit with on the first day? We can get into pairs." Tanya has a high, singsong voice.

There's no need to settle who goes with who, since we'll sit two by two and make an impenetrable square. But it's true that the dresses look out of place. So it's decided. The moment of metamorphosis has arrived. As long as no one forces me to wear the gray uniform with the pleated skirt, my larva will do its gestating in the cocoon of a boy.

I go home feeling brave and look for a bag of hand-me-down clothes, eighties and boyish, that I've never wanted to wear. But this place doesn't just have a swimming pool, old sweat suits, and classmates. I've finally found two new issues of *El Víbora* on the shelf by the bed. I'm strung out on those images. I can't live without them. Between the excitement about my new life and about the new *Víboras*, spending the weekend at Grandma's has never seemed less appealing. I want to keep exploring. The parents are fairly confident that this area is safe. Kids have more freedom here, so now I do too, since that's how the system works. Being shut in with Grandma and taking care of her plants is over. Now that she has Felipe she doesn't need me as much.

I'd like to delve into the magazines right away, but it's not quiet enough at home. I'd have to wait until they're asleep, and today I don't have the energy. In the morning I'm on alert, but Mom gets up in a cranky mood, makes me do the dishes, and sends me to the store three times but then doesn't feel like making lunch, so she takes me to a bar for some fillets with potatoes and egg. I start getting tired of thinking about it so I put the idea on hold. When we get back from the bar I call Prado to get her to come down to the pool, and Mom is pleased. I can't remember her face too well. I want to see her again. Her mom answers the intercom.

"Hi, is Prado there?"

"Who's asking?"

"Marina."

"Well look, Marina, Prado can't go down right now. Not until five."

"OK, sorry."

She hangs up. She seemed pretty annoyed, but it's not unusual to come across party poopers like that among parents. They're easy to handle, you just have to get the information you need and then ignore them. Tanya, however, is coming out of her building in a bikini. I look at her for a few seconds and she waves at me. She's so pretty – a bit plump, rosy-cheeked, self-confident, a little puppy blooming with health. We go to the pool together and sit under the shade of an umbrella that leans to one side. Now we can talk. She enjoys being questioned, and that helps things along. She's the oldest of three, and her middle brother is really naughty. The littlest is called Lydia, with a Y just like her, and looks a lot like their mom, who was a swimsuit model in the Continente catalog when she was younger. A bunch of people must have jerked off looking at her. Tanya soon starts telling me about different boys she likes in the neighborhood. She kissed one of them this summer. I sit up in a snap.

"What was it like, what was it like?" I ask eagerly. She laughs mischievously, showing her crooked teeth. Her natural colors look wintery, even though she has a tan. No wonder everyone notices how beautiful she is, she looks so pure, innocent, and saucy at the same time. She has the gross motor skills of a champion, her turquoise bikini looks fabulous on her, and she isn't snotty with me even though she could be. She points to the right to show you'd have to pass a few buildings to find the place.

"You know those arcades over there, near the freeway?"

"Where the video store is."

"Yeah, yeah, a bit further, but around there."

"Yeah, there are some brick buildings, I saw them yesterday."

"Yeah, yeah, around there, well it happened there two weeks ago!"

"But was it just once?"

"No, a few times, but all in the same place."

"Got it. So what did you do?"

"We kissed with our tongues and he touched my boobs through my shirt. Mine are really small, but I liked it."

My eyes hurt from being open so wide. She's the best person at answering questions I've ever met. She gets straight to the point, gives the most complete and relevant information, and delivers it efficiently.

"What was your T-shirt like?"

"White. Tight."

"You don't wear a bra yet, do you?"

"Of course not. Do you?"

"No, no. And I don't want to either."

"Exactly, fuck that. Such a pain in the ass."

Tanya swears a lot but doesn't care if I don't.

"Was it your first kiss?"

"The first with tongues. He gave me a few on the lips before that, but that's nothing. It doesn't count as making out."

"Right."

Three or four boys come out of nowhere, shake the umbrella, and run off. Tanya peers out.

"Dickheads!" she yells at them, putting our hideout back in its place.

"Who are they?"

"A bunch of jerks. One of them's the one I just told you about."

"And he wasn't like that with you?"

"No. Or that's not why I dumped him. I dumped him cause I found out he was kissing someone else behind my back. But he wasn't a jerk like that with me."

"What was he like with you?"

"He was cool with me. Boys seem dumb but they're different when you get them alone."

"But why can't they be like that all the time? You're cool all the time."

"Because they have to show off in front of their friends. But you should've seen how much he cried when I dumped him. Two-timing bastard!"

She yells her last comment so the boys spying on us hear it loud and clear.

I laugh. She makes it look so easy to be in control. The qualities I value most in a friend are, in this order: being wildly curious about forbidden subjects, being fun, and not standing me up when we have a playdate. Tanya represents an important contact on my journey. She doesn't seem like she'd be too punctual, but she was there for me today at the perfect moment, and I'll never forget the way she accepted me into her space. A mean, snot-nosed kid swoops in to our right and shoots a slimy gob of spit onto my leg.

"You little shit!" she yells, running after him. She gives him a shove and throws him onto the ground.

"You're really getting on my tits!"

The boys scurry away, and I go to the showers to rinse off my leg. When I come back, she's taking a deck of cards out of its packet.

"Sorry, that was my brother. He's the worst of all of them, you have no idea."

I breathe a sigh of relief. Being friends with that spiteful brat's older sister is going to save me a whole lot of misery. Tanya checks her waterproof watch and I get ready to try calling on Prado again. This time she answers the intercom. Her voice sounds unnatural and childish, which tells me she's being watched. She says she's about to have a snack, that I should come have one with her. She buzzes the door open. As soon as I walk in with my wet ponytail, I'm gripped by the certainty that this is the happiest moment of my life. The floor, the brown-and-silver wall, the tropical plant, the steps, the mirror, the mailboxes, the smell. Please, Lord, let me come back to this entryway lots of times, and if one day I have to stop coming, please send me here in my dreams. Come on, give it your best shot, is it really that hard? Just this entryway, I won't ask for anything more. What's the apartment going to be like? What are we going to have for our snack? Prado answers the door, her mom standing next to her. It's dark and silent inside. Her dad is taking a siesta. She's an only child too. They say hello with polite restraint. We go straight to the kitchen, which is packed with utensils, dishes, cereal, and canned food. The mom cheers up as soon as she opens the fridge, listing possible sandwich fillings. Some of them are really obscure.

"I want spicy sausage, Mom," says Prado.

"Me too!" I cry.

The mom looks down at us, standing straight as a crane. "Today's Friday."

"Oh yeah. Cheese then."

"What's going on?" I ask, puzzled. The mom stiffens further and nudges Prado.

"Meat isn't allowed on Fridays," Prado answers, like she's telling me off.

"Meat isn't allowed on Fridays? Why not?"

"Because Jesus died on a Friday," the mom answers sternly. And then I understand it all. They're Catholics, the kind that are actually serious about it. I must look like a disrespectful heathen not knowing this stuff, which explains why they're being so uptight. People like this are so easy to annoy, their ways will always surprise me, no matter how carefully I tread. I ask for a cheese sandwich too, and keep my mouth shut until we're alone. The mom tells us to be good and goes out. Prado is transformed as soon as she's gone. Her freckles get darker, her teeth sharpen, and she does a whole range of impressions, from Disney villains to the Hound of Dracula. She also likes being silly. I hope she never loses this talent for turning into someone her family wouldn't approve of. We finish our sandwiches in the living room. Her communion photo is on the table, blown up and framed along with a bunch of other portraits.

"You had your communion last year, right?"

"Yeah."

"And how was it?"

"It was cool."

"Did you like the dress?"

"Yeah, but then I changed into a prettier one for the party."

"There was a party after?"

"Of course, there's always a party, and you get gifts, that's the best part."

"You didn't like the church part?"

"Yeah, I liked that too. Haven't you done yours?"

"No."

"Well, a bunch of people do it when they're ten and it's no big deal. Don't worry, it's embarrassing but you get over it quickly."

"I'm not worried. I don't think I'm going to do it."

"But you're already late."

"Who cares, you don't have to do it if you don't want to."

"But it's not about what you want, it's about what you're supposed to do."

We have contradictory worldviews, and I suspect we'll have lots of disputes like this one, because there's no question that we're drawn to each other somehow, that we like to talk. I'd rather we agreed on everything and that I was welcome in her home, but that's no reason to pass up a potential friend like this one. Only two of the photos are bigger than the one of her communion, and they're of her parents' wedding and her grandpa dressed as a soldier. I adjust my glasses to look at his black-and-white uniform up close.

"That picture was taken in Africa, that's why the place looks so weird." Prado is showing off.

"Africa, huh?"

"Yeah, he spent a lot of time there. He was a general."

"When was that?"

"During Franco."

We both go quiet. Another issue that's going to cause us problems in the short, medium, and long term.

"Are your parents PP supporters?" I ask, trying to go back to the subject.

"Yeah."

"So they like Aznar."

"Of course."

Well, here are the Popular Party voters, at last.

"Does your family support the Socialist Party?"

"Yeah, my grandma's in love with Felipe González."

"The one who was with you?"

"Yeah."

"Well, I don't mind about her, she's a grandma. But they're a bunch of shameless thieves."

"I'd better not say what I think of your grandpa, the Francoist general in Africa."

"Yeah, OK, you'd better not. I don't care."

"One more thing, Prado."

"What?"

"Betis or Sevilla?"

"Betis."

"Oof, that's a relief."

"My dad has a video on the end of the TV stand that says it's a Betis match but it's really a porno."

"For real?"

"Yeah."

"And d'you think we could watch it some time when your parents are out?"

"Sure, I think so. My dad sleeps like a log and my mom just went out. Shall we put it on now?"

"Yes," I answer emphatically, preparing for a new happiest moment of my life in the same building within the same half hour. She's glad I'm interested and gives me a naughty smile. I don't care where she comes from, this girl is clearly my type. I wait in the living room for her to make sure the coast is clear, studying the photo of her honorable grandpa.

How's it going, Mr. General? I don't know how I've ended up at your house, but congratulations on your granddaughter, she's a first-rate find, and I'm sure she'll show up to all our playdates on time. I wonder what you'd think of the cover of *Cannibal Holocaust*. Prado and I like porn and Betis, who cares about anything else? The excitement is making it hard to answer. I can't let the same thing happen to me as that other morning in the bathroom. This is way easier. I have to snap into action, seize my chance. I'm going to watch porn with this girl. I can do it, I can do it, I can do it.

"All right, be quiet just in case," she whispers, beckoning me to follow her down the hall. I nod and obey. We go into the smaller living room and close the door. She opens a closet and starts taking out videos until she gets to the last row.

"He keeps it here at the back so my mom won't see it." We crease up in silence and she raises a finger to her lips.

"Shhh, we have to keep the volume down so we can hear if anyone's coming."

"Got it."

She puts the video in the player and the Betis match comes on.

"Dad always leaves part of the match at the beginning, just in case."

I'd explode with laughter and excitement if I could, but I don't want to ruin the moment, so I hold it all in as hard as I can. Prado fast-forwards and the players run around at high speed until suddenly there's a scene with a cheap kind of oriental backdrop. This is the porno. A bronze-skinned girl is dancing in front of a hairy man, next to a bed swathed in sheer canopies. You can see the hunger in his eyes. She sways seductively. He gets up and starts tearing her clothes off. Once she's naked, he throws her onto the bed, opens her legs, and starts sucking on her pussy.

"Here comes the best part," Prado explains in a whisper. The camera is now inside a kind of cave, and we see the guy stick his tongue in, but it's like we're inside the pussy. I shake my right hand and cover my mouth with my left. There's a noise. Prado looks at me on full alert. Her mom went out on a quick errand and now she's back. With ultrasonic reflexes, Prado rewinds the video, leaving it at the part with the soccer match, takes it out, replaces it at the back of the shelf and puts all the others in front of it in the same order. She's a pro. By the time her mom opens the door to the small living room, we're sitting on the couch, completely calm and collected.

"Didn't you want to go down to the pool?"

"Yes," Prado answers with the face of a little angel. "We've just finished our sandwiches."

"Very good, come on then, a quick dip in the pool!"

Everything's worked out, and this time the mom seems nicer. We squeal in the elevator on our way down, skip through the entry hall – the happiest place on earth – and run out to the lawn. We've just taken shelter under Tanya's umbrella and haven't managed to tell her about our epic adventure yet when Domingo shows up at the pool with a backpack in his hand, desperately searching for me. Already? Seriously, this already? My success here has lasted how long? Three days? I do my duty and go over to him, prepared for whatever it is. He looks at the ground and stumbles over his words.

"See, Partner, when I got home from work your mom was in pretty bad shape so we're taking a cab to the hospital. D'you have a little friend you can stay with? If her parents know you, even better. We've got to figure this out, we have to hurry. Don't be scared, it'll only be for a while, but it's best if she gets seen as soon as possible."

I'm not scared, but after yesterday I'd die of sadness if I never saw her dance again. The memory of the porno gives me strength and I cling to it. They have to go to the hospital as soon as possible. I've got to be practical. Within five minutes, Domingo has explained the situation in confused but technical terms at Prado's house, left me the backpack with a change of clothes and my toothbrush, and disappeared. Prado's mom is welcoming and puts a warm arm around my shoulders, telling her daughter to try and distract me for the rest of the afternoon. One of the things that worries me most about this unpredictable situation is that we might have fish for dinner tonight. The minutes seem to be going by at several different speeds. I really like Prado's room because it's messy and the whole closet is covered in Chabel doll stickers, the ones that used to come free with chewing gum back when I wasn't allowed to chew gum – alas – but I can't focus on anything. She shows me a bunch of books and dolls, and she has no fear of physical contact. We can't get the talk flowing, so we lie back quietly on her bed, trying to come up with another kind of connection to entertain us. It's not hard after sharing such an intense moment just a while back.

"Look, lie down on your side like this," she says. I obey. She lies close behind me and puts her hand around my waist.

"Like this?" I ask.

"Yeah. Now pretend I'm a boy you like."

Her leg slips between mine and her knee pushes upward. I'm facing away from her so it's easy, like it's not happening. She's also a little bit shy in her way and knows all the tricks to make things straightforward. We hear steps coming down the hall and sit up quickly. Her mom opens the door without knocking.

"How are you two? Marina, do you like cod?"

"Yes," I say, feeling flustered.

"Good with fried potatoes, right?"

"Yes, really good, thank you."

She goes off leaving the door open a crack. Prado closes it again.

"Do you want to play fighting without making any noise?"

I couldn't care less if her family is full of fascists or if they eat cheese and fish on Fridays. I knew it, I knew she was the kind of girl I was looking for. We wrestle on the floor in slow motion, trying to keep quiet, hearing the frying pan sizzle. We jab each other with our elbows a few times and it's hard to hold back the groans. She's obviously stronger than me and likes to give more than receive, but the exercise does me a lot of good anyway. At dinner, I can't take my eyes off the TV cabinet, knowing the porn is inside it, camouflaged at the back. We're still at the table when the intercom rings. It's Domingo. He comes in saying he's sorry to bother them and for showing up again so late, claiming they've just got back and Mom wants me home for the night, and whatever she says goes, and so on. His stuttering is off the charts and nothing he says makes any sense, so I grab the backpack, translate his words into a basic summary, and we hurry downstairs and through the entryway. It still smells good but feels spookier, and I have a feeling that if I come back in my dreams it'll look like this and not the way it did earlier. We don't have far to go, but it's long enough for him to bug me with his usual verbal diarrhea. He seems to be explaining things but he's pussyfooting around, not saying anything specific. We get inside the apartment, still full of unopened boxes, and I go straight to her room. She's lying down, resting. I'm feeling brave, ready to tackle all the subjects I normally just leave turning over inside me.

"Mom! What happened?"

"Don't be scared, sweetie, it's just the usual, it doesn't mean anything. It's one problem one day and another the next, remember how I felt shitty this morning?"

"But what was it? You were fine yesterday! You were dancing!"

"Well, I felt a bit funny but they gave me a few injections and now I'm better. We'll be dancing again in a couple of days."

"You should stop smoking!"

"Not now, kid. Don't start being a pain in the ass when I've had such an awful day. Come here, for fuck's sake, and tell me how it went at your friend's place."

I get in bed and let her squeeze me like I'm a pet or a teddy bear.

"What shall I tell you?"

"What's that little girl like?"

"Her name's Prado and I like her. I like her a lot!"

"Oh yeah? No kidding, that's great."

"Yeah, yeah."

"What's she like?"

"She's really funny and really pretty. She has freckles, her room's a disaster, and I saw a lot of records at her place."

"That's great. What did they give you for dinner?"

"Cod and fried potatoes."

"I'll have to say thank you. And what was their apartment like?"

"Their balcony faces the pool and they're PP supporters."

"Ooof, oh boy."

"But they're Betis fans."

"Well then, all right. If you like her then it's settled, they can't be all that bad if they're Betis fans."

"Yeah, don't worry Mom, I had a good time and I wasn't scared. If you get sick again you can leave me there. But listen."

"Tell me, sweetie."

"You're not dying yet, are you?"

"Not this again."

"But I have to ask!"

"Yes, of course, don't worry. I'll tell you."

"OK."

"Look, I've been way worse, a few months ago those fuckers thought I was a goner, but now? No ma'am, I'm not going to die of any of this, even if I have to spend all night at the hospital. You'll see."

"Are you sure?"

"I promise."

"All right, well, promise me something else too."

"Tell me."

"I want you to promise that if you're about to die, you'll tell Domingo to come get me in a cab so I can go see you."

"For God's sake, sweetie, don't say that."

"But you have to understand! When you get worse you get all proud and don't want me to see you! I'm always thinking you'll get worse any moment and I'll never see you again!"

"You're right, I understand."

"Promise?"

"Yes."

"And another thing."

"Jeez."

"No, this one's easier."

"All right then."

"I want you to get me a Diana Ross tape and a bottle of your perfume so I can have my own."

"Huh?"

"In case you die, so I'll be prepared and have something to hold on to, that I can count on."

"Ah. Like a survival kit."

"Yeah."

"Those are the things you want in case I die. A tape of Diana Ross songs and a bottle of my perfume."

"Yeah."

Mom bursts into tears and squeezes me tight.

"But don't cry, it's only just in case!"

"All right, just in case. Don't you worry about it, I'll get them for you."

Domingo comes into the room, hunched over, hand to his forehead, and collapses on the other side of the bed in exhaustion. He hugs Mom and Mom hugs me. Pretty soon they fall asleep, but I'm still wired, their two snores booming behind me. It's all worked out, we've weathered the storm one more time, and I was brave enough to say what I needed without dying of embarrassment. I get up quietly and go back to my room. Only now do I allow myself the luxury of softly humming the theme tune to *The Land Before Time.* Like a baby dinosaur staring a meteorite in the face, I shed a few tears while I look at the floor, then at the window, and think of the shot from inside the pussy Prado showed me this afternoon. The greatest hope of my days. Nothing is lost yet, absolutely nothing.

I blow my nose and sit straight up in bed, ready to gather the strength to keep on going. Right now my priority is to give myself over to Monica, who's been waiting for me all day and is the only one who can give me relief from the state I'm in. I take a deep breath and go find the magazine, which is still on the nightstand. Monica is the heroine of *Rubber Flesh* but she's also Beatriz's best friend. While they're still snoring deeply in the room next door, I put the pages up against the window and trace them both, Monica and Bea, calling upon them as future friends who I hope won't judge me if I emerge from my chrysalis looking like a pile of shit with impaired motor skills. I slide the pencil gently over the pictures so I don't leave a mark, then I go over the line with a felt tip pen. Here they are, drawn by my own hand. I plant an invisible kiss on the page, crumple it into a ball, and throw it out of the window. An anonymous salute to the people who wander around at night, who walk with me on this uncertain, alluring path. The ones who fuck, the ones who shoot up, even the ones who want to fuck with me.

Dear readers,

As well as relying on bookshop sales, And Other Stories relies on subscriptions from people like you for many of our books, whose stories other publishers often consider too risky to take on.

Our subscribers don't just make the books physically happen. They also help us approach booksellers, because we can demonstrate that our books already have readers and fans. And they give us the security to publish in line with our values, which are collaborative, imaginative and 'shamelessly literary'.

All of our subscribers:

- receive a first-edition copy of each of the books they subscribe to
- are thanked by name at the end of our subscriber-supported books
- receive little extras from us by way of thank you, for example: postcards created by our authors

BECOME A SUBSCRIBER,
OR GIVE A SUBSCRIPTION TO A FRIEND

Visit andotherstories.org/subscriptions to help make our books happen. You can subscribe to books we're in the process of making. To purchase books we have already published, we urge you to support your local or favourite bookshop and order directly from them – the often unsung heroes of publishing.

OTHER WAYS TO GET INVOLVED

If you'd like to know about upcoming events and reading groups (our foreign-language reading groups help us choose books to publish, for example) you can:

- join our mailing list at: andotherstories.org
- follow us on Twitter: @andothertweets
- join us on Facebook: facebook.com/AndOtherStoriesBooks
- admire our books on Instagram: @andotherpics
- follow our blog: andotherstories.org/ampersand

THIS BOOK WAS MADE POSSIBLE
THANKS TO THE SUPPORT OF

A Cudmore
Aaron McEnery
Aaron Schneider
Abi Webb
Abigail Howell
Abigail Walton
Adam Clarke
Adam Lenson
Adrian Astur Alvarez
Adrian Perez
Aifric Campbell
Aisha McLean
Ajay Sharma
Alan Baldwin
Alan Donnelly
Alan Felsenthal
Alan McMonagle
Alan Stoskopf
Alastair Gillespie
Alastair Whitson
Albert Puente
Alecia Marshall
Alex Fleming
Alex Liebman
Alex Lockwood
Alex Pearce
Alex Ramsey
Alexander Williams
Alexandra Citron
Alexandra Stewart
Alexandra Stewart
Alexandra Tammaro
Alexandra Tilden
Alexandra Webb

Alfred Birnbaum
Ali Ersahin
Ali Smith
Ali Usman
Alice Morgan
Alice Radosh
Alice Smith
Alice Wilkinson
Alicia Medina
Alison Hardy
Alison Winston
Aliya Rashid
Alyse Ceirante
Alyssa Rinaldi
Amado Floresca
Amaia Gabantxo
Amalia Gladhart
Amanda
Amanda Dalton
Amanda Maria
  Izquierdo Gonzalez
Amanda Read
Amelia Lowe
Amine Hamadache
Amy and Jamie
Amy Arnold
Amy Benson
Amy Bessent
Amy Bojang
Amy Finch
Amy Kitchens
Amy Tabb
Ana Novak
Anastasia Carver

Andra Dusu
Andrea Barlien
Andrea Brownstone
Andrea Oyarzabal
  Koppes
Andrea Reece
Andrew Marston
Andrew McCallum
Andrew McDougall
Andrew Ratomski
Andrew Reece
Andrew Rego
Andy Corsham
Andy Turner
Angela Everitt
Angela Lopez
Angelica Ribichini
Angus Walker
Anita Starosta
Ann Rees
Anna Finneran
Anna French
Anna Gibson
Anna Hawthorne
Anna Milsom
Anna Zaranko
Anne Barnes
Anne Carus
Anne Craven
Anne Edyvean
Anne Frost
Anne O' Brien
Anne Ryden
Anne Sticksel

Anne Withane
Anne Boileau Clarke
Annette Hamilton
Annie McDermott
Anonymous
Anonymous
Anthony Alexander
Anthony Brown
Antonia Lloyd-Jones
Antonia Saske
Antony Osgood
Antony Pearce
Aoife Boyd
Archie Davies
Aron Negyesi
Arthur John Rowles
Asako Serizawa
Ash Lazarus
Audrey Mash
Audrey Small
Barbara Bettsworth
Barbara Mellor
Barbara Robinson
Barbara Spicer
Barry Norton
Bea Karol Burks
Becky Cherriman
Ben Buchwald
Ben Schofield
Ben Thornton
Ben Walter
Benjamin Judge
Benjamin Pester
Beth Heim de Bera
Bethan Kent
Bhakti Gajjar
Bianca Duec
Bianca Jackson

Bianca Winter
Bill Fletcher
Björn Warren
Bjørnar Djupevik
    Hagen
Blazej Jedras
Briallen Hopper
Brian Anderson
Brian Byrne
Brian Callaghan
Brian Conn
Brian Smith
Bridget Maddison
Brigita Ptackova
Buck Johnston
Burkhard Fehsenfeld
Caitlin Halpern
Callie Steven
Cameron Adams
Camilla Imperiali
Carla Castanos
Carol Quintana
Carole Parkhouse
Carolina Pineiro
Caroline Perry
Caroline Smith
Caroline West
Catharine Braithwaite
Catherine Cleary
Catherine Lambert
Catherine Tandy
Catherine Tolo
Catherine Williamson
Cathryn Siegal-
    Bergman
Cathy Galvin
Cathy Sowell
Catie Kosinski

Catriona Gibbs
Cecilia Rossi
Cecilia Uribe
Chantal Lyons
Chantal Wright
Charlene Huggins
Charles Fernyhough
Charles Kovach
Charles Dee Mitchell
Charles Rowe
Charlie Errock
Charlie Levin
Charlie Small
Charlotte Bruton
Charlotte Coulthard
Charlotte Durnajkin
Charlotte Holtam
Charlotte Ryland
Charlotte Whittle
Charlotte Woodford
Cherilyn Elston
China Miéville
Chris Holmes
Chris Johnstone
Chris Köpruner
Chris Potts
Chris Stergalas
Chris Stevenson
Chris Thornton
Christian Schuhmann
Christina Moutsou
Christine Bartels
Christine Humphreys
Christopher Allen
Christopher Homfray
Christopher Smith
Christopher Stout
Ciara Ní Riain

Ciarán Schütte
Claire Adams
Claire Brooksby
Claire Hayward
Claire Mackintosh
Claire Morrison
Claire Morrison
Claire Smith
Claire Williams
Clarice Borges
Clarissa Pattern
Cliona Quigley
Colin Denyer
Colin Hewlett
Colin Matthews
Collin Brooke
Cornelia Svedman
Cortina Butler
Courtney Lilly
Craig Kennedy
Cynthia De La Torre
Cyrus Massoudi
Daisy Savage
Dale Wisely
Dan Martin
Dan Parkinson
Dana Lapidot
Daniel Arnold
Daniel Gillespie
Daniel Hahn
Daniel Hester-Smith
Daniel Stewart
Daniel Syrovy
Daniel Venn
Daniela Steierberg
Darina Brejtrova
Darryll Rogers
Dave Lander

David Anderson
David Coates
David Cowan
David Darvasi
David Davies
David Gould
David Greenlaw
David Gunnarsson
David Hebblethwaite
David Higgins
David Hodges
David Johnson-Davies
David Leverington
David F Long
David McIntyre
David and Lydia Pell
David Reid
David Richardson
David Shriver
David Smith
Dawn Bass
Dean Taucher
Deb Hughes
Deb Unferth
Debbie Enever
Debbie Pinfold
Deborah Banks
Declan Gardner
Declan O'Driscoll
Deirdre Nic Mhathuna
Denis Larose
Denise Bretländer
Denton Djurasevich
Derek Taylor-
  Vrsalovich
Desiree Mason
Diana Baker Smith
Diarmuid Hickey

Dietrich Menzel
Dina Abdul-Wahab
Dinesh Prasad
Dominic Nolan
Dominick Santa
  Cattarina
Dominique Brocard
Dominique Hudson
Dorothy Bottrell
Doug Wallace
Duncan Clubb
Duncan Macgregor
Duncan Marks
Dustin Hackfeld
Dyanne Prinsen
Earl James
Ebba Aquila
Ebba Tornérhielm
Ed Tronick
Ekaterina Beliakova
Elaine Frances
Elaine Juzl
Eleanor Maier
Elena Esparza
Elif Aganoglu
Elina Zicmane
Elisabeth Cook
Eliza Mood
Elizabeth Braswell
Elizabeth Coombes
Elizabeth Draper
Elizabeth Franz
Elizabeth Guss
Elizabeth Leach
Elizabeth Seals
Elizabeth Wood
Ellen Wilkinson
Ellie Goddard

Emeline Morin
Emily Armitage
Emily Dixon
Emily Jang
Emily Paine
Emily Webber
Emily Williams
Emma Bielecki
Emma Dell
Emma Louise Grove
Emma Page
Emma Post
Emma Teale
Erica Mason
Erin Cameron Allen
Esmée de Heer
Esther Donnelly
Esther Kinsky
Ethan Madarieta
Eugene O'Hare
Eunji Kim
Eva Oddo
Eve Corcoran
Ewan Tant
F Gary Knapp
Fawzia Kane
Fay Barrett
Faye Williams
Felicity Williams
Felix Valdivieso
Finbarr Farragher
Fiona Mozley
Fiona Quinn
Fran Sanderson
Frances Spangler
Frances Thiessen
Francesca Brooks
Francesca Hemery

Francis Mathias
Frank Rodrigues
Frank van Orsouw
Frauke Matthes
Freddie Radford
Friederike Knabe
Gabriel Colnic
Gabriel and Mary de
    Courcy Cooney
Gala Copley
Garan Holcombe
Gavin Aitchison
Gavin Collins
Gavin Smith
Gawain Espley
Gemma Doyle
Genaro Palomo Jr
Genevieve Lewington
Geoff Thrower
Geoffrey Cohen
Geoffrey Urland
George McCaig
George Stanbury
George Wilkinson
Georgia Panteli
Georgia Shomidie
Georgia Wall
Georgina Norton
Gerry Craddock
Gill Boag-Munroe
Gillian Grant
Gina Heathcote
Glenn Russell
Gordon Cameron
Gosia Pennar
Grace Cohen
Graham Blenkinsop
Graham R Foster

Graham Page
Grant Rintoul
Gregory Philp
Hadil Balzan
Halina Schiffman-
    Shilo
Hamish Russell
Hannah Bucknell
Hannah Freeman
Hannah Harford-
    Wright
Hannah Morris
Hannah Procter
Hannah Rapley
Hannah Jane
    Lownsbrough
Hanora Bagnell
Hans Lazda
Harriet Stiles
Haydon Spenceley
Hayley Cox
Hazel Smoczynska
Heidi James
Helen Bailey
Helen Berry
Helen Coombes
Helen Moor
Helena Buffery
Henriette Magerstaedt
Henrike Laehnemann
Henry Patino
Hilary Munro
HJ Fotheringham
Holly Barker
Holly Down
Howard Robinson
Hugh Shipley
Hyoung-Won Park

Ian Hagues
Ian McMillan
Ian Mond
Ian Randall
Ian Whiteley
Ida Grochowska
Ilona Abb
Ines Alfano
Iona Preston
Iona Stevens
Irene Croal
Irene Mansfield
Irina Tzanova
Isabella Garment
Isabella Weibrecht
Isobel Foxford
Jacinta Perez Gavilan
 Torres
Jack Brown
Jacqueline Haskell
Jacqueline Lademann
Jacqui Jackson
Jade Yiu
Jadie Lee
Jake Baldwinson
James Attlee
James Beck
James Crossley
James Cubbon
James Elkins
James Kinsley
James Lehmann
James Leonard
James Lesniak
James Norman
James Portlock
James Scudamore
James Silvestro

Jamie Cox
Jan Hicks
Jan Leah Lowe
Jane Anderton
Jane Dolman
Jane Fairweather
Jane Leuchter
Jane Roberts
Jane Roberts
Jane Willborn
Jane Woollard
Janelle Ward
Janne Støen
Jasmine Gideon
Jason Montano
Jason Timermanis
JE Crispin
Jeanne Guyon
Jeff Collins
Jeff Goguen
Jen Hardwicke
Jenifer Logie
Jennifer Arnold
Jennifer Fisher
Jennifer Higgins
Jennifer Leech
Jennifer Mills
Jennifer Watts
Jenny Barlow
Jenny Huth
Jenny Newton
Jeremy Koenig
Jeremy Wellens
Jess Hazlewood
Jess Wood
Jesse Coleman
Jesse Hara
Jesse Thayre

Jessica Cooper
Jessica Gately
Jessica Kibler
Jessica Mello
Jessica Queree
Jethro Soutar
Jill Harrison
Jo Cox
Jo Elliot
Jo Heinrich
Jo Keyes
Joanna Luloff
Joanne Smith
Joao Pedro Bragatti
 Winckler
JoDee Brandon
Jodie Adams
Joe Gill
Joe Huggins
Joel Garza
Joel Swerdlow
Joelle Young
Johanna Eliasson
Johannes Holmqvist
Johannes Menzel
Johannes Georg Zipp
John Bennett
John Betteridge
John Bogg
John Carnahan
John Conway
John Down
John Gent
John Guyatt
John Hanson
John Hodgson
John Kelly
John Reid

John Royley
John Shaw
John Steigerwald
John Walsh
John Winkelman
John Wyatt
Jolene Smith
Jonathan Blaney
Jonathan Fiedler
Jonathan Harris
Jonathan Huston
Jonny Kiehlmann
Jordana Carlin
Jorid Martinsen
Jose Machado
Joseph Novak
Joseph Schreiber
Joseph Thomas
Josh Calvo
Josh Sumner
Joshua Davis
Joshua McNamara
Judith Gruet-Kaye
Judith Virginia Moffatt
Judy Davies
Julia Rochester
Julia Sanches
Julia Von Dem
  Knesebeck
Julian Hemming
Julian Molina
Julie Winter
Julienne van Loon
Juliet Birkbeck
Jupiter Jones
Juraj Janik
Justine Goodchild
Justine Sherwood

Kaarina Hollo
Kaelyn Davis
Kaja R Anker-Rasch
Karl Chwe
Kasper Haakansson
Kataline Lukacs
Katarzyna
  Bartoszynska
Kate Attwooll
Kate Beswick
Kate Carlton-Reditt
Kate Gardner
Kate Procter
Kate Shires
Katharina Liehr
Katharine Robbins
Katherine Mackinnon
Katherine Sotejeff-
  Wilson
Kathryn Edwards
Kathryn Williams
Kathy Gogarty
Katia Wengraf
Katie Brown
Katie Freeman
Katie Grant
Katie Kline
Katie Smart
Katy Robinson
Keith Walker
Kelly Mehring
Ken Barlow
Kenneth Blythe
Kenneth Michaels
Kent McKernan
Kerry Parke
Kevin Tole
Kieran Rollin

Kieron James
Kim McGowan
Kim White
Kirsty Doole
Kirsty Simpkins
KJ Buckland
KL Ee
Kris Ann Trimis
Kristen Tcherneshoff
Kristin Djuve
Krystale Tremblay-
  Moll
Krystine Phelps
Kyra Wilder
Kysanna Shawney
Lacy Wolfe
Lana Selby
Lara Vergnaud
Larry Wikoff
Laura Batatota
Laura Clarke
Laura Ling
Laura Pugh
Laura Zlatos
Lauren Pout
Lauren Rea
Laurence Laluyaux
Laurie Rosenblatt
Leah Cooper
Leah Zamesnik
Leanore Ickstadt
Lee Harbour
Leon Geis
Leona Iosifidou
Leslie Jacobson
Liliana Lobato
Lily Blacksell
Linda Jones

Lindsay Brammer
Lindsey Ford
Line Langebek
  Knudsen
Linette Arthurton
  Bruno
Lisa Agostini
Lisa Barnard
Lisa Bean
Lisa Dillman
Lisa Leahigh
Lisa Simpson
Lisa Weizenegger
Liz Clifford
Liz Starbuck Greer
Lorna Bleach
Lottie Smith
Louise Evans
Louise Greenberg
Louise Hoelscher
Louise Jolliffe
Louise Smith
Luc Daley
Luc Verstraete
Lucie Taylor
Lucy Banks
Lucy Gorman
Lucy Huggett
Lucy Leeson-Smith
Lucy Moffatt
Ludmilla Jordanova
Luke Healey
Luke Loftiss
Lydia Trethewey
Lynda Graham
Lyndia Thomas
Lynn Fung
Lynn Martin

Maeve Lambe
Magdaline Rohweder
Maggie Kerkman
Maggie Livesey
Manu Chastelain
Marcel Inhoff
Marcel Schlamowitz
Marco Medjimorec
Margaret Cushen
Margaret Dillow
Margaret Jull Costa
Margo Gorman
Mari-Liis Calloway
Maria Ahnhem Farrar
Maria Hill
Maria Lomunno
Maria Losada
Marie Donnelly
Marina Castledine
Mario Sifuentez
Marisa Wilson
Marja S Laaksonen
Mark Harris
Mark Huband
Mark Sargent
Mark Sheets
Mark Sztyber
Mark Walsh
Mark Waters
Marlene Simoes
Martin Brown
Martin Munro
Martin Price
Martin Eric Rodgers
Mary Angela
  Brevidoro
Mary Heiss
Mary Wang

Maryse Meijer
Mathieu Trudeau
Matt Davies
Matt Greene
Matt O'Connor
Matthew Adamson
Matthew Armstrong
Matthew Banash
Matthew Eatough
Matthew Francis
Matthew Gill
Matthew Lowe
Matthew Warshauer
Matthew Woodman
Matthias Rosenberg
Maura Cheeks
Max Cairnduff
Max Longman
Maya Chung
Meaghan Delahunt
Meg Lovelock
Megan Holt
Megan Wittling
Mel Pryor
Melissa Beck
Melissa Quignon-
  Finch
Melissa da Silveira
  Serpa
Melissa Stogsdill
Melissa Wan
Meredith Jones
Meredith Martin
Mia Khachidze
Michael Aguilar
Michael Bichko
Michael Boog
Michael James

Eastwood
Michael Floyd
Michael Gavin
Michael Kuhn
Michael Moran
Michael Roess
Michelle Perkins
Miguel Head
Mike Turner
Miles Smith-Morris
Misa Sekiguchi
Moira Garland
Moira Sweeney
Moira Weir
Molly Foster
Mona Arshi
Moray Teale
Morayma Jimenez
Moremi Apata-
  Omisore
Morgan Lyons
Moriah Haefner
Muireann Maguire
Myles Nolan
N Tsolak
Nan Craig
Nancy Foley
Nancy Jacobson
Nancy Oakes
Nancy Sosnow
Nanda Griffioen
Natalia Reyes
Natalie Ricks
Nathalie Adams
Nathalie Atkinson
Nathalie Karagiannis
Nathan McNamara
Nathan Rowley

Nathan Weida
Neferti Tadiar
Nguyen Phan
Nicholas Brown
Nicholas Rutherford
Nicholas Smith
Nick James
Nick Love
Nick Nelson & Rachel
  Eley
Nick Sidwell
Nick Twemlow
Nicola Cook
Nicola Hart
Nicola Sandiford
Nicola Scott
Nicole Joy
Nicole Matteini
Nigel Fishburn
Niki Sammut
Nina Alexandersen
Nina de la Mer
Nina Nickerson
Nina Todorova
Nudrat Siddiqui
Odilia Corneth
Ohan Hominis
Olivia Scott
Olivia Turon
Pamela Ritchie
Pamela Tao
Pat Winslow
Patricia Aronsson
Patrick Hawley
Patrick Hoare
Paul Cray
Paul Jones
Paul Munday

Paul Myatt
Paul Nightingale
Paul Robinson
Paul Scott
Paul Segal
Paul Thompson and
  Gordon McArthur
Paula McGrath
Pauline Drury
Pauline France
Pavlos Stavropoulos
Penelope Hewett-
  Brown
Peter Goulborn
Peter Griffin
Peter Halliday
Peter Hudson
Peter McBain
Peter McCambridge
Peter Rowland
Peter Taplin
Peter Van de Maele
  and Narina Dahms
Peter Watson
Peter Wells
Petra Stapp
Phil Bartlett
Philip Herbert
Philip Warren
Philip Williams
Philipp Jarke
Phillipa Clements
Phoebe McKenzie
Phoebe Millerwhite
Phyllis Reeve
Pia Figge
Piet Van Bockstal
PRAH Foundation

Prakash Nayak
Rachael de Moravia
Rachael Williams
Rachel Dolan
Rachel Gregory
Rachel Matheson
Rachel Van Riel
Rachel Watkins
Ralph Cowling
Ramona Pulsford
Ranbir Sidhu
Raymond Manzo
Rebecca Braun
Rebecca Fearnley
Rebecca Ketcherside
Rebecca Moss
Rebecca O'Reilly
Rebecca Peer
Rebecca Rosenthal
Rebecca Servadio
Rebecca Shaak
Rebekka Bremmer
Renee Thomas
Rhiannon Armstrong
Rich Sutherland
Richard Catty
Richard Clark
Richard Ellis
Richard Gwyn
Richard Mansell
Richard Padwick
Richard Priest
Richard Shea
Richard Soundy
Richard Stubbings
Richard White
Riley & Alyssa
  Manning

Rishi Dastidar
Rita Kaar
Rita O'Brien
Rob Kidd
Robert Gillett
Robert Hannah
Robert Sliman
Roberto Hull
Robin McLean
Robin Taylor
Rogelio Pardo
Roger Newton
Roger Ramsden
Rory Williamson
Ros Woolner
Rosalind May
Rosalind Ramsay
Rose Crichton
Rose Pearce
Ross Beaton
Ross MacIntyre
Rowan Bowman
Roxanne O'Del Ablett
Roz Simpson
Ruby Thiagarajan
Rupert Ziziros
Ruth Deyermond
Ruth Field
Ryan Day
Sabine Griffiths
Sabine Little
Sally Arkinstall
Sally Baker
Sally Bramley
Sally Ellis
Sally Warner
Sam Gordon
Sam Reese

Samantha Walton
Samuel Crosby
Sara Bea
Sara Kittleson
Sara Sherwood
Sara Warshawski
Sarah Arboleda
Sarah Blunden
Sarah Brewer
Sarah Duguid
Sarah Farley
Sarah Goddard
Sarah Lucas
Sarah Pybus
Sarah Roff
Sarah Spitz
Sasha Dugdale
Scott Astrada
Scott Chiddister
Scott Henkle
Scott Simpson
Sean Kottke
Sean McDonagh
Shane Horgan
Shannon Knapp
Sharon Dogar
Shauna Gilligan
Shauna Rogers
Sheila Duffy
Sheila Packa
Shira Lob
Sienna Kang
Simon James
Simon Pitney
Simon Robertson
Simone Martelossi
SK Grout
Sonia McLintock

Sophie Church
ST Dabbagh
Stacy Rodgers
Stefanie Schrank
Stefano Mula
Stephan Eggum
Stephanie Lacava
Stephanie Miller
Stephanie Shields
Stephanie Smee
Stephen Pearsall
Steve Chapman
Steve Dearden
Steve James
Steve Raby
Steve Tuffnell
Steven Norton
Steven Vass
Steven Williams
Stewart Eastham
Stu Hennigan
Stu Sherman
Stuart Phillips
Stuart Wilkinson
Su Bonfanti
Sunny Payson
Susan Bamford
Susan Clegg
Susan Edsall
Susan Jaken
Susan Winter
Suzanne Colangelo
  Lillis
Suzanne Kirkham
Sydney Hutchinson

Tamara Larsen
Tania Hershman
Tara Pahari
Tara Roman
Tasmin Maitland
Teresa Werner
Teri Hoskin
Tess Cohen
Tess McAlister
Tessa Lang
Thom Cuell
Thom Keep
Thomas Mitchell
Thomas Phipps
Thomas Rasmussen
Thomas Smith
Thomas van den Bout
Thomas Andrew
  White
Tian Zheng
Tiffany Lehr
Tim Kelly
Tim Schneider
Tim Scott
Tim Theroux
Tina Rotherham-
  Winqvist
Toby Halsey
Toby Ryan
Tom Darby
Tom Doyle
Tom Franklin
Tom Gray
Tom and Ben Knight
Tom Stafford

Tom Whatmore
Tory Jeffay
Tracy Northup
Tracy Shapley
Trevor Wald
Ursula Dawson
Val & Tom Flechtner
Vanessa Fernandez
  Greene
Vanessa Fuller
Vanessa Heggie
Vanessa Nolan
Victor Meadowcroft
Victoria Eld
Victoria Goodbody
Victoria Larroque
Vijay Pattisapu
Vikki O'Neill
Wendy Langridge
Will Stolton
William Black
William
  Brockenborough
William Dennehy
William Franklin
William Mackenzie
William Schwaber
William Sitters
Yoora Yi Tenen
Zachary Hope
Zachary Maricondia
Zachary Whyte
Zara Rahman
Zareena Amiruddin
Zoë Brasier

CURRENT & UPCOMING BOOKS

ELISA VICTORIA was born in Seville in 1985. She has published two books of short stories, *Porn & Pains* in 2013, and *La sombra de los pinos* in 2018, and has contributed to several anthologies. Her debut novel, *Oldladyvoice*, was published in Spanish in 2019 to great critical acclaim and was selected as Book of the Week by *El País*.

CHARLOTTE WHITTLE has translated works by Silvia Goldman, Jorge Comensal and Rafael Toriz, among others. Her translation of Norah Lange's *People in the Room* was longlisted for the American Literary Translators Association prize and shortlisted for both the Warwick Prize for Women in Translation and the Society of Authors' TA First Translation Prize. Her translation of *Notes from Childhood*, also by Norah Lange, was published by And Other Stories in 2021. She lives in New York.